BOOTS AND STILETTOS

THE SPYKER RANCH
BOOK TWO

KIRK VOCLAIN

DEDICATION

I want to thank my wife, Tammy Voclain, for being my preliminary editor and my sounding board throughout this entire process. Your patience, sharp notes, and steady belief carried this book from first spark to final period. This one, like all of them, is for you.

Next, I would like to acknowledge Bob and Lisa Spyker, our very good vacation friends. When I shared my love of writing, they challenged me to write this novel, with two conditions: the main characters would be loosely inspired by parts of their personalities, and the romance between Jake and Annie would remain G rated. With that nudge, I started down this path. Thank you, Bob and Lisa, for the spark and for helping me get started.

PRAISE FOR BOOTS AND STILETTOS

It's easy to get lost in the rich prose of this book...it's a rich, warm, deeply satisfying read.

— CONSTANCE-NH

To me, it is like a poem to be savored. The words depicting the scenes are amazingly sharp, clear, concise, like a painter that can make a scene come alive with a few brush strokes, yet that scene is perfect.

— MOMTOC

This novel is heart-warming, electric, and hard to put down. If you're looking for next-level Hallmark story-telling, this is it!

— JFNOONE

If you love Western romance with heart, competence, and a true happily ever after, Boots and Stilettos is absolutely worth reading. A story about love that works as hard as the people living it.

— JADE

The descriptions were vivid, and gave the reader a clear view; the scenery, the imagery, the scent of a budding relationship.

— ERIC REDMON

Everybody loves a movie with horses and romance. I for one am a forever fan. Read this book!!!

— LISA

CONTENTS

DUST AND INHERITANCE

A NOTE FROM THE AUTHOR

If you found this book during a promotion, thank you for taking a chance on my work.

If you enjoy **Boots and Stilettos**, I'd truly appreciate an honest review on BookBub or Goodreads. Even a few words can help other readers decide if this story is right for them.

You can find more about my books at **KirkVoclain.com**, and you're welcome to join my newsletter for updates on new stories, bonus content, and future promotions.

PROLOGUE

THE PLANE TICKET

*S*he almost didn't board the plane.

Her boarding pass sat there on the gate counter, mocking her. Row 12C, economy, no champagne, no silk pillow, no carefully curated playlist of Italian opera.

Just a one-way ticket to Montana.

Montana.

An entire state that sounded like it had more cows than people and absolutely no concept of designer anything.

Antoinette Contadelucci, heiress to one of Europe's most luxurious fashion empires, stood alone at Gate 28, now with a boarding pass in one hand and a thousand doubts in the other.

This wasn't a vacation. It wasn't a business trip. This was exile. Sent to "learn the family business," her father said. Sent to "grow up," Ricardo had sneered.

But deep down, if she was honest, she'd bought this ticket herself. Not with money. With pride. With stubbornness. With something that ached just beneath her ribs, something she couldn't quite name.

The gate agent called final boarding.

Antoinette took a breath. She looked at her reflection in the airport window. Mascara flawless. Lipstick sharp. But her eyes…

They didn't look ready.

Still, she walked forward.

She didn't know she was stepping off that plane into dirt roads and disaster, or that the man waiting at the gate would look at her like she was a puzzle he didn't want to solve. She boarded anyway.

CHAPTER ONE

BIG SKY COLLISION

The sun dipped low over the Montana plains, casting a golden glow across the rugged land. Jake Spyker leaned against the weathered post of the corral, his hat tipped back just enough to reveal blue eyes as dark as the black coffee he started his day with. The evening breeze carried the familiar scents of sage and prairie grass, mixed with the earthier notes of cattle and leather from the nearby barn. He was wiry, the kind of skinny that comes from years of hard work under the sun, with a quiet strength hidden beneath the dust on his shirt. Life out here didn't leave room for much more than cattle and long stretches of silence, broken only by the occasional lowing of cattle or cry of a hawk riding the thermals above. That was fine by him... until she showed up.

Antoinette Contadelucci stepped out of the truck like a dream misplaced, the setting sun catching her arrival like nature's own spotlight. Her golden hair caught the breeze, tumbling in waves over her shoulders, and her every movement carried the effortless grace of her Italian roots. The contrast between her and the rustic ranch setting was almost jarring, like finding a pearl in a feed bucket. Jake had seen her kind before, at least, he thought he had. The tourists who came through Montana every summer looking for adventure, snapping photos of wide-open spaces before retreating to their big city lives, leaving nothing behind but tire tracks and forgotten coffee cups from the local diner. But there was something different about Antoinette, or Annie, as she preferred to be called. She wasn't a tourist. She was here for something more, and that something glinted in her eyes like steel beneath silk.

She walked toward him, her heels crunching on the gravel with each deliberate step, a sharp contrast to the soft melody of her accent when she said, "You must be Jake? Or do you prefer Jacob?" She met his gaze with eyes as blue as the big Montana sky. Her words were warm, yet he sensed a spark of challenge, as if she'd already decided she wasn't impressed by the man in dusty boots, wearing his dad's old belt buckle stamped with "SPIKE."

Jake straightened and tipped his hat in greeting, feeling the familiar weight of responsibility that came with the ranch pressing down on his shoulders. He knew why she was here. It had all been arranged by her father, Dante. Emails, phone calls, payments, arrangements, everything had been set weeks ago. Jake didn't know why his ranch had been chosen, only that he needed the money they were willing to pay. Whatever had brought her to this exact stretch of nowhere, he couldn't say, but he had a feeling she was about to turn his world upside down.

"Jake's fine," he said, his voice rough from disuse. The ranch didn't offer much opportunity for conversation beyond the occasional grunt at the feed store or quick words with the veterinarian. Even the weekly supply runs into town had become exercises in efficiency rather than social calls. He studied her carefully, noting the designer label on her jacket that probably cost more than his monthly feed bill. The jacket was beautiful, he had to admit, but about as practical for ranch work as snow shoes in July. "Your father called ahead. Said you needed to learn about ranch operations."

Annie's perfectly shaped eyebrows arched slightly, a gesture that managed to be both elegant and slightly defensive. "Ah, so you know why I'm here. Did he tell you everything?" There was something in her tone that suggested layers of meaning, stories untold, and Jake found himself curious despite his better judgment.

"Just that you're taking over the family's agricultural investment division, and he wants you to understand the business from the ground up." Jake pushed away from the post, gesturing toward the sprawling ranch behind him, where the evening light painted the pastures in shades of gold and amber. A small herd of cattle grazed in the distance, their shapes dark against the sunset. "Though I got to say, seems like an awful long way to come from Milan just to look at some cows."

A flash of irritation crossed her face, like lightning in clear skies. "Milano," she corrected automatically, then caught herself and smiled, transforming her face from merely beautiful to something that made Jake's chest tight. "And there's more to it than just looking at cows, Mr. Spyker. My father may see this as just another investment, but I..." She paused, looking out across the vast expanse of land, something vulnerable flickering across her features. The wind caught her hair again, and for a moment she looked less like an Italian heiress and more like someone searching for solid ground. "I need to prove something."

The wind picked up, and Jake watched as Annie pulled her jacket closer, her citified perfume mixing with the earthy smells of the ranch. She wasn't dressed for what was coming, neither the weather nor the work ahead. Her delicate shoes already showed signs of defeat from the rough ranch ground.

"Storm's rolling in," he said, nodding toward the darkening western sky, where clouds were building like a mountain range of their own. "Best get you settled in the guest house before it hits. We can start your... education tomorrow morning. Five AM sharp."

Annie's eyes widened slightly, feeling the full weight of the distance and time zones she had just traveled. She wasn't sure she heard him correctly. "Five? In the morning?"

"Cattle don't care much for sleeping in," Jake replied, the ghost of a smile tugging at his lips. A nearby horse nickered softly, as if agreeing. "And if you're serious about learning this business, you'll need to see it all, including the parts that don't make it into your father's quarterly reports."

Secretly wishing she could have just one day to settle in, she lifted her chin, meeting his gaze with a determination that seemed to come from somewhere deeper than her polished exterior. "I'll be ready."

Jake doubted that, but he kept the thought to himself. Instead, he watched as she turned back to her truck, presumably to gather her things. Her confident stride faltered slightly as her heel sunk into a patch of soft earth, and he found himself moving forward instinctively to steady her, his rancher's instincts overriding his intention to maintain distance. His hand caught her elbow, and for a brief moment, they were close enough for him to see the flecks of gold in her blue eyes and smell her soft floral perfume.

"Careful," he murmured, quickly stepping back, trying to ignore the warmth that lingered on his palm. "Ground can be treacherous out here."

"I'm beginning to see that," Annie replied softly, and Jake had the distinct impression she wasn't just talking about the dirt beneath her feet. Something passed between them then, quick as a shadow from a passing cloud, but just as real.

Thunder rumbled in the distance as Jake helped her with her luggage, three expensive-looking suitcases that seemed better suited for a European fashion week than a working ranch. The leather was butter-soft, the hardware gleaming gold, and he tried not to think about how they'd look after a few weeks of ranch dust. The guest house was simple but clean, with a small covered porch and windows that looked out over the western pasture. It had been his grandmother's house once, before she passed, and something about seeing this polished city woman ascending those worn wooden steps made his chest tight with an emotion he couldn't quite name.

"It's... rustic," Annie said, taking in the modest accommodations. But there was no judgment in her voice, only curiosity, and perhaps a touch of appreciation for the way the setting sun painted the weathered wood in shades of honey and gold. A hummingbird darted past, checking out the feeder his grandmother had hung years ago, and Annie's face lit up at the sight.

"It's home," Jake replied simply, watching her reaction to the tiny bird. "Or it will be, for the next few months at least." He set her bags inside the door and stepped back onto the porch, breathing in the storm-heavy air. "There's coffee and basic supplies in the kitchen. Bathroom's down the hall. If you need anything else, my house is just over that rise." He pointed to the slightly larger structure about a quarter-mile away, where smoke curled from the chimney despite the warm evening.

Annie followed his gesture, then turned back to him with an unreadable expression. "You live alone?"

"Just me and Blue," he answered, referring to his aging cattle dog who was probably already curled up by the fireplace, keeping watch over the ranch in his own way. "And Spike," he added, a slight smile touching his lips as he thought of the stubborn black stallion he'd named after his father. The horse had been his faithful partner through every cattle drive and midnight emergency for the past decade. The horse was more friend than livestock, with a personality as big as the Montana sky. "And about three hundred head of cattle, give or take."

He hesitated, then added, "I couldn't do it without Maria. She lives next door. She cooks more than I ask her to."

Annie tilted her head. "You have a cook?"

"She'd laugh if she heard you say that," Jake said. "She's been around since my mom was alive. Decided somewhere along the way that I'd starve without her." He shrugged. "Her husband Carlos doesn't mind, and she hardly charges me. Closest thing to family out here, I guess. After Blue."

"No wife? No family?" The question seemed to surprise her as much as it did him, and she quickly added, "I'm sorry, that's none of my business." A blush colored her cheeks, making her look younger, more vulnerable.

Jake adjusted his hat, buying time before responding, feeling the worn leather band that had molded to his head over countless days under the Montana sun. "No ma'am. Never found anyone who loved this land as much as I do." The words came out more honest than he'd intended, carrying the weight of lonely nights and quiet mornings, and he cleared his throat awkwardly. "But I guess Maria, and Tommy who helps out around here, would qualify as family. Anyway, I'll leave you to get settled. Remember, five AM."

"I won't forget," she said, and there was that challenge in her eyes again, mixed with something softer that made him want to linger on the porch longer than he should. The first stars were beginning to appear in the eastern sky, and for a moment, they were reflected in her eyes.

The first fat drops of rain began to fall as Jake made his way back to his own house, his boots leaving deep prints in the increasingly muddy ground. Behind him, lights began to glow in the windows of the guest house, warm and inviting against the gathering storm. He tried not to think about how those lights would shine across the pasture every evening now, or how they might make the ranch feel a little less empty.

Blue greeted him at the door with a questioning look, as if to ask what he made of their new guest. Jake scratched behind the dog's ears, considering the same question himself. Annie Contadelucci was clearly out of her element here, armed with designer clothes and big city expectations. She'd probably last a week, maybe two, before running back to her comfortable life in Italy. And yet...

And yet there had been something in her eyes when she looked out across the ranch, something that reminded him of the way he'd felt the first time he'd seen this land. Like she was searching for something she couldn't quite name, something that might just be hidden in the vast spaces between earth and sky.

Thunder cracked overhead, and Blue pressed closer to his leg, his warm presence a comfort against the growing storm. Jake moved to the window, watching as rain swept across the plains in silvery sheets, transforming the dusty ranch into something wild and mysterious. The lights in the guest house remained steady and bright, a beacon in the gathering darkness, like a promise or a warning, he wasn't sure which. Whatever Annie was looking for, whatever she needed to prove, to her father or to herself, Jake had a feeling the next few months were going to change them both in ways neither of them could predict.

He just hoped his heart was ready for the storm that was coming.

CHAPTER TWO

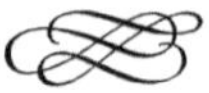

FASHION EMERGENCY

$\mathcal{A}$nnie showed up at the barn at exactly 5:15 AM, and Jake nearly choked on his morning coffee. She stood there in yoga pants that probably cost more than his saddle, pristine white tennis shoes, and what appeared to be a silk blouse in a shade of pink that would send his bulls running. Her golden hair was pulled back in a neat ponytail, and she'd even put on makeup. At five in the morning. For ranch work.

"You're late," he said, instead of commenting on her outfit. "And you're not dressed for this."

"I'm wearing athletic clothes," Annie protested, gesturing at her ensemble. "These are top-of-the-line performance wear. They wick moisture and everything." She pronounced it 'ev-ery-thing' in that Italian way that shouldn't have been charming but somehow was.

Jake set his coffee mug down on a fence post and crossed his arms. "Those fancy pants won't last ten minutes in the saddle, and those shoes..." He shook his head. "You'll ruin them in the first muddy patch you hit. And that shirt..." He couldn't even finish the sentence.

"What's wrong with my shirt?" Annie lifted her chin defiantly. "It's practical and breathable."

"It's silk," Jake said flatly. "And pink. Bright pink."

"So?"

"So the bulls hate pink. Makes 'em aggressive. And silk doesn't exactly hold up to barbed wire."

Annie's eyes widened slightly. "Barbed wire? Nobody said anything about barbed wire."

Jake couldn't help the small smile that tugged at his lips. "Welcome to ranch life, princess. Wait here." He turned and headed toward the house, calling over his shoulder, "And don't go near the bull pen in that outfit!"

Twenty minutes later, he returned with a cardboard box, dust floating off the top as he set it down. "These were my mother's. They should work until we can get you proper gear in town."

Annie peered into the box with the same expression she might use to examine a rattlesnake. She pulled out a pair of faded jeans, worn soft with age and work. "These are... vintage."

"They're practical," Jake corrected. "There's boots in there too. And some work shirts."

Annie lifted a plaid flannel shirt, holding it at arm's length. "This is... very... rustic."

"That's one word for it." Jake leaned against the barn door, watching her sort through the box with perfectly manicured fingers. "There's a bathroom in the barn. Get changed. We're already behind schedule."

Annie gathered the clothes, then paused. "Turn around."

"What?"

"Turn around. I know it's a bathroom, but it's a barn bathroom, and I don't trust that door to lock properly."

Jake rolled his eyes but turned his back. "No one out here cares what you're wearing, much less what you look like changing."

"I care," Annie shot back. He heard the bathroom door close firmly.

Ten minutes later, the door creaked open, and Jake turned to find Annie swimming in his mother's old clothes. The jeans were rolled up at the ankles, the shirt was tucked and belted to keep it from looking like a dress, and she'd managed to stuff her feet into the boots. She looked ridiculous. She looked adorable.

"Don't say a word," she warned, pointing a finger at him.

"Wasn't going to." But he was grinning now, unable to help himself. "But you might want to do something about that hair."

Annie's hand flew to her perfect ponytail. "What's wrong with my hair?"

"Nothing, if you want it full of hay and horse slobber by noon." He reached into the box and pulled out a battered straw hat. "Here."

She took it gingerly. "Please tell me you're joking."

"Nope. Sun protection is serious business out here." He adjusted his own hat. "Besides, can't have you getting freckles on that perfect nose of yours."

"I'll have you know freckles are very fashionable right now," Annie said, but she put the hat on anyway, adjusting it with surprising style.

"Alright, city girl. Let's see what you're made of. First lesson is feeding, and we're already behind because of your fashion show."

"I prefer to think of it as a wardrobe consultation," Annie replied primly, then ruined the effect by tripping slightly in the too-big boots. Jake caught her elbow, steadying her, and for a moment they were too close again, her looking up at him with those challenging blue eyes.

"You're going to be trouble, aren't you?" he murmured.

Annie's smile was bright and fierce. "Oh, you have no idea, cowboy. No idea at all."

The morning that followed was a comedy of errors that tested Jake's patience and, though he'd never admit it, his ability to keep a straight face. Annie insisted on naming every cow she saw. She shrieked when she stepped in something unpleasant. She tried to pet the chickens. But she never quit, never complained about the work itself, and when she managed to properly measure out feed portions on her first try, her triumphant smile made something warm unfurl in Jake's chest.

"Not bad," he admitted as they headed back to the barn. "For a beginner."

"High praise indeed," Annie said dryly. She was dusty, disheveled, and had a piece of hay stuck in her hair despite the hat. "I suppose tomorrow we tackle the barbed wire?"

"Nah, that was just to scare you." Jake reached over and plucked the hay from her hair before he could think better of it. "Tomorrow we start with the horses."

Annie's eyes lit up. "Horses? Real ones?"

"No, we keep imaginary ones out here for atmosphere," Jake drawled. "Yes, real ones. But if you show up in yoga pants again, you'll be mucking stalls instead."

"These clothes smell like mothballs," Annie complained, plucking at the flannel shirt.

"We'll go into town this weekend, get you properly outfitted." Jake paused, then added, "Though I got to say, you make mothballs look pretty good."

Annie's cheeks flushed pink, and for a moment Jake thought he'd overstepped. But then she smiled, slow and warm. "Careful, cowboy. A girl might think you're flirting with her."

Before Jake could respond to that dangerous observation, Annie had already turned and started walking toward the guest house, her stride more confident now in the borrowed boots. She called over her shoulder, "Same time tomorrow? I promise no silk!"

Jake watched her go, shaking his head. She was going to be trouble all right. The kind of trouble that could break a man's heart if he wasn't careful. And Jake Spyker had never been particularly careful when it came to matters of the heart.

Blue ambled up beside him, looking between Jake and Annie's retreating figure.

"Don't say it," Jake told the dog. "Don't say it."

Blue's expression clearly said he didn't need to. They were both thinking the same thing: this summer just got a whole lot more interesting.

Back in the guest house, Annie found a folded slip of paper in the flannel's pocket. Old. Soft at the edges. Pencil, faded.

She smoothed it under the lamp. Most of it was gone, names and dates rubbed into nothing, but one line still held.

Debt settled in full.

She crumpled the note and tossed it in the trash, like that ended it.

It didn't.

Lying in the dark a few minutes later, she kept seeing the words, and wondering what this debt must have cost.

CHAPTER THREE

LEARNING CURVES

"You can't keep wearing my mother's old clothes forever," Jake said over breakfast, watching Annie try to roll up sleeves that were three inches too long. "Town's got a decent Western wear store. We can head in after morning chores."

Annie looked up from her coffee, suspicious of the offer. After two days of his gruff instructions and minimal conversation, this sudden suggestion of a shopping trip seemed out of character. "We?"

"Someone's got to make sure you get proper work gear, not those fashion boots that'll get you killed." But there was a hint of amusement in his voice that made her heart do a little flip.

The Western wear store in town turned out to be nothing like the boutiques Annie was used to. The Three Rivers Trading Post occupied an old brick building on Main Street, its windows displaying sturdy boots and practical hats rather than the latest fashion trends. A bell jingled as they entered, and the smell of leather and denim wrapped around them.

"Jake Spyker!" A woman with silver-streaked hair pulled into a practical braid emerged from behind a display of work gloves.

"Haven't seen you in here since..." She trailed off, her eyes landing on Annie. "Well, now. This must be the Italian lady everyone's talking about."

"Mrs. Harrison," Jake nodded. "Annie needs a proper ranch wardrobe. Figured you'd know best what she'll need."

Mrs. Harrison's eyes lit up with the joy of a true clothier presented with a challenge. She circled Annie slowly, taking in her borrowed outfit and designer boots. "Honey, we're going to need to start from the ground up. Literally." She pointed at Annie's feet. "Those pretty things might work in I-tally," she drawled, mangling the word with the confident incorrectness of someone who'd never left Montana, "but they'll snap your ankle out here faster than a rattler strikes."

What followed was two hours of the most practical shopping Annie had ever experienced. Mrs. Harrison didn't just sell clothes, she educated. Each item came with an explanation of its purpose, its proper care, how it would protect Annie from the elements and hazards of ranch work.

"These jeans?" Mrs. Harrison held up a pair. "Triple-stitched seams, reinforced knees. They'll last through fence mending and cattle work. And this denim's pre-softened, won't have to break it in like the old days."

Jake leaned against a support post, watching with poorly concealed amusement as Annie emerged from the dressing room in various combinations of practical ranch wear. But when she stepped out in a pair of well-fitted jeans, properly broken-in boots, and a Western-cut shirt that actually fit, his expression changed. Something flickered in his eyes before he quickly looked away.

"Better," was all he said, but Annie caught Mrs. Harrison hiding a knowing smile.

The final bill would have bought a single designer handbag back in Milano. Instead, Annie had a complete working wardrobe: jeans, shirts, boots, work gloves, rain gear, and a hat that Mrs. Harrison insisted was essential for sun protection.

"Now then," Mrs. Harrison said as they finished loading their purchases into Jake's truck. "You'll be wanting something special for dancing tonight."

Annie blinked. "Dancing?"

"Saturday night at the Silver Dollar," Mrs. Harrison continued, ignoring Jake's warning look. "Best dance hall in Missoula. Jake used to be quite the dancer, before..." She caught herself. "Well, it's been a while."

The drive to Missoula was quiet, but not uncomfortably so. Annie watched the Montana landscape roll past, occasionally stealing glances at Jake. He seemed more relaxed away from the ranch, one hand loose on the steering wheel, the other resting on the seat between them.

The Silver Dollar was already buzzing when they arrived. Country music spilled out into the parking lot, along with laughter and the sound of boots on wooden floors. Annie smoothed down her new dress, a simple blue cotton thing that Mrs. Harrison had insisted would be perfect, suddenly nervous.

"Ready?" Jake asked softly.

Inside, the dance hall was a whirl of movement and music. Couples spun across the floor in complicated patterns that made Annie's head spin. But before she could feel too out of place, she noticed something. These weren't polished ballroom dancers executing perfect steps. These were real people, having real fun, laughing when they missed steps and holding each other closer than strictly necessary.

"Jake Spyker, as I live and breathe!" A tall man in a pearl-snap shirt approached them. "Thought you'd sworn off dancing for good."

"Evening, Bill." Jake's hand found the small of Annie's back, a gesture that felt both protective and possessive. "Annie, this is Bill Cooper. Owns the largest cattle operation this side of the divide."

Bill's weathered face broke into a genuine smile. "So you're the I-tallian lady," he said, mangling the word just like Mrs. Harrison had, "who's got the whole county talking. Welcome to Montana." He turned to Jake, eyes twinkling with mischief. "You going to show this pretty blonde gal how we dance out here, or do I need to find her a partner who remembers how?"

Something sparked in Jake's eyes, pride maybe, or competition. Without a word, he held out his hand to Annie just as the band started a slow song.

"I should warn you," Annie said as he led her onto the floor. "I only know formal ballroom steps."

"Forget everything you learned in those fancy studios," Jake murmured, pulling her close. "This is simpler. Just follow my lead."

And somehow, it was simpler. Jake's hand was warm on her waist, his movements sure and steady. Annie found herself relaxing into the rhythm, letting him guide her through the steps. When he spun her, she caught glimpses of other dancers watching them, smiling approvingly.

"They're staring," she whispered after a particularly smooth turn.

"Not at your dancing," Jake replied, his voice low near her ear. "At how beautiful you look in that dress."

The compliment, delivered so matter-of-factly, made her cheeks warm. Before she could respond, the music changed to something faster. Jake's eyes lit with challenge.

"Trust me?"

What followed was a crash course in country swing dancing. Annie lost count of how many times she stepped on Jake's boots, but he never stopped smiling, never loosened his hold on her hand. Between dances, he bought her a Bud Light from the bar, and Annie found herself staring at the blue aluminum can like it was some exotic specimen. She'd never had beer before, her world had been all crystal champagne flutes and carefully aged wines. But something about the cold, crisp taste felt right here, simpler and somehow more honest than all the expensive champagne she'd sipped at Milano galas. By the end of the night, she was breathless, laughing, and feeling more alive than she had in years, though whether that was from the dancing, the beer, or the way Jake kept looking at her when he thought she wouldn't notice, she couldn't quite say.

The drive back to the ranch was quiet again, but this time the silence hummed with something new. Annie's hand rested on the seat between them, and somewhere along the dark highway, Jake's fingers brushed against hers. Neither of them moved away.

Sunday morning dawned clear and warm. Annie woke to the smell of coffee and bacon drifting from the main house. She dressed in her new clothes, appreciating how much easier everything was when it actually fit.

Jake was at the stove when she entered his kitchen, looking surprisingly domestic in worn jeans and a soft flannel shirt. "Thought you might want a real ranch breakfast before your first riding lesson."

The spread he'd prepared was nothing like her usual continental breakfast: fluffy pancakes, crispy bacon, eggs over easy, and coffee strong enough to stand a spoon in. They ate on his back porch, watching the sun climb over the eastern pastures.

"My father would have a heart attack if he saw me eating like this," Annie said, swiping a piece of bacon through egg yolk.

"Your father might have a lot of heart attacks in the coming weeks," Jake replied, but his tone was gentle.

After breakfast, they walked to the barn together. The morning air was sweet with hay and possibility. Jake led out a gentle gelding named Rusty, explaining each piece of tack as he demonstrated proper saddling technique.

"Always check your cinch twice," he said, running his hands along the saddle straps. "A loose saddle can roll, and that's a quick trip to the hospital."

Annie tried to focus on the technical details, but she kept getting distracted by Jake's hands, strong and sure on the leather, capable of such gentleness with the horse. When it was her turn to try saddling, he stood close behind her, guiding her movements.

"Like this," he murmured, his hands covering hers on the leather straps. Annie was suddenly very aware of his chest against her back, his breath stirring her hair.

The round pen lesson that followed was both easier and harder than she expected. Easier because Rusty was patient, responding to the slightest cue. Harder because Jake's instructions, delivered in that deep voice of his, kept making her lose focus.

"You're a natural," he said as she successfully guided Rusty through a series of turns. "Just remember to keep your heels down and your eyes up."

Eyes up. Annie stole a glance at him, leaning against the round pen fence in the Sunday morning light. He was watching her with an expression that made her breath catch, pride mixed with something warmer, something that made her think of dark dance halls and shared silence on long drives home.

"I think that's enough for today," Jake said finally, helping her dismount. His hands lingered on her waist a moment longer than necessary. "Don't want to overdo it your first time."

As they led Rusty back to the barn, Annie realized something had shifted between them. The gruff rancher who'd greeted her arrival with skepticism had been replaced by someone else, someone who danced and cooked breakfast and taught with infinite patience. Someone who looked at her like she was more than just an Italian heiress playing at ranch life.

Someone who made her heart race with a simple touch, made her laugh with a raised eyebrow, made her feel more herself than she had in years.

"Thank you," she said softly as they finished untacking Rusty. "For everything."

Jake paused in coiling a lead rope, meeting her eyes. "You're doing all the hard work. I'm just showing you the way."

But they both knew he was showing her more than that. He was showing her a whole new world, a new way of living, a new way of being. And somewhere between designer boots and practical ones, between formal ballroom steps and country swing, between Milano sophistication and Montana simplicity, Annie was discovering who she really wanted to be.

The fact that this discovery seemed tied to the quiet rancher beside her was something she'd have to examine later. How had she not noticed his eyes and how stunningly handsome he was? For now, she was content to help him finish the barn chores, stealing glances at him in the Sunday morning light, wondering if he felt it too, this sense that something important was beginning, as natural and unstoppable as the Montana sunrise.

CHAPTER FOUR

STORM WARNING

*J*ake knew something was wrong the moment he stepped onto his front porch at dawn. The air felt heavy, charged with an electricity that had nothing to do with the weather, and Blue was pacing instead of settling down for his usual morning nap. Then he heard it, the distinctive bawling of cattle in distress.

He was already running toward the south pasture when he spotted Annie hurrying from the guest house, this time properly dressed in the new ranching clothes they'd bought in town over the weekend. At least she was learning.

"What's happening?" she called out, jogging to catch up with him. Her boots were actually laced properly this time, and she'd forgone makeup for their early start.

"Trouble," he said grimly. "Sounds like the herd's spooked. Could be wolves, could be a broken fence." He whistled for Blue, who was already racing ahead of them. "You should stay here."

Annie's jaw set in that stubborn way he was coming to recognize. "I didn't come to Montana to stay inside when things get difficult."

There wasn't time to argue. They crested the hill together, and

Jake's heart sank at what he saw. The fence along the south pasture was down in three places, probably from the storm two nights ago, and at least thirty head of cattle had pushed through. Even worse, they were heading toward Miller's Creek, dangerous in the best conditions, deadly after heavy rains.

"We need to head them off before they reach the creek," he said, already turning toward the stables. "You remember your riding lessons from yesterday?"

"Enough to stay on and steer," Annie replied, keeping pace with him. "Probably."

"That'll have to do." They reached the barn. Jake threw a saddle on Spike while Annie went to Rusty, the gentle gelding he'd been using to teach her. To his surprise, she saddled him almost perfectly, fumbling only a little at the cinch.

"Stay behind me," he instructed as they mounted up. "If I tell you to pull back, you pull back immediately. No questions."

"What about the rest of the herd?" Annie asked, adjusting her seat with more confidence than he'd expected.

"They're still contained, but spooked. We get the strays first, then repair the fence before the others follow." He looked at her seriously. "This isn't a lesson, Annie. This is real ranching. Things can go wrong fast out here."

Something flickered in her eyes, not fear, but understanding. "I know the risks, Jake. My father didn't just invest in ranches; he worked them when he was young. Before he became... what he is now." She squared her shoulders. "I'm not here just to prove something to him. I'm here to prove something to myself."

The admission caught him off guard, but there wasn't time to dig deeper. The cattle were moving fast, and the sound of rushing water was getting closer. They spurred their horses forward, Blue running alongside them, as the first drops of rain began to fall.

What followed was the kind of controlled chaos that Jake had trained for but never wanted to experience. The cattle were panicked, slipping in the mud as they tried to navigate the steep creek bank. One cow had already lost her footing, bellowing in distress as she slid toward the rushing water.

"Circle wide!" Jake shouted over the rain, which was falling harder now. "Don't let them bunch up at the bank!"

To his amazement, Annie didn't hesitate. She guided her horse in a wide arc, just as he'd taught her, helping to turn the cattle back toward safer ground. She was soaked through, her hair plastered to her face, but her expression was pure concentration.

Then everything went sideways. A crack of thunder spooked both cattle and horses. Annie's gelding reared, and for a heart-stopping moment, Jake thought she would fall. But she grabbed the saddle horn and held on, somehow keeping her seat. The real problem, though, was that the noise had sent several more cows scrambling toward the creek.

"Annie!" Jake called out. "Stay with the main group. Blue and I will get the others!"

But Annie was already moving, guiding her horse carefully along the creek bank. "They're going to slip!" she shouted back. "We need to get closer!"

Before Jake could stop her, she had dismounted and was approaching the stranded cattle on foot. His heart nearly stopped when she slipped in the mud herself, but she caught herself on a tree branch. Moving with surprising grace for someone in her first week of ranch work, she managed to get behind the stranded cows, using her voice and presence to urge them away from the creek bank.

It was either the bravest or stupidest thing he'd ever seen. Probably both.

Together, they managed to herd the cattle back toward safer ground. By the time the last cow was clear of the creek, they were both exhausted, covered in mud, and soaked to the bone. But when Annie looked at him, her eyes were bright with triumph.

"Still think I'm just a city girl?" she asked, trying to wipe mud from her face but only managing to smear it more.

Jake dismounted Spike and walked over to her, his boots squelching in the mud. "That," he said slowly, "was either incredibly brave or incredibly foolish."

"Is there a difference out here?"

"Not always." He reached out without thinking and wiped a streak of mud from her cheek with his thumb. "But what you did... that was pure rancher. Your father would be proud."

Something complicated crossed her face. "My father hasn't been proud of me since I told him I wanted to actually work the ranches instead of just managing them from an office in Milano."

"His loss," Jake said softly, his hand still lingering near her face. They were standing very close now, the rain falling softer around them, and for a moment the whole world seemed to hold its breath.

Then Blue barked, reminding them they still had work to do.

"We should get back," Jake said, stepping away. "Check the rest of the herd, repair those fences before dark."

Annie nodded, already moving toward her horse. "I'll help. I'm already filthy, might as well make it count."

Jake watched her mount up with practiced ease, as if she'd been riding all her life instead of just two days. She was full of surprises, this one. And with each surprise, the walls he'd built around his heart developed another crack.

"Coming, cowboy?" she called back to him, already turning her horse toward the broken fence.

"Right behind you," he replied, and he was, right behind her, falling for her, and completely unable to stop either one.

CHAPTER FIVE

FATHER'S DAUGHTER

*A*nnie sat on the porch of the guest house, watching the sunset paint the mountains in shades of purple and gold. Her muscles ached from the day's work, Jake had her mending fences all afternoon, but it was a good kind of pain, the kind that meant you'd accomplished something real. Her phone buzzed for the third time that evening, her father's name flashing on the screen. With a sigh, she finally answered.

"Pronto, Papa."

"Antoinette." Her father's voice was crisp, professional. Always professional these days. "I've been trying to reach you all day."

"I was working, Papa. Actually working. You know, like you used to?"

The silence that followed was heavy with decades of expectations and disappointments. "The board meeting is next week. I need you back in Milano."

"No." Annie stood, pacing the weathered boards of the porch. "We had an agreement. Three months here, learning the operation from the ground up. It's barely been two weeks."

"Things have changed. The Rossi merger... "

"The Rossi merger can wait." Annie caught movement near the main house, Jake leading his horse to the stable for the night. Even from this distance, his movements held a grace that came from absolute belonging. "I'm not coming back until I understand this business. Really understand it."

"You understand plenty," her father countered. "Top of your class at Bocconi University, MBA from London Business School. You've sat in on every major acquisition meeting since you were twenty-two."

"I understand spreadsheets and profit margins," Annie said, watching Jake disappear into the stable. "But I don't understand this." She gestured at the ranch around her, even though her father couldn't see it. "The land, the animals, the people who make it all work. How can I make decisions that affect their lives when I've never lived it myself?"

"Ah." Her father's voice took on that knowing tone she hated. "This is about Ricardo."

Annie's grip tightened on her phone. "This has nothing to do with Ricardo."

"No? The timing seems convenient. He announces his engagement to that Brazilian heiress, and suddenly you need to 'find yourself' on some ranch in Montana?"

"That's not fair." But the words stung, probably because there was a grain of truth in them. Ricardo's engagement had been the final push, the thing that made her realize how empty her life in Milano had become. All the parties, the social obligations, the carefully orchestrated business meetings, none of it felt real anymore.

"Life isn't fair, *piccola*." Her father's voice softened, just slightly. "Look, two things. First, I've spoken with Ricardo. He's having second thoughts about the engagement. I think he's starting to come to his senses about his relationship with you."

He paused.

"And second, you have responsibilities. To the company. To our family name."

"Like you did?" The words came out sharper than she intended. "You used to tell me stories about working the ranches in Tuscany, about how much you loved it. What happened to that man, Papa?"

The silence stretched between them, filled with all the things they never talked about, her mother's death, the way her father had thrown himself into building his empire afterward, the growing distance between them as Annie tried desperately to be the daughter he wanted while losing sight of who she wanted to be.

"That man," her father finally said, "learned that dreams don't pay bills. Dreams don't secure your future."

"No," Annie agreed, "but maybe they make that future worth having." She watched as Jake emerged from the stable, pausing to look toward her house. Even in the growing darkness, she could feel the weight of his gaze. "I'm learning things here, Papa. Important things."

"About ranching?" Her father's skepticism was clear.

"About everything." About herself, about what she really wanted, about the kind of person she could be when she wasn't trying to live up to someone else's expectations. "The board meeting can proceed without me. The merger documents are all prepared. I reviewed them myself before I left."

She paused, then added, "Plus, that was our agreement. Three months of learning on a real ranch, and an 'optional' return for board meetings."

Another pause, deliberate this time.

"I'm executing my optional return," she said. "I'm staying here."

"And what am I supposed to tell the board when they ask why my heir apparent is playing cowgirl in America?"

"Tell them..." Annie straightened her spine, channeling the

strength she'd felt earlier when she'd successfully herded cattle through a storm. "Tell them that the future CEO of Contadelucci Agricultural Investments is conducting hands-on research into our largest sector. Tell them I'm not just following in your foot-steps, I'm blazing my own trail."

"You sound like your mother." It wasn't quite an accusation, but it wasn't quite a compliment either.

"Good." Annie felt tears prick at her eyes. "Mama would have understood this."

Another long silence. Then, "Two more weeks, Antoinette. Then I expect you back in Milano."

"Three months, Papa. Like we agreed. I'm not asking for your blessing anymore, I'm telling you how it's going to be."

She ended the call before he could respond, her hands shaking slightly. When she looked up, Jake was standing at the bottom of her porch steps, a concerned expression on his face.

"Everything okay?" he asked softly. "I was coming to check if you wanted to join me for dinner, but I heard... well, I heard enough to know it might not be a good time."

Annie wiped at her eyes, surprised to find herself smiling despite everything. "Actually, it's a perfect time. I could use a reminder of why I'm here."

"And why is that?" Jake climbed the steps slowly, keeping a respectful distance but close enough that she could smell hay and horses and honest work on him.

"To become who I am," she said, "instead of who everyone expects me to be." She met his eyes in the gathering dusk. "Does that sound crazy?"

"Sounds like the most sensible thing I've heard all day." He gestured toward his house. "Come on. Blue makes a great listener, and I've got soup on the stove. Nothing fancy, but... "

"Perfect," Annie interrupted. "Fancy is exactly what I'm trying to get away from."

As they walked toward his house, Annie felt something settle in her chest. Her father was wrong about this place, about her reasons for being here. Ricardo's engagement might have been the catalyst, but this journey was about so much more than a failed romance. It was about finding the piece of herself that had gotten lost somewhere between board meetings and charity galas.

And maybe, just maybe, it was about finding something, or someone, she never knew she was looking for.

CHAPTER SIX

ALMOST PERFECT

The soup was simple, beef, vegetables, and barley, but Annie couldn't remember the last time food had tasted this good. Maybe it was the honest hunger earned from a day's work, or maybe it was the way Jake watched her from across his worn kitchen table, his eyes holding hers a moment longer than necessary each time she looked up.

"So," she said, tearing off a piece of crusty bread, "do you cook for all your ranch hands, or am I special?"

The corner of Jake's mouth quirked up. "Don't have many ranch hands who show up wearing silk shirts on their first day."

"Are you ever going to let me live that down?"

"Not likely." He leaned back in his chair, relaxed in a way she rarely saw him during working hours. The kitchen was warm from the stove, and he'd rolled up his sleeves, revealing tanned forearms corded with muscle. "Though I have to admit, you've improved since then."

"High praise from the man who spent twenty minutes this morning teaching me the proper way to coil rope."

"Important skill out here." His eyes crinkled at the corners.

"Never know when you might need to lasso something. Or someone."

Annie felt heat rise to her cheeks that had nothing to do with the soup. "Are you implying I need corralling, Mr. Spyker?"

"I think we both know you're untameable, Miss Contadelucci."

The way he said her name, with that slight drawl, sent a shiver down her spine. She covered it by reaching for her water glass, but her fingers brushed his as he moved to refill it. Neither pulled away immediately.

"It's getting dark," she said softly, though the sun had set hours ago.

"It is." He still hadn't moved his hand.

"I should probably head back to the guest house."

"Probably."

Neither of them moved. Blue, who had been dozing by the wood stove, lifted his head to watch them with what Annie swore was amusement.

"Or," Jake said, his voice low, "you could stay for coffee."

"Coffee sounds nice." Annie wasn't thinking about coffee at all. She was thinking about the way the lamplight caught his eyes, how his shirt stretched across his shoulders, the quiet strength in his hands that could be so gentle with injured calves.

Jake stood, moving to the counter where an old percolator sat. Annie found herself following him, drawn like a magnet. He reached for the coffee tin on a high shelf, and she noticed a scar on his arm.

"What's this from?" She traced it lightly with her finger before she could think better of it.

Jake went still under her touch. "Barbed wire. First year running the ranch on my own. Made some rookie mistakes."

"And now?" She was standing very close to him now, close enough to feel the heat radiating from his body.

"Now I make entirely different kinds of mistakes." He turned to face her, and suddenly the kitchen felt very small. His eyes dropped to her lips, then back to her eyes. "Annie..."

She tilted her face up to his, her heart thundering in her chest. One of his hands came up to cup her cheek, callused fingers impossibly gentle against her skin. She could feel his breath, count his eyelashes, sense the slight tremor in his hand that told her he was just as affected as she was.

"Jake," she whispered, and she barely recognized her own voice.

Then Blue erupted in a series of sharp barks, springing up from his place by the stove. Before either of them could move, the front door burst open.

"Boss!" Tommy, the teenage boy who helped with weekend work, stumbled into the kitchen. "There's, oh, sorry, I didn't..." He flushed bright red at finding them standing so close.

Jake stepped back, his rancher's instincts taking over. "What's wrong?"

"Lights out in the north pasture," Tommy panted. "Bunch of 'em. Moving fast. Jenkins from up the road called, says two of his bulls went missing today. Thinks it might be rustlers."

The warm, intimate atmosphere of moments ago evaporated. Jake was already reaching for his jacket. "Get the trucks started. I'll call the sheriff." He turned to Annie. "You should... "

"If you tell me to stay here, we're going to have our first real fight," she cut in, already pulling on her boots.

A ghost of a smile crossed his face despite the situation. "Was going to say you should get the rifles from the gun safe. You remember the combination?"

Annie nodded, her pulse quickening for entirely different reasons now. "Like you taught me yesterday."

"Good girl." He caught himself, meeting her eyes. "Good ranch manager," he corrected softly.

Then they were both moving, the almost-kiss hanging between them like smoke, impossible to catch and impossible to forget. Whatever was happening in the north pasture would have their full attention, but Annie had a feeling she'd be replaying those moments in the kitchen for a long time to come.

And judging by the look Jake gave her as they headed out into the night, she wasn't the only one.

CHAPTER SEVEN

DARK NIGHT, BRIGHT STARS

nnie's heart refused to slow as they drove through the darkness, and it had nothing to do with the potential danger ahead. Jake sat beside her in the truck, one hand on the wheel, the other resting on the rifle between them, and even in the crisis, she couldn't help but be aware of every inch of space between them. The almost-kiss in the kitchen played on repeat in her mind, like a movie she couldn't stop watching. The way his hand had felt on her cheek, the warmth of his breath, the look in his eyes that made her knees weak, all of it haunted her even now.

The truck bounced over the rutted ranch road, and her shoulder brushed against his. Even that slight contact sent electricity coursing through her body. This was madness. They were heading toward what could be dangerous criminals, and all she could think about was how his aftershave mixed perfectly with the leather of his jacket and the crisp Montana night air.

"You okay?" Jake's voice was low, concerned, and it did nothing to help her racing pulse.

"Fine," she managed, though she was anything but fine. How

could she be fine when every cell in her body seemed to be reaching for him like a flower turning toward the sun?

The headlights cut through the darkness, illuminating fence posts and scrub brush. In the distance, Tommy's truck followed them, Blue riding in the back. Annie gripped the door handle tighter, trying to focus on the task at hand instead of the way Jake's profile looked in the starlight, all sharp angles and quiet strength.

"Sheriff's ten minutes out," Jake said, checking his phone. "We'll park up ahead and wait."

Annie nodded, not trusting her voice. They were heading into potential danger, and yet she felt safer than she ever had in Milano. Jake's presence beside her was like a shield, solid and reassuring. When had that happened? When had this man, this place, become somewhere she felt so completely protected?

The truck slowed as they approached the north pasture. Jake killed the engine but left the keys in the ignition, always prepared. The silence that fell was deafening. Annie could hear her own heartbeat, the soft whisper of Jake's breath, the distant sound of crickets.

"See those lights?" Jake whispered, pointing toward the far end of the pasture.

Annie leaned closer to follow his gesture, caught a whiff of his skin, sage and sunshine and something uniquely Jake, and nearly forgot what she was supposed to be looking for. But then she saw them: pinpricks of light moving in the distance, too steady to be stars.

"Flashlights," she whispered back. Her hand found his arm in the darkness, squeezing gently. "What's the plan?"

Jake turned to answer her and their faces were suddenly very close. In the dim light from the dashboard, she could see the flecks of black in his dark blue eyes, count each of his eyelashes, trace the curve of his lips with her gaze. Time seemed to stop, the potential danger forgotten for one endless moment.

"Annie..." The way he said her name was like a prayer and a warning all at once.

A tap on the window made them both jump. Tommy stood outside, pointing urgently toward the lights, which were now moving faster. The spell broke, but the electricity between them remained, crackling like static in the air.

They slipped out of the truck, and Jake immediately took charge, all business now. But as he outlined the plan to Tommy, Annie saw his eyes keep drifting back to her, as if he couldn't help himself. The knowledge that he was just as affected as she was made her feel powerful and vulnerable all at once.

"Annie, you stay with the trucks," Jake said, but there was a gentleness in his voice that hadn't been there two weeks ago. "If you hear anything that sounds like trouble... "

"I'll call the sheriff and then come after you with the rifle," she finished. At his look, she added, "What? I'm a quick study."

The ghost of a smile crossed his face, and for a moment she saw the echo of their kitchen moment in his eyes. "That you are."

Then he and Tommy were moving into the darkness, leaving Annie with her racing thoughts and the memory of almost-kisses. She watched Jake's figure disappear into the night, her heart reaching after him like a compass needle finding true north. When had this happened? When had this quiet, strong man become the center of her world?

The Montana night stretched endless above her, stars scattered like diamond dust across black velvet. So different from the hazy skies of Milano, just as Jake was different from any man she'd ever known. Ricardo, with his polished manners and calculated charm, seemed like a character from another life now. Jake was real in a way no one else had ever been, as solid and true as the mountains themselves.

A noise in the darkness snapped her back to attention. Annie gripped the rifle, her body tense, ready for whatever came next. But her mind kept drifting back to the kitchen, to the way Jake's hand had felt on her cheek, to the look in his eyes that told her he wanted to kiss her as badly as she wanted to be kissed.

Blue whined softly from Tommy's truck, and Annie reached over to scratch his ears. "I know, boy," she whispered. "I'm worried about him too."

The confession felt big in the quiet night, not just that she was worried, but that she cared enough to worry. That somehow, in just two weeks, this man and this place had worked their way into her heart like roots growing through rich soil. Whatever happened tonight with the rustlers, Annie knew one thing for certain: she was falling hard for Jake Spyker, and there wasn't a thing in the world she could do about it.

More concerning still was the fact that she didn't want to do anything about it. For the first time in her life, she was exactly where she wanted to be, falling for exactly the right person at exactly the right time. If only they could get through this night, if only they could find their way back to that perfect moment in the kitchen...

A gunshot cracked through the night, shattering her thoughts.

Annie was moving before she could think twice, her heart in her throat. Somewhere in the darkness was the man she was falling in love with, and nothing, not rustlers, not her father's expectations, not her own fears, was going to keep her from making sure he was safe.

The night swallowed her up as she ran toward the sound, the rifle steady in her hands, her boots sure on the familiar ground. And with every step, every breath, every beat of her heart, she knew with growing certainty that her life would never be the same after tonight. Whether that was because of the danger they faced or the love blooming in her chest, she couldn't say.

Maybe it was both. Maybe that's what real love was, being ready to face any danger, any challenge, any storm, as long as you could face it together.

CHAPTER EIGHT

WORTH THE RISK

Annie's heart pounded as she moved through the darkness, every sense heightened. The gunshot had come from the direction of the old north barn, and a sick feeling churned in her stomach at the thought of Jake in danger. She'd never fired a gun at anything but paper targets, but her grip on the rifle was steady. For Jake, she'd find the courage to do whatever was necessary.

A hand grabbed her arm from behind, and she nearly screamed before a familiar scent, sage and sunshine, registered. Jake pulled her behind a large oak tree, his body shielding hers.

"What happened to staying with the trucks?" he whispered, his breath warm against her ear.

"What happened to not getting shot at?" she countered, trying to ignore how his proximity made her pulse race even in the midst of danger.

A flash of movement caught their attention. Two figures were running from the old barn toward an idling pickup truck. Tommy appeared from behind the barn, clutching his arm.

"Tommy's hurt," Annie gasped, starting to move, but Jake held her back.

"Wait," he breathed. "There might be more of them."

As if on cue, a third figure emerged from the shadows, raising what looked like a rifle. Without thinking, Annie shoved Jake hard, sending them both tumbling to the ground as a shot cracked overhead. They rolled together, Jake taking the brunt of the fall, one arm cradling her head protectively.

For a split second, their eyes met in the darkness. Despite the danger, despite everything, Annie felt that familiar electricity spark between them. Then Jake was moving, rolling them again so she was behind him as he raised his own rifle.

"That's far enough!" Jake's voice boomed across the pasture. "Next shot won't be a warning!"

The third figure froze, then bolted toward the pickup. Annie, still on the ground, saw what Jake couldn't, a fourth man emerging from behind them with a raised weapon.

"Jake!" She grabbed his belt and yanked hard, pulling him down just as another shot split the night. In the distance, Blue's barking grew closer, and red and blue lights began to flash on the horizon. The would-be rustlers apparently saw them too, because the pickup's engine roared to life.

"You okay?" Jake's hands were suddenly on her face, checking for injuries, his touch sending shivers through her despite the adrenaline coursing through her veins.

"I'm fine," she assured him, her own hands moving to his chest, needing to verify he was unharmed. "Tommy... "

"Here, boss!" Tommy called out, jogging toward them while still holding his arm. "Just grazed me. Tried to stop them loading up the cattle, but... "

"But you did exactly right," Jake cut in, finally pulling away from Annie though his hand lingered on her shoulder. "Getting yourself killed wouldn't have helped the cattle."

The sheriff's cars were pulling up now, and in their headlights Annie could see the pickup truck disappearing over the ridge.

She started to stand, but her legs were shaking from the after-math of adrenaline. Jake's arm slipped around her waist, steady and strong.

"I've got you," he murmured, and she knew he meant more than just physically supporting her.

The next hour passed in a blur of sheriff's questions, para-medics checking Tommy's arm (just a deep graze, thankfully), and calling neighboring ranches to warn them about the rustlers. Through it all, Jake stayed close to Annie, his hand finding excuses to touch her, guiding her over rough ground, passing her coffee from a thermos, brushing hair from her face when the wind kicked up.

Finally, they were alone again, leaning against his truck and watching the last of the sheriff's cars disappear down the ranch road. The adrenaline had faded, leaving behind a bone-deep exhaustion and something else, something electric and unavoidable.

"You could have been killed," Jake said softly, turning to face her. "When I heard that gunshot and knew you'd left the trucks..."

"You could have been killed too," Annie replied, meeting his intense gaze. "I wasn't going to just wait there while you were in danger."

"Annie." Her name was rough in his throat. His hand came up to cup her cheek, just like in the kitchen hours ago, but this time there was an urgency to his touch. "When I saw that rifle aimed at you..."

"I know." She leaned into his touch, her own hand coming up to cover his. "I felt the same way when I saw the man behind you. I've never been so scared. Or so sure."

"Sure?"

"Sure that I'd do anything to protect you." The words came out in a rush. "Sure that whatever this is between us, it's worth any risk."

Jake's other hand found her waist, pulling her closer. The night air was cool, but Annie felt like she was burning anywhere he touched her. His eyes searched hers, asking a question they both knew the answer to.

A distant howl made them both jump, then laugh softly at their own nerves. Blue, who had been patrolling the perimeter, came trotting up to them, his tail wagging.

"Some guard dog you are," Jake murmured, but his eyes never left Annie's face. "Showing up after all the excitement's over."

"Maybe he just knows when to give people a moment alone," Annie suggested, her fingers playing with the collar of Jake's jacket.

"Maybe." Jake's thumb brushed over her cheekbone. "Though our track record with moments alone isn't great tonight."

"Then maybe we should stop waiting for the perfect moment." Annie raised herself up on her toes, bringing their faces close enough that she could feel his sharp intake of breath. "Maybe we should just... "

The rest of her words were lost as Jake's lips finally found hers. The kiss was gentle at first, tentative, but quickly deepened into something that made Annie's knees weak. His arms wrapped around her waist as hers wound around his neck, and the whole world seemed to disappear except for this, the taste of him, the solid strength of his body against hers, the way her heart felt like it might burst from too much feeling.

When they finally broke apart, they were both breathing hard. Jake rested his forehead against hers, his hands spanning her back like he couldn't bear to let her go.

"Worth the wait?" he asked, his voice husky.

Annie smiled, playing with the hair at the nape of his neck. "Worth everything."

Blue barked once, as if in agreement, and they both laughed. But as Jake pulled her in for another kiss, Annie knew she'd spoken nothing but truth. This man, this place, this life, it was all worth any risk, any danger, any challenge the world might throw at them.

She just prayed the world would throw fewer armed rustlers their way in the future. Though with Jake's arms around her and his heart beating steady against hers, she had a feeling they could face anything together.

CHAPTER NINE

GHOSTS AND DOUBTS

*D*awn found Jake already in the barn, methodically brushing down Midnight even though she'd been brushed the night before. He hadn't slept. Every time he closed his eyes, he felt Annie's lips on his, tasted the sweetness of her mouth, heard the soft sound she'd made when he'd pulled her closer. The memory was both heaven and torture, heaven because it had been perfect, torture because he couldn't stop wondering if he'd made a terrible mistake.

The kiss had been everything. And that was exactly the problem.

He'd known Annie less than three weeks, but she'd somehow worked her way under his skin, into his blood, becoming as essential as breathing. The way she'd faced down danger last night, the way she'd protected him without hesitation, the way she'd looked at him in the starlight, it was all too much, too fast, too real.

The brush caught on a knot in Midnight's mane, and Jake forced himself to gentle his strokes. The mare shifted, sensing his unease.

"Sorry, girl," he murmured. "Got a lot on my mind."

As if on cue, Annie's phone rang from the direction of the guest house. Even at this distance, the sound carried across the quiet morning air. Jake's hands stilled on the brush. After their kiss last night, after walking her to her door and sharing one more soft goodnight kiss, he'd promised to make her breakfast. But now, in the harsh light of day, doubts gnawed at him.

What could he possibly offer someone like her? She was Italian aristocracy, educated at Europe's finest schools, heir to an agricultural empire. And he was... what? A rancher with dirt under his nails and barely two nickels to rub together. The bank note on the ranch was due for renewal soon, and the rustlers last night were just another reminder of how precarious this life could be.

Blue nudged his hand, whining softly.

"I know, boy," Jake sighed. "I'm overthinking it."

The sound of tires on gravel made Jake look up. A sleek black rental car rolled toward the guest house, the kind you didn't see on these roads unless someone was lost or someone was trying not to be. Jake stepped to the barn door and watched a man climb out of the driver's side.

Even at this distance, everything about him signaled money. A tailored suit that didn't wrinkle, shoes that hadn't met mud, a casual elegance that suggested he expected the world to accommodate him.

Annie appeared on her porch, phone still in hand, and Jake saw her freeze.

"Ricardo?"

The name hit him hard, not because he knew it, but because she did. Her voice tightened around it, as if it had teeth. Jake's hand closed on the barn door while he watched the scene unfold.

"Surprise, *cara mia!*" The man's voice carried easily in the morning air, cultured and confident. He spread his arms wide, like he expected her to run into them. "Your father told me where to find you."

Annie didn't move. "What are you doing here?"

"Coming to my senses." Ricardo started toward the porch steps. "This engagement to Sophia, it's a mistake. I've known it all along, but seeing you run away to this…" He gestured at the ranch with elegant disdain. "This wilderness. It made me realize what I was losing."

Jake should've looked away. He should've gone back to his chores and pretended he couldn't hear every word. Instead, he stayed rooted, heart thumping in a way that made him angry with himself.

"Ricardo." Annie's voice was tight. "You shouldn't have come."

"No?" Ricardo reached the steps. "Then why did you go so far? Why hide out here if not to make me chase you?"

"I didn't run from you." The words came quick, but Jake caught the slight wobble under them. "This isn't about you."

Ricardo smiled, like he'd heard that line before and already owned the ending. "Everything has always been about us, *cara*. Since we were children." He took another step up. "I know I hurt you. Let me make it right."

Jake turned away. He couldn't watch it anymore.

His movements went mechanical as he finished with Midnight and moved on to Spike and the other horses. The kiss from last night suddenly felt foolish, like a dream he'd been naïve to believe in.

He didn't know what Ricardo was to her, not fully, but he knew what he looked like standing there in that suit. He looked like a past with roots. Like a man who'd been in her life long before Montana, long before Jake. A man who could offer her a world that didn't involve busted fence posts and storm repairs.

Jake kept his head down and worked, forcing his hands to stay steady while his chest did everything but.

The morning passed in a blur. Jake threw himself into work, taking the most difficult tasks, the ones that required all his concentration. He moved cattle to the south pasture, mended the fence damaged in last night's confrontation, anything to keep his mind off the scene he'd witnessed.

But every quiet moment brought it all rushing back, not just Ricardo's arrival, but everything that had come before. The way Annie's eyes sparkled when she mastered a new skill. How her laugh seemed to brighten the whole ranch. The fierce determination she'd shown last night, protecting him without hesitation. The softness of her lips, the way she'd melted into him, the perfect rightness of holding her.

"Jake?"

He startled, nearly dropping the fence post he was setting. Annie stood a few yards away, looking uncertain. She'd changed into work clothes, his mother's old jeans, a flannel shirt, boots that were starting to show real wear. The sight made his heart ache.

"Busy day," he said, turning back to the fence. "Lot to repair after last night."

"Jake." Her voice was closer now. "About Ricardo… "

"None of my business." The words came out harder than he'd intended. He softened his tone. "You don't owe me any explanations."

"Yes, I do." She moved into his line of sight, forcing him to look at her. "After last night… "

"Last night was…" He couldn't find the right words. Amazing. Terrifying. Everything. "Last night was intense. We'd both been through something dangerous. Emotions were high."

He saw the hurt flash across her face before she masked it. "Is that all it was to you? Adrenaline?"

No, he wanted to say. It was everything. It was the moment I realized I could fall in love with you. Instead, he said, "Maybe it's better if we keep things professional."

"Professional?" Annie's voice rose slightly. "You're going to stand there and tell me that kiss was professional?"

"Annie… "

"No." She stepped closer, fire in her eyes. "You don't get to dismiss what happened. Not after everything we've been through. Not after... "

"Cara!" Ricardo's voice carried across the pasture. He was walking toward them, somehow managing to make even ranch mud look like his natural environment. "There you are. I thought we could continue our conversation over lunch."

Jake watched something complicated cross Annie's face, irritation, confusion, maybe a hint of their shared history. And why shouldn't there be? She and Ricardo probably had years of inside jokes, shared memories, a common world that Jake could never understand.

"I have work to do," Annie said, but her voice wasn't as firm as before.

"All this can wait, surely?" Ricardo gestured at the fence. "I've come all this way..."

"The cattle can't wait," Jake cut in, his voice professional, distant. "And Miss Contadelucci has responsibilities here." He turned to Annie. "But you should take the afternoon off. Catch up with your... friend."

"Jake... " Annie started, but he was already walking away, each step feeling like lead in his boots.

"I'll finish up here," he called over his shoulder. "Blue and I can handle it."

He could feel Annie's eyes on him as he walked away, could feel the weight of everything unsaid hanging in the air between them. But he didn't look back. Couldn't look back. Because if he did, if he saw the hurt in her eyes, he might forget all the reasons this could never work.

The rest of the day passed in a fog of work and memories. Jake threw himself into physical labor, pushing his body until his muscles screamed, trying to drown out the thoughts that wouldn't leave him alone. But every time he closed his eyes, he saw Annie, Annie laughing as she learned to rope cattle, Annie facing down danger without flinching, Annie in his arms under the stars.

Evening found him on his front porch, nursing a beer he didn't really want, watching the lights in the guest house. He could see shadows moving, two of them. Annie and Ricardo, probably reminiscing about their shared past, their sophisticated world, everything they had in common.

Blue rested his head on Jake's knee, whining softly.

"I know, boy." Jake scratched behind the dog's ears. "I'm being an idiot."

But was he? Annie was here temporarily, three months at most, she'd said. Then she'd return to her real life, to board meetings and charity galas and everything she'd been born to. And he'd stay here, working the land, fighting the bank, living the only life he knew how to live.

Last night's kiss had been perfect. But maybe that's all it could ever be, one perfect moment, preserved in memory, untouched by the complications of reality. Better to step back now, before either of them got in too deep. Before the inevitable goodbye hurt even more than it already would.

The lights in the guest house went out, one by one. Jake stood, his joints protesting the long day's work. Tomorrow would be another day of careful distance, of professional courtesy, of pretending his heart didn't race every time she was near. It would be hard, but it was necessary.

Because the truth was, Annie Contadelucci deserved more than a hardscrabble ranch and a man with calloused hands. She deserved Ricardo's world of ease and elegance. She deserved someone who could give her everything, not someone who had to count every penny just to keep his dream alive.

As Jake headed inside, he caught one last glimpse of the guest house. A single light still burned in an upstairs window. Was she thinking of him? Of Ricardo? Of the choice she'd have to make?

It didn't matter, he told himself firmly. He'd already made the choice for both of them. Better a clean break now than a shattered heart later.

But as he lay in bed, staring at the ceiling, Jake couldn't quite convince himself he was doing the right thing. The memory of Annie's kiss haunted him, sweet and perfect and possibly the biggest mistake of his life.

Or maybe, whispered a treacherous voice in his heart, the only mistake was letting her go.

CHAPTER TEN

HEARTS APART

Annie stood at the guest house window, watching Jake move across the pasture in the early morning light. Even from this distance, she could tell he was deliberately taking the long route to the barn, avoiding his usual path that would bring him closer to her house. Her fingers touched her lips unconsciously, remembering their kiss from two nights ago. How had everything gone so wrong so fast?

"Cara mia, you're up early." Ricardo's voice from the doorway made her shoulders tense. He'd insisted on staying at the bed and breakfast in town, but he'd been showing up at dawn every morning, trying to recreate their old routine from Milano. As if bringing her espresso in a fancy travel cup could somehow erase everything that had changed.

"Ranch work starts early," she said, not turning around. In the distance, Jake disappeared into the barn. She waited, hoping to see him emerge, even as she told herself to stop watching.

"Ah yes, your... experiment." Ricardo moved closer, the subtle scent of his expensive cologne jarringly out of place among the ranch's morning smells of coffee and hay. "You've proven your point, surely? Shown your father you can rough it with the cowboys?"

Annie finally turned to face him, really looking at him for the first time since his arrival. He was exactly as she remembered, perfectly groomed, devastatingly handsome, completely sure of himself. Once, that confidence had drawn her like a moth to flame. Now it just made her tired.

"This isn't an experiment, Ricardo. Or a game. Or whatever you think it is." She moved to the kitchen, pulling on her work boots. They were scuffed now, broken in, comfortable. Like this life was becoming. "This is my life."

"For three months," he reminded her, watching with barely concealed distaste as she tied her boots. "Then you return to your real life. To Milano, to the company, to... "

"To you?" The words came out sharper than she intended. "Is that why you're really here? Because your perfectly arranged engagement isn't fulfilling enough?"

Ricardo set the coffee cup down, his movements deliberate. "Sophia was a business decision. You know how these things work in our world. But you and I..." He stepped closer, and Annie caught herself backing away. "We have history, cara. Real feeling."

"Had," she corrected. "We had history." Through the window, she saw Jake leading his horse from the barn. His head turned slightly toward the guest house, then deliberately away. The small gesture felt like a physical pain in her chest.

"Because of him?" Ricardo's voice held a note she'd never heard before, uncertainty mixed with something darker. "This cowboy who can barely string two sentences together?"

Anger flared hot and sudden in Annie's chest. "Don't. Don't you dare judge him. Jake Spyker has more integrity in his little finger than... " She stopped herself, drawing in a sharp breath. "I have work to do."

She grabbed her jacket, her work jacket now, tough canvas

instead of designer labels, and headed for the door. Ricardo caught her arm.

"Annie, wait. I'm sorry." His voice softened to the tone that used to make her melt. "I just don't understand what's happened to you. This isn't you, the boots, the manual labor, the isolation. You're meant for more than this."

"That's just it," Annie said quietly, gently pulling her arm free. "For the first time in my life, I'm figuring out exactly what I'm meant for. What I want, not what everyone else wants for me."

"And what is that?"

The question hung in the air between them. Through the open door, Annie could hear the morning sounds of the ranch, cattle lowing, horses nickering, the distant sound of Jake's voice giving instructions to the morning crew. Her heart ached at how familiar it all was, how right it felt.

"I want to matter," she finally said. "Not because of my name or my father's company, but because of what I can do. What I can learn." She looked at Ricardo steadily. "When was the last time you really had to learn something new? To be completely vulnerable and uncertain and push through anyway?"

"We're not meant for uncertainty, cara. People like us… "

"That's exactly what I'm talking about." Annie stepped onto the porch. "Maybe I don't want to be 'people like us' anymore."

She walked away before he could respond, heading toward the barn. But as she approached, she saw Jake emerge and quickly mount his horse, spinning the animal away before she could reach him.

"He's headed to the north pasture," Tommy called from where he was mucking stalls. "Said to tell you to work on the fence repair in the south section today."

Annie's heart sank. The south pasture was as far from the north as you could get on the ranch. Jake was making sure their paths wouldn't cross.

She threw herself into work, focusing on each task with fierce determination. The physical labor helped quiet her mind, but it couldn't entirely silence the questions that plagued her. Why was Jake pulling away? Was it Ricardo's presence? Doubt about their kiss? Fear of what people might think about them together?

Around noon, she saw Jake's horse approaching and her heart lifted, only to fall again as he changed direction, taking the long way around to the barn. The deliberate avoidance hurt worse than anything Ricardo could say or do.

Blue trotted up to her as she worked on the fence, whining softly.

"At least you're still talking to me," she told the dog, scratching behind his ears. "Your master's being a bit of a coward, you know that?"

Blue's tail wagged as if in agreement, and Annie felt tears prick at her eyes. Everything had been so perfect during their kiss. The way Jake had held her, like she was precious but not fragile. The way he'd looked at her, like he was seeing straight through every layer of polish to the real her underneath.

Now he wouldn't look at her at all.

The sun was setting by the time she finished the fence repair. Her muscles ached, and her hands were blistered despite her work gloves, but she'd done it right. Jake had taught her how, after all.

As she walked back to the guest house, she saw Ricardo's rental car in the drive. He was leaning against it, jacket off, sleeves rolled up in what she supposed was his conception of casual ranch wear.

"Have dinner with me," he called out. "In town. Real food, real wine, civilized conversation."

Annie looked down at her dirty clothes, her blistered hands, her scuffed boots. A month ago, she would have been mortified to be seen like this. Now she felt a strange pride in the evidence of honest work.

"Thank you, but no." She was surprised by how easy the refusal was. "I have an early start tomorrow."

"Annie." Ricardo's voice stopped her on the porch steps. "What happened to us?"

She turned to look at him, really look at him, and suddenly she knew exactly what had happened.

"Life happened," she said softly. "Real life. Not the carefully arranged version we grew up with, but messy, complicated, beautiful real life. And once you've tasted that..." She shook her head. "There's no going back to pretty illusions."

"He'll never understand your world," Ricardo said quietly. "Never fit into it."

Annie looked toward the main house, where a light burned in Jake's kitchen window. "Maybe I don't want that world anymore. Maybe I'm finding a new one."

"He's avoiding you," Ricardo pointed out, an edge in his voice. "I've seen it. Whatever happened between you… "

"Is between us," Annie cut in firmly. "Go home, Ricardo. Go back to Milano, back to Sophia. Build whatever pretty illusion makes you happy. But please... let me build something real."

She went inside before he could respond, her heart pounding but her mind clearer than it had been in days. Yes, Jake was avoiding her, and yes, it hurt like hell. But she'd fought for everything she'd learned on this ranch, fought through blisters and bruises, through exhaustion and fear, through her own preconceptions and others' doubts.

She could fight for this too. For him. For them. For whatever was growing between them that was strong enough to terrify them both.

First, though, she had to figure out why he was running. And then... then she had to make him stop.

CHAPTER ELEVEN

SNAKE IN THE GRASS

*R*icardo Valentini stood at the edge of the north pasture, his Italian leather shoes already ruined by the morning dew, watching Jake Spyker check the fencing near the creek. The rancher moved with the easy confidence of a man on his own territory, completely unaware he was being observed. Ricardo's lip curled slightly. Such a simple man, this cowboy who'd caught Annie's attention. So trusting. So... predictable.

He pulled out his phone, checking the email from Annie's father again. The bank note on the ranch was indeed coming due for renewal. One well-placed call from Contadelucci Agricultural Investments suggesting the ranch was a poor risk, and Jake Spyker's dream would crumble like the dry Montana dirt beneath Ricardo's feet.

But that would be too obvious, too traceable. No, what this situation needed was something more... unfortunate. An accident, perhaps.

Ricardo watched Jake climb down into the creek bed to check a support post. The recent rains had made the banks treacherous, and that particular section of fence kept cattle from wandering onto a dangerous stretch of unstable ground. One loose fence post, one spooked herd...

He waited until Jake moved further down the creek before approaching the fence. His manicured hands looked absurd gripping the rough wood, but growing up on Italian estates had taught him enough about fence construction to know exactly how to weaken the post without making it immediately obvious. Just enough that a good push from a full-grown steer would send the whole section tumbling.

"Looking for something?"

Ricardo spun around to find Tommy, the teenage ranch hand, watching him suspiciously.

"Ah, young man." Ricardo smoothed his features into a practiced smile. "Just admiring your American ranching techniques. In Italia, we do things quite differently." He gestured vaguely at the fence. "The construction is fascinating."

Tommy's eyes narrowed slightly. "Fence is a fence. Not much fascinating about it."

"Perhaps not to you." Ricardo brushed dirt from his hands with exaggerated care. "Though I'm sure Annie finds it all quite captivating. She always did have a taste for... rustic charm."

He watched satisfaction as uncertainty flickered across the boy's face. Everyone on the ranch knew about the kiss between Annie and Jake, ranch gossip traveled faster than Italian tabloids. And everyone had noticed Jake's subsequent withdrawal.

"Speaking of Annie," Ricardo continued smoothly, "I should check on her. These long days of manual labor must be wearing on her. She's used to a more... refined lifestyle."

He walked away, knowing the seeds of doubt had been planted. Behind him, Tommy stared at the fence post for a long moment before shrugging and heading back to his chores. Young minds were so easily distracted.

Later that afternoon, Ricardo found Annie by the barn, brushing down her horse. The sight of her in worn jeans and a work shirt still jarred him. She'd been the toast of Milano society, turning heads at every gala. Now she was covered in dust and horse hair, and somehow looking more alive than he'd ever seen her.

"I have something for you," he announced, approaching with practiced confidence.

Annie barely glanced up. "I'm busy, Ricardo."

"Too busy for this?" He pulled out a small blue box with familiar gold lettering. Tiffany & Co. Her one weakness, once upon a time.

Now she just looked annoyed. "Ricardo..."

"The one you always wanted," he pressed, opening the box to reveal a stunning sapphire ring. "Remember? You saw it in the window in New York last year. Said it reminded you of the Mediterranean."

"That was a different person," Annie said quietly. "A different life."

"It could be your life again." He moved closer, holding out the ring. "All of it, the galas, the yacht parties, the winter chalets. No more dirt and cattle and endless physical labor."

Annie stared at the ring for a long moment. Then, to his surprise, she started laughing. Not the polite social laugh she'd perfected over years in high society, but a real, deep laugh that bent her double.

"Oh, Ricardo," she gasped, wiping tears from her eyes. "You really don't understand at all, do you? This?" She gestured at her dirty clothes, the barn, the ranch spreading out around them. "This isn't punishment. It's freedom."

"Freedom?" He couldn't keep the disdain from his voice. "Freedom to what? Break your back? Ruin your hands? Live in the middle of nowhere with a man who can barely... "

"A man who sees me," Annie cut in, her laughter fading to something harder. "Not the version of me you created in your head, not the perfect society wife your family wanted, but me. The real me."

"The real you belongs in our world," Ricardo insisted, reaching for her hand. "Not playing cowgirl with some American farmer who... "

What happened next was so fast Ricardo barely registered it. Annie's horse, normally the gentlest animal in the stable, suddenly reared up, nearly trampling him. He stumbled backward, dropping the ring box, his perfect suit splattered with mud.

"Careful," Annie said, calming the horse with practiced ease. "They can sense when someone's being a snake."

From the corner of his eye, Ricardo caught movement. Jake stood in the barn doorway, his expression dark as a storm cloud. Had he seen Ricardo reaching for Annie? Heard her laughing? Either way, the rancher turned and stalked away before Annie noticed him.

Perfect.

"Think about it," Ricardo said, retrieving the muddy ring box. "About who you really are, what you really want." He backed away, letting his voice carry just enough to reach any listening ears. "I'll be here when you're ready to be honest with yourself."

Annie's dismissive snort followed him across the yard, but it didn't matter. He'd seen Jake's face, seen the doubt and anger there. The fence post was compromised, the seeds of jealousy planted. Now all he had to do was wait.

He reached his rental car and pulled out his phone, dialing a familiar number.

"Signor Contadelucci? Yes, everything is proceeding as planned. Though I must say, your daughter seems quite... attached to this place." He listened for a moment, smiling. "No, no, nothing we can't handle. You were right, a few well-placed pressures, and this little ranch fantasy will collapse under its own weight."

He ended the call and looked back toward the barn. Annie

was visible in the doorway, watching Jake's retreating figure with longing she probably didn't even realize she was showing. Soon she'd learn that some dreams weren't meant to last. Soon she'd remember who she really was, who she belonged with.

And if Jake Spyker happened to have an unfortunate accident in the process... well, ranch work was dangerous. Everyone knew that.

Ricardo started his car, the engine purring to life with European precision. As he pulled away, he saw Jake in his rearview mirror, staring after Annie with equal longing. Such a shame, really. They might have been quite the love story, in another life.

But Ricardo Valentini hadn't gotten where he was by letting other people's love stories interfere with his plans. By this time next week, that weakened fence would prove just how dangerous ranch life could be. And Annie would need someone to comfort her, someone to help her see that this had all been a beautiful but impossible dream.

He smiled as the ranch disappeared behind him. Sometimes love stories needed a villain. He was happy to oblige.

What he didn't notice was Blue, Jake's faithful cattle dog, watching his departure with unusual intensity. Animals, after all, could sense a snake in the grass. And Blue had been watching the fence post too.

CHAPTER TWELVE

FINDING HOME

Annie woke before her 4:30 alarm, her body now naturally attuned to the ranch's rhythm. The pre-dawn quiet wrapped around her like a familiar blanket as she breathed in the crisp Montana air through her open window. A month ago, she would have found this hour barbaric. Now it felt like a gift, these peaceful moments before the world fully woke.

She padded to the kitchen in her sock feet, starting the coffee, real cowboy coffee now, strong enough to stand a spoon in, not the fancy Italian espresso she once couldn't live without. The rich aroma filled the guest house, mixing with the early morning smells drifting in from outside: sage, wet earth, and the sweet scent of fresh hay from the barn. Funny how tastes could change. Funny how everything could change.

Standing at the window, cradling her coffee mug in both hands, Annie watched the first hints of dawn touching the eastern sky. Stars still glittered overhead, and the mountains were dark shadows against the lightening horizon. A coyote's distant call echoed across the ranch, answered by a chorus of dogs from neighboring properties. Even Blue, normally quiet this early, offered a single bark in response.

Annie smiled, remembering how that wild sound had unnerved her during her first weeks here. Now it was just another note in the ranch's morning symphony, as natural as breathing. She took another sip of coffee, savoring the bitter warmth, and moved to get dressed.

Her morning routine had evolved into something that would have shocked her Milano friends. Gone were the hour-long makeup sessions and careful hair styling. Instead, she pulled her hair into a practical braid, splashed cold water on her face, and reached for her work clothes with practiced ease: worn jeans, a flannel shirt soft from washing, boots that had molded perfectly to her feet. Her designer clothes hung untouched in the closet, looking like artifacts from another life, beautiful, expensive artifacts that had nothing to do with the woman she was becoming.

She caught her reflection in the window and paused, really looking at herself in the dim light. The woman looking back at her was lean and strong, sun-kissed and confident. Her hands, once perfectly manicured, now showed calluses from rope work and horse riding. Her face, free of makeup, glowed with health and purpose. Even the way she held herself had changed, gone was the society posture of her past, replaced by the balanced stance of someone who knew her place in the world and was comfortable in it. She looked real, solid, and true.

The first message arrived as she was lacing her boots. Her phone lit up with her father's name, the bright screen harsh in the pre-dawn dimness. Annie sighed, knowing this was just the beginning. Sure enough, as she watched, more notifications began to appear:

From Papa: "Board meeting scheduled for next week. Your presence is non-negotiable. The Rossi merger depends on family unity. Call me."

From Aunt Sophia: "Darling, you're breaking your father's heart. This rebellious phase has gone on long enough. Think of the family name."

From Uncle Marco: "Your father built this company from nothing. You owe him more than this childish behavior."

From Cousin Giulia: "The Milano social papers are having a field day. Come home before you completely ruin your reputation."

Each message felt like a small weight, trying to drag her back to her old life. But Annie squared her shoulders and silently thanked Jake for teaching her about bearing up under heavy loads. She switched off the phone without responding and headed for the door, pausing only to check her reflection one final time.

"Sorry, Papa," she whispered to her image, "but I'm not that perfectly polished doll anymore. I'm something better. Something real."

The morning air carried a bite that promised autumn wasn't far off, mixing the scent of sage and wet earth from last night's rain with the earthier notes of horses and cattle. Annie breathed deeply, letting the authentic smells of ranch life fill her lungs. Once, she would have wrinkled her nose at such common odors. Now each scent told her a story: the sweetness of fresh hay meant the morning feed was ready, the musty warmth from the barn meant the horses were already stirring, the hint of wood smoke suggested Jake was already up and had his fire going.

Jake. Her heart did that familiar little flip it always did when she thought of him, followed by the now-familiar ache. He'd been avoiding her for days now, ever since Ricardo showed up. Even now, she could see him in the distance, deliberately taking the long way to the barn rather than pass near her house.

"Morning, boss lady!" Tommy's cheerful voice broke through her thoughts. He was jogging toward her from the barn, his breath visible in the cold air. "Got a situation with the new foal. She's being stubborn about her medicine, and Doc Wilson says she needs it before breakfast."

Annie's heart lifted. Just a month ago, she wouldn't have

known the first thing about handling a difficult foal. Now she found herself moving with purpose toward the barn, already planning her approach. "Got the halter ready?"

"Yes, ma'am. The red one you worked with yesterday."

Inside the barn, the morning light filtered through dusty windows, creating golden beams that caught the floating hay particles. The warmth and animal smells wrapped around Annie like a familiar embrace. Various ranch hands called out greetings as she passed, no more awkward stares or doubtful glances. She'd earned her place here, one blister and bruise at a time.

The foal, a beautiful little paint they'd named Stella, was indeed being difficult, tossing her head and shying away from Tommy's attempts to approach. But Annie had learned the trick of it, had spent hours watching Jake with the horses before he started avoiding her. She approached with quiet confidence, speaking in low, soothing Italian that seemed to calm the nervous animal.

"Piano, piano, piccola," she murmured, letting Stella catch her scent. "Tranquilla, bella ragazza." Slowly, steadily, she worked her way closer until she could slip the halter on. "There you go, that's not so bad, is it?"

"You've got the touch," came Jake's voice from behind her. Her heart jumped, but when she turned, he was already moving away, his shoulders stiff. She caught just a glimpse of his face, the shadows under his eyes suggesting he was sleeping about as well as she was.

"He's hurting himself more than you," Tommy said quietly, taking advantage of Annie's distraction to administer the medicine. "Whole ranch can see it."

Annie swallowed hard and focused on praising Stella, who was taking her medicine like a champion now. "Sometimes people have to figure things out for themselves."

The morning progressed with the familiar routine she'd come to love. She helped Tommy muck out stalls, her movements efficient now where they'd once been awkward. She checked feed levels in the grain room, making notes in the inventory log with the same attention to detail she'd once given to corporate spreadsheets. When it came time to move cattle to fresh pasture, she mounted her horse, no more nervous fumbling with the reins or uncertain seat. Her body knew what to do now, moving in harmony with the animal beneath her.

"Watch the lead steer," called Carlos, one of the senior ranch hands. "He's been ornery lately."

Annie nodded, already noting the way the big steer was holding his head. A month ago, she wouldn't have known what to look for. Now she could read cattle like she used to read financial reports, noting the subtle signs that told her everything she needed to know.

She guided her horse with her knees, positioning herself perfectly to turn the steer. The rope swung out from her hand smooth as silk, settling exactly where she wanted it. A quick turn, a gentle but firm pull, and the whole herd was moving in the right direction.

"Nicely done," Carlos called out, genuine respect in his voice. "Jake teach you that rope work?"

"Jake taught me everything," Annie replied softly, more to herself than Carlos. And he had, whether he'd meant to or not. Taught her about the ranch, about horses and cattle, about working through pain and exhaustion because the animals depended on you. About being real in a way she'd never been in her old life.

Most importantly, he'd taught her about having the courage to be exactly who you were, no matter what anyone else thought you should be.

Her moment of reflection was interrupted by her phone buzzing again, this time her mother's youngest sister, Francesca: "Darling, I've just had lunch with your father. He's beside himself.

The Milano society papers are starting to talk. Come home before you ruin everything."

Annie was about to delete the message when her father's name flashed on the screen. With a deep breath that smelled of sage and honest work, she answered.

"Papa."

"Enough." His voice was steel, the tone he used in hostile takeovers. "This little adventure has gone on long enough. I have investors asking questions, the board losing confidence. Your absence suggests family instability."

Annie dismounted, patting her horse's neck as she replied. "No, Papa. My absence suggests family humanity." She squared her shoulders, feeling the strength she'd built from weeks of physical labor. "I'm learning our business from the ground up, just like you did."

"I did not spend years building an empire so my daughter could play cowgirl with some American rancher!" His voice rose, and Annie could picture him pacing his marble-floored office in Milano, designer shoes clicking on imported stone. "The Rossi merger will fall apart without a show of family unity. Your cousin Giulia says you're all over the social media gossip sites. Ricardo tells me... "

"Ricardo?" Annie's voice sharpened. "So that's what this is really about? Did he tell you about his constant visits to the ranch? About how he shows up uninvited, trying to pressure me back to a life I don't want anymore?"

"He tells me you're throwing away everything for some romantic fantasy about ranch life. About this Jake Spyker... "

Movement caught her eye, a figure in expensive clothes skulking near the equipment barn. Her breath caught as she recognized the familiar silhouette.

"Papa, I have to go."

"Antoinette Contadelucci, don't you dare... "

"I'm not finished," she cut in, her voice steady as she began walking toward the barn. "You taught me to understand this business from all angles. That's what I'm doing. You taught me to trust my instincts. That's what I'm doing. You taught me to recognize value beyond numbers on a spreadsheet. That's what I'm doing."

"I taught you responsibility to this family!"

"And I'm honoring that responsibility by becoming someone worthy of it. Someone real." The figure disappeared around the corner of the barn. Annie quickened her pace. "The board meeting will have to proceed without me. I'm doing important work here, Papa. Real work."

"This isn't about work." His voice softened slightly, taking on the tone he'd used when she was small and had skinned her knee. "Piccola, you can't throw away everything for some romantic fantasy. Come home. We'll find you a proper position in the company. Something... dignified."

Annie reached the equipment barn just as Tommy came running around the corner, out of breath. He gestured urgently at her to come closer.

"One moment, Papa." She covered the phone. "What is it?"

"Someone was messing with the tractor," Tommy panted. "Saw them running off toward the creek. Looked like... "

"Ricardo," Annie finished grimly. "But you're not sure?"

Tommy shook his head. "Too far away. But who else wears Italian leather shoes out here? Found these beside the tractor." He held up a pair of wire cutters. "The fuel line's been tampered with. Not cut through, but weakened. Could've caused a real accident if someone tried to use it."

Annie's blood ran cold, then hot with anger. She put the phone back to her ear. "Papa, listen to me. Really listen. I'm not throwing anything away. I'm finding something. Finding myself. And if you ever truly want to understand our business, come see what I'm learning. Come see who I'm becoming."

"Antoinette... "

"And one more thing." Her voice hardened. "Tell Ricardo that if anything happens to this ranch, anything at all, I'll know exactly who to blame. And I'll make sure the entire agricultural investment community knows too."

She ended the call before he could respond and turned to Tommy. "Get Jake, and find Blue, that dog's got a nose for trouble. I want every piece of equipment checked before anyone uses it."

As Tommy ran off, Annie surveyed the ranch spreading out before her. The morning sun had burned off the last of the dawn mist, revealing the patchwork of pastures, the cattle dotting the hillsides, the distant mountains standing guard. All of it feeling more like home than Milano ever had.

Movement in the creek bed caught her eye, another glimpse of expensive clothing disappearing into the brush. Ricardo was getting bolder, more desperate. She'd seen the paperwork on Jake's desk about the upcoming bank note renewal. One wrong word from Contadelucci Agricultural Investments about the ranch's stability...

Her phone buzzed again, the family group chat exploding with messages of concern, manipulation, and thinly veiled threats about her inheritance. Annie silenced it without reading them. Let them talk. Let them worry. Let them try to pressure her back into their gilded cage.

She wasn't going anywhere.

The morning sun warmed her face as she started toward the stable, her boots sure on the familiar path. Time to show everyone exactly who she'd become. Starting with a certain skulking ex-fiancé who needed to learn that some things, some people, some places, some dreams, weren't for sale at any price.

She had chosen her path, chosen her life, chosen her heart. Now all she had to do was fight for it. And if there was one thing ranch life had taught her, it was how to fight for what mattered.

CHAPTER THIRTEEN

BREAKING POINT

Jake sat at the kitchen table with the ranch spread out in paper. Statements. Notes. Repairs. The math didn't bend. The last cattle sale came in light, the equipment kept breaking, and the bank note coming due felt heavier every time he looked at it.

Blue whined softly from his place by the wood stove, sensing his master's distress.

"I know, boy," Jake muttered, running a hand through his already disheveled hair. "Don't see a way out of this one."

The coffee in his cup had gone cold, forgotten during hours of trying to make the numbers add up differently. His grandmother had always said the ranch was built on blood, sweat, and prayer. Lately, it felt like they were running short on all three.

Earlier a light flickered on in the guest house, catching his eye. Annie would be starting her day, probably already dressed in those worn jeans that somehow made her look more elegant than any designer outfit ever had. His chest tightened at the thought of her. Keeping his distance these past few days had been hell, but watching her with Ricardo was worse.

The Italian's sleek car had been parked at her place when Jake rode in yesterday, their laughter carrying across the yard. The sound had hit him like a physical blow. Of course she was laughing with Ricardo, they shared a world Jake could never be part of. A world of wealth and sophistication, of knowing which fork to use at fancy dinners and how to talk about wine vintages. A world where ranch mud was something to avoid, not wear as a badge of honor.

Movement outside caught his attention. Tommy was racing across the yard toward the barn, something clutched in his hand. The boy had been acting strange lately, watching the shadows like he expected trouble. Jake pushed back from the table with a sigh. Time to see what new crisis the day had brought.

The morning air bit at his face as he stepped outside, reminding him that winter wasn't far off. Another worry to add to his growing collection, they needed to repair the north barn roof before the snow came, and that wasn't in the budget either.

"Boss!" Tommy called out, spotting him. "Found something you need to see."

The boy held out what looked like a piece of metal pipe. Jake's stomach dropped as he recognized it, part of the brake line from the hay baler.

"Found it behind the equipment barn," Tommy said, his young face serious. "It's been cut clean through. And boss... this is the third piece of equipment I've found tampered with this week."

Jake turned the metal over in his hands, feeling the smooth edges of the cut. This wasn't wear and tear or accident, this was deliberate sabotage. His mind flashed to Ricardo's perfectly polished shoes, recently spotted near the equipment barn. But that was crazy, wasn't it? Even Ricardo wouldn't stoop to damaging equipment. Would he?

"Keep this quiet," Jake instructed Tommy. "But check everything before it's used. And I mean everything."

"Yes, sir." Tommy hesitated. "Boss... about Miss Annie..."

"Not now, Tommy." Jake's voice was sharper than he intended, but he couldn't handle hearing about Annie right now. Couldn't handle thinking about her smile, her determination, the way she'd kissed him that night under the stars before everything went sideways.

The sound of hooves made them both turn. Annie was riding in from the east pasture, her seat perfect now, hair catching the early morning sun like spun gold. She rode past without looking their way, but Jake saw her shoulders stiffen. She knew he was watching. She always knew.

"She misses you, you know."

Jake's head snapped up at Tommy's quiet words. The boy was scuffing his boot in the dirt, not meeting Jake's eyes.

"You don't know what you're talking about," Jake said roughly, but the words felt hollow even to him. He did know. He saw it in the way Annie's eyes followed him across the yard, in how she started to speak when their paths crossed, only to fall silent when he turned away.

"All I know is," Tommy pressed on, "when Miss Annie thinks nobody's watching, she looks at that fancy Italian fella like he's something stuck to her boot. But when she looks at you..." He trailed off as a sleek black car pulled into the ranch yard, gravel crunching under expensive tires.

Speak of the devil. Ricardo emerged from his rental car looking like he'd stepped off a magazine cover, not a speck of ranch dust daring to settle on his perfectly pressed suit. Jake's hand tightened on the piece of cut brake line until his knuckles went white.

"Ah, Mr. Spyker." Ricardo's voice was smooth as aged whiskey and twice as expensive. "Just the man I wanted to see. Might we have a word? In private?"

Tommy took the hint and disappeared toward the barn, but not before giving Jake a meaningful look. Jake merely nodded, tucking the brake line piece into his pocket.

"Beautiful morning, isn't it?" Ricardo gestured at the landscape. "Though I imagine the view is less beautiful when you're worried about bank notes coming due."

Jake went still. "How do you know about that?"

"Oh, I make it my business to know everything about Annie's... investments." Ricardo's smile didn't reach his eyes. "It would be a shame if something happened to this place. Accidents can be so costly, especially when a ranch is already struggling financially."

The threat was clear as mountain air. Jake took a step forward, his voice dropping low. "You want to run that by me again?"

"Merely an observation." Ricardo held up his manicured hands in mock surrender. "Though I must say, if something were to happen, equipment failures, accidents, that sort of thing, it might help Annie see reason. Help her understand where she truly belongs."

"She belongs wherever she chooses to belong."

"Does she?" Ricardo's eyes glittered. "And you think she'll choose this?" He gestured dismissively at the ranch. "Dust and mud and financial ruin? Please. I saw you watching us yesterday. Did you hear her laughing? That's the Annie I know. The real Annie. Not this... cowgirl fantasy she's playing at."

Jake's fists clenched. He thought of the cut brake line in his pocket, of other mysterious equipment failures, of perfectly polished shoes seen near the barn at odd hours.

"If I find out you've been anywhere near my equipment..."

"You'll what?" Ricardo's smile turned sharp. "Prove it? To whom? The local sheriff? The bank? The investment board preparing to review your loan? Face it, Mr. Spyker. You're out of your depth. In every possible way."

A door slammed, making them both turn. Annie stood on her porch, watching them with narrow eyes. The morning sun caught her hair, and for a moment Jake's heart stopped at how natural she looked there, how right. Then he remembered her laughter with Ricardo, remembered the world of difference between them.

"Think about what I said," Ricardo murmured, already turning toward Annie with a brilliant smile. "Some dreams aren't worth the price of holding onto them."

He strolled away, leaving Jake with the weight of cut brake lines in his pocket and unspoken words in his throat. Blue pressed against his leg, growling softly at Ricardo's retreating figure.

"Yeah," Jake said quietly. "I don't trust him either, boy."

The rest of the morning passed in a blur of work and worry. Jake threw himself into physical labor, trying to quiet his mind with exhaustion. But every task seemed to lead back to Annie. The new fence she'd helped mend, her work growing stronger each day. The horse she'd gentled when no one else could get near it. The coffee cup she'd left in the barn office, lipstick still on the rim.

His phone buzzed, the bank manager again. Jake ignored it, just like he'd been ignoring Annie's attempts to talk to him. Some conversations were better put off, even if putting them off only made things worse.

"Jake!" Carlos's shout cut through his thoughts. "We got trouble at the north creek!"

Jake was running before Carlos finished speaking. The north creek was where he'd spotted Ricardo earlier, where the fence had been mysteriously weakening. He rounded the barn at full speed, then stopped dead.

Annie was already there, ankle-deep in creek mud, trying to help a fallen calf. But something was wrong. The usual calm precision of her movements was off, and even from this distance, Jake could see blood on her arm.

"Barbed wire," she called out when she saw him, her voice tight with pain. "Someone removed the warning flags. I was checking the fence line when… " She broke off with a hiss of pain as the calf struggled.

Jake was moving before he could think better of it, splashing into the creek beside her. Up close, he could see the nasty gash on her arm where the hidden wire had caught her. Could also see how she was favoring her left leg. But she hadn't let go of the calf, hadn't called for help until Carlos spotted her.

"Let me," he said gruffly, carefully taking her place. Their hands brushed, sending that familiar spark through his body. "You're hurt."

"I'm fine." But she swayed slightly as she stepped back, her boots slipping in the mud. Jake caught her with his free arm, pulling her against him even as he steadied the calf with his other hand.

For a moment, they were pressed together, both breathing hard. She smelled like sunshine and hay, and something that was only Annie, something that made his heart ache. This close, he could see the depth in her eyes, count her lashes, feel the trembling in her body that had nothing to do with pain.

"Jake," she whispered, and his name on her lips was almost his undoing. "We need to talk about… "

"Miss Annie!" Ricardo's voice shattered the moment. He was picking his way down the creek bank in his expensive shoes, face a mask of concern. "I saw you were hurt. I've called a doctor."

Jake let go of Annie as if burned, focusing on the calf. But he felt her eyes on him, felt the weight of everything unsaid between them.

"The warning flags," she said quietly. "They were here yesterday. I checked them myself."

"Probably animals," Ricardo offered smoothly. "Or the wind."

"All of them?" Annie's voice held an edge Jake had never heard before. "Every single flag, at exactly the height where someone might check the fence line?"

Silence fell, broken only by the calf's distressed noises and the creek's gentle burble. Jake worked methodically, freeing the animal while his mind raced. The cut brake line. The weakened fence posts. The missing warning flags. And always, Ricardo nearby, watching with those calculating eyes.

"You should get that arm looked at," Jake said finally, not meeting Annie's gaze. "Ricardo's right, a doctor… "

"Don't." The word was soft but fierce. "Don't you dare agree with him. Don't you dare push me away again."

The calf struggled free and bolted up the bank, but Jake barely noticed. Annie was still watching him, blood dripping slowly from her arm, waiting for something, some word, some sign that he was still the man she'd kissed under the stars.

But Ricardo's words echoed in his head: Some dreams aren't worth the price. He looked at Annie's injured arm, thought of the cut brake line, the bank note coming due. How many accidents would it take before someone got seriously hurt?

"Go with Ricardo," he said roughly. "Get that arm treated. Then…" He swallowed hard. "Then maybe it's time you started thinking about where you really belong."

The hurt that flashed across her face was worse than any physical injury. She took a step back, then another, mud sucking at her boots.

"You're a coward, Jake Spyker," she said quietly. "And you're a fool if you think I don't know exactly where I belong."

She turned and walked away, head high despite her limping gait. Ricardo hurried after her, shooting Jake a smile that held more triumph than concern. Jake watched them go, his hands clenched into fists at his sides.

Blue appeared at his feet, whining softly at Annie's retreating figure.

"I know, boy," Jake whispered. "I'm breaking both our hearts. But better broken hearts than broken bodies."

He pulled the cut brake line from his pocket, studying it in the morning light. One way or another, this had to end. He just hoped he had the strength to see it through, even if it meant watching Annie walk away for good.

The bank note sat heavy in his back pocket, a reminder that some dreams came with too high a price. But as he watched Annie disappear into the morning sunshine, Jake wondered if losing her might cost him something worth far more than money.

CHAPTER FOURTEEN

THUNDER AND LIGHTNING

A steady rain rolled in just before sunset, turning the Montana sky a bruised shade of gray. Annie stood on her porch, watching lightning dance between towering thunderheads, her injured arm throbbing in time with the distant thunder. The doctor had used eight stitches to close the barbed wire gash, but the emotional wound of Jake's dismissal cut far deeper.

Movement near the main barn caught her eye. Jake was rushing to secure equipment before the storm hit, his movements precise despite the growing wind. Even now, watching him hurt, but not watching him was impossible. She knew every line of his body, every gesture, every habit. Knew he was favoring his right shoulder, probably from helping that calf in the creek. Knew he'd been up since dawn, worrying over papers she wasn't supposed to know about.

But she did know. She'd seen the bank notices, the equipment repair bills, the dwindling balance sheets. The ranch was in trouble, and Jake was too proud to admit it, too stubborn to accept help. Especially from her.

Lightning cracked overhead, startlingly close, and Annie saw

Blue race into the barn. But Jake remained outside, struggling with a piece of equipment that had chosen the worst possible moment to jam.

"Damn stubborn man," she muttered, already moving down her porch steps. The first fat drops of rain began to fall as she jogged across the yard, her boots slipping slightly in the mud. By the time she reached Jake, the rain was coming down in sheets.

"You need help," she called over the wind. Not a question, a statement of fact.

Jake's head snapped up, water streaming down his face. "Annie, go back inside. Your arm... "

"Isn't going to get any worse from a little rain." She moved to the other side of the equipment, a hay baler that had seen better days. "Tell me what you need."

For a moment, she thought he'd send her away again. But another crack of lightning made the decision for them. "The lever's stuck," he shouted over the thunder. "Need to get it covered before the motor floods."

They worked together in the growing storm, their bodies remembering the rhythm they'd developed over weeks of ranch work. Annie braced while Jake pulled, their hands brushing occasionally, sending sparks that had nothing to do with the lightning above.

Finally, the lever gave way with a grinding sound. Jake threw his weight into pushing the baler toward the barn. Annie grit her teeth against the sharp pull of her fresh stitches and matched him step for step. They were nearly there when her boots slipped in the mud. Jake caught her before she could fall, pulling her against his chest. For a heartbeat, they stood frozen, rain pouring down around them, bodies pressed together, breath mingling in the electric air.

His hands were warm despite the cool rain, one at her waist, the other carefully avoiding her injured arm. This close, she could see the droplets clinging to his eyelashes, the pulse beating in his throat, the way his eyes darkened as they dropped to her lips.

"Annie," he breathed, and her name was both a prayer and a curse. She felt him sway forward slightly, felt her own body rise to meet him, felt the years of society polish fall away until she was nothing but nerve endings and want and…

A massive thunderclap made them jump apart. The moment shattered like glass, leaving them both breathing hard, staring at each other in the rain.

"We need to get inside," Jake said roughly, already turning away. "Storm's getting worse."

They made it into the barn just as another lightning bolt split the sky. The familiar smells of hay and horses wrapped around them, but something had changed in the air between them. The almost-kiss hung there like smoke, impossible to ignore.

"Jake." Annie's voice was quiet but firm. "We need to talk about this."

"Nothing to talk about." He moved to check on the horses, his back to her. "Storm's got them spooked."

"I'm not talking about the horses." She followed him, refusing to let him retreat this time. "I'm talking about whatever this is between us. About why you're pushing me away."

A nervous whinny from his favorite mare gave Jake an excuse to delay answering. He moved to soothe the animal, his hands gentle on her neck. Annie watched him, seeing the tension in his shoulders, the careful way he avoided looking at her.

"It's Ricardo, isn't it?" she pressed. "You saw us laughing the other day and thought… "

"Doesn't matter what I thought." His voice was rough. "What matters is keeping this ranch afloat. And lately, seems like every-thing's working against that."

As if on cue, his phone buzzed. Jake pulled it out, his face darkening as he read the message.

"Bank wants to move up the loan review," he said, more to

himself than her. "And the Miller brothers just pulled out of the cattle deal."

Annie's head snapped up. "The winter grazing contract? But that deal was solid."

"Was. Until someone mentioned to them that the ranch might not be operational come spring." His laugh was bitter. "Three guesses who that someone was."

"Ricardo." Annie's hands clenched. "Jake, you have to know I had nothing to do with… "

"Ma'am?" Tommy's voice interrupted them. He stood in the barn doorway, rain dripping from his hat. "Sorry, but Mr. Davidson from the bank is on the phone. Says it's urgent."

Jake moved to take the call outside, but Annie caught his arm. "Put it on speaker."

He started to protest, but something in her face stopped him. He answered the call, his voice carefully neutral. "Davidson. What can I do for you?"

"Jake, wish I had better news." The banker's voice crackled with static from the storm. "But given recent... concerns about the ranch's stability, we're going to need to accelerate the loan review. And frankly, with the Miller contract falling through..."

"The Miller contract isn't final," Annie cut in smoothly, her voice shifting into what Jake had privately dubbed her 'board-room tone.' "In fact, I was just about to call them myself."

There was a startled pause on the line. "Miss Contadelucci? I didn't realize you were involved in the ranch's financial dealings."

"Oh, I'm very involved, Mr. Davidson. And I think you'll find that any concerns about the ranch's stability are greatly exaggerated. Perhaps we should schedule a meeting to discuss the actual numbers?"

Another pause. "I... yes, that might be helpful. Though I should warn you, given the current situation..."

"Given the current situation," Annie interrupted again, "you should know that three other ranches have expressed interest in our winter grazing program. The Millers may find themselves missing out on an excellent opportunity."

Jake stared at her. This was news to him.

"Is that so?" Davidson's voice held new interest. "And these other ranches are…"

"Eager to discuss terms," Annie finished smoothly. "I'd be happy to walk you through the projections tomorrow. Say, ten AM?"

After finishing the call, Annie turned to find both Jake and Tommy watching her with identical expressions of amazement.

"There aren't really three other ranches, are there?" Tommy asked.

Annie's smile was pure Milano steel. "Not yet. But there will be. Jake isn't the only one who can work cattle deals." She turned to Jake, her expression softening slightly. "Whether you want my help or not, this is my home too now. And I protect what's mine."

The word 'mine' hung in the air between them, heavy with meaning. Outside, the storm raged on, but inside the barn, something else was brewing, something that felt like hope and fear and possibility all mixed together.

The next few hours brought a steady stream of neighbors to the barn, seeking shelter from the storm. Old Jim Henderson from the next ranch over, the Peterson sisters from the feed store, Carlos's wife Maria with a thermos of hot coffee. Each brought news: the Miller brothers were already regretting their hasty decision. Word had spread about Ricardo's interference, and the community was pushing back.

"Told them Millers straight up," Jim growled, accepting a cup of coffee from Maria. "Any ranch that'd let some fancy-pants Italian turn them against good neighbors ain't worth dealing with anyway."

"Whole town's talking," Sarah Peterson added. "About the equipment accidents, the mysterious problems. People ain't stupid, Jake. We can see what's happening."

Annie watched Jake absorb this, saw the muscle working in his jaw. The barn had become an impromptu war room, with neighbors offering support, suggestions, and most importantly, their business. The Peterson sisters had feed contracts they were willing to extend. Carlos's cousin needed winter grazing for his small herd. Even Jim Henderson, notorious for his independence, was talking about sharing hay-cutting equipment.

"We take care of our own," Maria said simply, patting Jake's arm. "Always have."

Annie felt her throat tighten at the simple declaration. This was what Ricardo would never understand about ranch life. The connections here weren't built on profit margins and social advantages. They were forged in shared struggle, in helping hands and borrowed equipment, in coffee brought to storm shelters and feed contracts offered in hard times.

As the storm began to ease, their impromptu gathering broke up. Annie helped Maria collect the coffee cups, very aware of Jake watching her from across the barn. When the last neighbor had gone, leaving them alone with Tommy (who was pretending to be very interested in a stable door), the tension that had been building all evening finally broke.

"You don't have to save me, Annie." Jake's voice was low, intense. "Or the ranch."

"I'm not trying to save you." She turned to face him fully. "I'm trying to be your partner. There's a difference."

"A partner?" His laugh was harsh. "Like you and Ricardo were partners? All polished and perfect, understanding each other's worlds?"

"Is that what this is about?" Annie stepped closer, anger and hurt making her voice shake. "You think I want that life back? That perfectly scripted existence where every move was calculated, every relationship was a business arrangement?"

"It's your world, Annie. The world you grew up in. The world you'll go back to when... "

"When what?" She was properly angry now, advancing on him until they were toe to toe. "When Ricardo successfully drives you away? When you push me away to 'protect' me? When my father threatens to cut me off?"

Jake went still. "What?"

Annie let out a breath. "Papa called this morning. Said if I don't come home, if I don't 'stop this nonsense,' he'll cut off my trust fund. My inheritance. Everything."

"Annie..." The pain in his voice was worse than anger would have been. "You can't throw away your whole life for... "

"For what? For this ranch? For this community that's become more family to me than my blood relatives? For you?" Her voice broke slightly on the last word. "Or maybe the real question is, why won't you let me?"

"Because I can't give you what Ricardo can!" The words exploded out of him. "I can't give you security, or luxury, or... "

"I don't want security!" Annie's shout echoed off the barn walls, making the horses stir nervously. More quietly, she added, "I don't want luxury. I want this. The mud and the work and the community. I want morning coffee that tastes like coffee, not some fancy espresso that costs more than feed grain. I want to know my work matters, that it means something real." She stepped closer, her voice dropping to a whisper. "I want you, Jake Spyker, even when you're being an idiotic, noble, stubborn fool."

The silence that followed was electric. Even Tommy had stopped pretending to work on the door.

"I could help," Annie said softly. "One call to Papa, and the bank wouldn't dare foreclose. The equipment could be replaced. Everything Ricardo's done could be undone."

"No." Jake's voice was firm, but his eyes were softer now, watching her face like he was trying to memorize it. "If this ranch survives, it has to be on its own merits. Not because of your family's money or influence."

"Then let me help in other ways. Let me use what I know

about business, about contracts. Let me be your partner in this, Jake. Because whether you want to admit it or not, I'm already your partner in here." She pressed her hand to his chest, feeling his heart thunder under her palm.

For a long moment, Jake just looked at her, his eyes full of things he couldn't seem to say. Then, slowly, he covered her hand with his own, keeping it pressed against his heart.

"Partners," he said quietly, like he was testing the word. "Even knowing it might cost you everything?"

Annie smiled, feeling tears prick at her eyes. "Being here, doing this work, knowing you... it's already given me everything that matters."

Outside, the storm was finally passing, leaving behind that peculiar stillness that follows great turbulence. But inside the barn, something was just beginning to break open, something that felt like dawn after a long, dark night.

Tommy's discreet cough broke the moment, reminding them they weren't alone. Jake stepped back slightly, though his hand lingered over Annie's for one heartbeat longer.

Annie exhaled, steadying herself. "Tomorrow," she said quietly. "We deal with the bank, the Millers, all of it."

"We?" Jake raised an eyebrow, but there was a warmth in his voice that had been missing for days.

"Yes, we." She lifted her chin. "You know cattle and land. I know negotiations and contracts. Together, we can... "

The barn door burst open, cutting her off. Ricardo stood in the doorway, his perfect suit soaked, his usual smooth demeanor ruffled by more than just the storm.

"Annie, cara, I've been looking everywhere for you." His voice held an edge of desperation she'd never heard before. "Your father just called. The board is meeting tomorrow. If you're not there... "

"If I'm not there, what?" Annie's voice was steel wrapped in silk. "The merger will fail? The stock might drop? The Milano social papers will have something new to gossip about?"

"Your entire future is at stake!" Ricardo stepped forward, then stopped abruptly when Blue growled from his place near Jake's feet. "Everything we've worked for, everything your father built… "

"My father built an empire by understanding the land and the people who work it." Annie moved to stand beside Jake, her shoulder brushing his. "Something you seem to have forgotten. Or maybe never knew in the first place."

"The cut brake lines," Jake said quietly. "The missing warning flags. The equipment failures. That was all you, wasn't it?"

Ricardo's face went carefully blank. "I'm sure I don't know what you're talking about. Though accidents do tend to happen on these... rustic operations."

"Rustic operations that have security cameras?" Tommy piped up, unable to contain himself any longer. "Got some real interesting footage from behind the equipment barn. Sheriff might find it interesting too."

The color drained from Ricardo's face. "You're bluffing. There were no cameras… "

"Installed them last week," Jake said, his voice deadly quiet. "After the third 'accident.' Seems Annie isn't the only one who knows something about modern business practices."

Annie felt a fierce pride surge through her. While she'd been working on the financial side, Jake had been laying his own traps. Partners indeed.

"Get off my ranch," Jake continued, taking a step forward. "Don't come back. And if anything else happens here, anything at all, that footage goes straight to the sheriff."

"Annie," Ricardo tried one last time. "Think about what you're throwing away. The life you could have… "

"The life I have," she corrected him, "is right here. And if you ever try to hurt this ranch or the people I love again, I'll personally make sure every agricultural investment firm in Europe knows exactly what kind of man you really are."

For a moment, Ricardo stood frozen, looking between them. Then, without another word, he turned and walked out into the rain.

"Well," Tommy said into the silence that followed, "reckon that's gonna make tomorrow's negotiations with the Millers real interesting."

A surprised laugh burst out of Annie, and suddenly they were all chuckling, the release of tension almost dizzying in its intensity. Jake's arm slipped around her waist, natural as breathing, and she leaned into him.

"You know this isn't over," he murmured. "Your father, the bank, Ricardo..."

"I know." She turned to face him, not pulling away from his arm. "But we have something they don't."

"Oh? What's that?"

"A community that stands together. Real relationships, not business arrangements." She smiled up at him. "And a partnership that's worth more than any merger deal."

"Partners," Jake said again, and this time the word held a promise.

Tommy made a show of heading toward the door. "Think I'll go check on them horses in the south barn. Might take a while. Like, a real long while."

As his boots scuffed away through the scattered hay, Jake looked down at Annie. The storm had passed, leaving behind that peculiar gray-gold light that sometimes follows rain in Montana. It turned Annie's eyes to amber, made her skin glow like something precious.

"You're really staying?" he asked softly. "Even knowing what it might cost?"

Annie reached up, finally allowing herself to trace the line of his jaw with her fingers. "The only thing that would cost too much," she whispered, "would be leaving."

Outside, the sun was breaking through the clouds, turning the rain-washed world to diamonds. Inside the barn, two people who had been fighting their hearts finally surrendered to the inevitable. And somewhere in the distance, thunder rolled one last time, not an ending, but a beginning.

CHAPTER FIFTEEN

THE SPACE BETWEEN

The morning bit hard, like Montana had something personal against early risers. A heavy, cold mist clung to every wooden rail, every rusted nail, every inch of the ranch. Annie tugged her borrowed canvas jacket tighter and marched through the damp ground with boots that were not, in fact, designed for stealth or speed.

She'd woken up alone. She had hoped last night would turn into more today, but it seemed something was off.

After the kiss, Jake had slipped away, back to his house, back to silence. And in his place, the ache of unanswered questions.

That kiss! It had happened. Clear as the morning sky in front of her. Not just one. Not just thank you. Something else. Something deeper.

But they hadn't talked about it. Not a word. And that silence had bloomed overnight into something taut and breathless.

Now, under this pale morning light, everything felt unsure again.

Annie blinked against the wind as she reached the barn, her arms already sore from hauling water to the pens earlier. And that was just round one.

She now stood in the barn doorway, coffee in hand, pretending to check on the feed bins. In reality, she was stealing glances.

Jake was by the feed truck, his silhouette sharp against the early light. He moved like a man who had long since given up trying to impress anyone, fluid, no wasted motion, no effort spent where none was needed. He tossed a fifty-pound bag of feed onto the truck bed like it was a sack of flour. Next, he was heading across the yard. It was brutally obvious that he was going to be working the reins on a stubborn gelding. Jake seemed to be always so focused. Composed. Totally unreadable.

Which made it worse.

Because she didn't know what it *meant now*.

The second one. Not the sweet, thank-you-for-saving-my-Ranch. The one that came after. The one that had nothing to do with gratitude and everything to do with... something else.

She hadn't asked what he was thinking. He hadn't said. And now, here they were, orbiting each other like two magnets trying to figure out whether they were going to snap together or repel.

She hesitated.

They hadn't spoken since yesterday's… what? Kiss? Makeout? Whatever it was, she still wasn't sure what to call it. And even that felt generous. It had been mostly glances. Grunts. One questionable ear nibble. Or was it a nibble? Maybe just a brush of his stubble?

Annie offered a cautious wave. "Morning."

Jake looked over his shoulder, gave a barely-there nod, and turned back to his work.

Not icy, exactly. But not warm either.

He'd been doing that thing again, where he stared at her like she was a math problem with no solution. And every time she thought he might say something... he didn't.

She crossed the yard and grabbed a pair of gloves from the

supply bench. The fingers were too big and smelled faintly of horse. She made a face and shoved her hands in anyway.

Tommy appeared from the side barn with two buckets of grain and a smirk already plastered across his face.

"Well if it ain't Princess Boots," he said, tipping an imaginary hat. "You survived the frost? I thought y'all melted when it dropped below sixty."

Annie groaned. "I'm not a Disney villain. I'm just cold."

He looked her up and down. "Yeah, but those boots are tryin' real hard not to be."

"They're scuffed," she protested. "And broken in."

"They look like they cost more than my truck."

"They probably did."

Annie had put on the pretty boots hoping Jake would be impressed. But so far, it seemed he did not even notice.

Tommy let out a laugh loud enough to wake a few sleepy hens. "Girl, you are somethin' else. Yesterday you were wranglin' hoses like a garden gnome, and now you're tryin' to pretend you're just one of the boys."

"I'm adaptable."

"You're entertaining."

Jake didn't laugh. He was by the truck now, tying off the last sack of feed, eyes fixed on the tailgate like it had insulted his mama.

Annie glanced his way again. Still stone-faced.

"Is he always this chatty?" she muttered.

Tommy leaned closer, as if offering a secret. "He only gets quiet like that when he's thinkin'. Or brooding. Or possibly plotting to throw someone off the nearest cliff."

"Good to know."

"You wanna ride with him or take a four-wheeler?"

She looked at Jake, already climbing into the driver's seat of the flatbed. "Ride with him. Might as well keep working on his trust issues."

Tommy chuckled. "Brave woman."

Jake didn't speak when she climbed in. Just gave the wheel a hard crank, and the truck rumbled to life beneath them.

The cab was warm, at least. Smelled faintly of leather, cedar, and coffee that had long since gone cold. Annie stole a sideways glance. He was watching the road ahead, jaw tight, one hand resting on the wheel like it had offended him.

"I'm not trying to mess things up here," she said quietly.

Still nothing.

"I'm not trying to play cowgirl either. I know what it looks like. But I'm not."

He shifted gears, eyes still forward. "You don't have to explain."

"Clearly I do."

Jake exhaled through his nose. "We're just feeding cattle. No need to complicate it."

But it already was. Everything felt off-kilter. Like the air between them was full of static they were both too stubborn to acknowledge.

Annie folded her arms and leaned against the window. Frost framed the glass like lace, delicate and temporary.

"Fine," she murmured. "Let's just feed the cows."

And they did. In silence. A silence that said everything they weren't ready to.

The hum of chores finally gave way to mid-morning quiet. The cows had been fed, the gates checked, and Tommy had ridden off to the east pasture, whistling like he hadn't a care in the world.

Annie slipped into the tack room, letting the wooden door creak shut behind her. She leaned against it, letting out a breath she hadn't realized she'd been holding.

Jake was impossible. One minute he was warm, almost reachable, and the next... colder than the Montana frost. She felt a tear forming...

She pulled off her gloves and rubbed her hands together. They were red and stiff from the cold, her knuckles raw from the fencing wire. She didn't mind it. Pain had always been easier to deal with than doubt.

Her phone buzzed on the shelf behind her saddle bag.

Buzzed again.

And again.

She hesitated. Nothing good ever came from that many notifications all at once. Especially not from unknown numbers.

She picked it up.

Unknown Number:

Still playing cowgirl?

Buzz.

A little reminder of who you really are…

An image downloaded.

It took a second to load, just long enough for dread to start twisting in her stomach.

She tapped it open, and there it was.

A photo taken by someone across the ballroom floor. Flash-blown and glittering, but unmistakable. Annie in a curve-hugging gold satin gown, laughing beside her father on the marble steps of the Palazzo Vecchio. Her makeup flawless, her expression practiced. Diamonds hung from her ears like trophies. The kind of image publicists loved. The kind Ricardo hoarded.

Her stomach flipped.

She could feel the dress again. The way it clung to her. The way she couldn't breathe from the corset built into the bodice. The way she had smiled like she wasn't thinking about how long she'd be trapped there, standing still, speaking Italian she barely knew, shaking hands with men twice her age.

Beneath the photo, a single caption lit up her screen:

"Remember the real you?"

There was a scrape behind her. She jumped.

Jake stood in the doorway, brow furrowed, one gloved hand

still gripping the edge of the frame. His eyes dropped to her phone screen, still glowing in her hand.

He didn't ask.

He didn't have to.

She turned the phone face-down on the shelf, heart pounding louder than it had any right to.

Jake stepped inside, his boots dragging across the wooden floor. He didn't look at her. Didn't look at the phone again either. Just moved toward the far wall where the wire cutters were hanging.

"Fence line needs mending," he said.

His voice was flat. Like he was reading from a script.

Annie stood frozen for a second, then forced her body to move. She tucked the phone into her jacket pocket, zipped it up, and grabbed a coil of wire from the shelf.

They walked back out into the daylight without a single word.

They didn't speak as they loaded the tools into the ATV. Didn't speak when they rode out past the barn and down the trail that edged the property.

But the silence wasn't empty.

It was loaded. Dense.

The further they drove, the more Jake's jaw tightened. His knuckles were white on the steering wheel, his eyes locked ahead.

She knew by the way he was acting that he had seen the photo on her phone before she could hide it.

She wanted to say something. Anything.

That Ricardo didn't matter. That the girl in that photo wasn't who she wanted to be. That she had never smiled like that because she was happy.

But the words stayed trapped. They rattled around inside her, loud and useless.

Blue trotted behind them, tail wagging, totally oblivious.

The day before she thought they had fixed this. Their talk, the kiss… What was happening now? She was so confused.

It wasn't until they reached the broken section of fence that Jake finally cut the engine.

"You ever fix barbed wire?" he asked, stepping down.

"No."

He handed her a pair of thick gloves. "You're about to learn."

It wasn't kind. But it wasn't cold either. It was… something in between.

The space between.

The southern fence line stretched like a tired thread across the landscape, sagging in places, twisted in others, worn down by time and weather. Wind rustled through the dry grasses, and the sun had finally shown up, just in time to glare off the bits of broken wire like polished silver.

Jake jumped down from the ATV without a word, grabbed a shovel and a fence stretcher, and motioned for her to follow.

Annie adjusted her gloves and slid down carefully, boots crunching on gravel and brittle grass. She hated that her legs still ached from yesterday. Hated that Jake noticed, even though he didn't say a word. Especially because he didn't say a word.

"This post's split," he muttered, tapping the old cedar with the handle of the shovel. "We'll need to reset it before we run new tension."

Annie nodded, even though she wasn't sure what that meant exactly. She just mirrored him, grabbed a tool, knelt beside the post, and pretended like she knew what she was doing.

Jake said nothing. He handed her a pry bar, and together they dug out the broken support. He moved fast, precise, like his hands had done this a thousand times. She followed as best she could, mud splattering up her jeans and onto her coat.

They dropped a new post into place. Jake packed it down with tight, clean stomps. Annie tried to help, but her boot sank deep into the wet ground and stuck.

She tugged, wobbled, and let out a very un-rancherlike "Ugh!"

Jake didn't laugh. He didn't help her out either.

There was dirt on her cheek, hay in her hair, and she was fairly certain one of her socks was halfway off inside her boot. But she held her ground. Glared at him until he offered a quiet, amused, "You're improving. But where are your work boots?"

"High praise."

"You didn't fall. But I think your Princess Boots are ruined."

She yanked her foot free with a dramatic pop and stood tall. "I am a graceful and dignified creature."

"You're muddy."

"I'm adaptable," she said again, brushing off her jeans.

Jake handed her the coil of barbed wire. Their gloves touched. Just for a second. Just a brush.

But it was enough.

She looked up.

So did he.

They froze, close enough to hear each other breathing, close enough that the air between them seemed to tighten like the fence line they were about to pull.

Jake's hand lingered a second too long on the wire.

Annie's fingers trembled slightly.

His eyes dropped to her mouth, then back up. Searching. Guarded. Wanting. Afraid.

He leaned in, just enough to feel the warmth of his breath, just enough for the world to still...

And then...

BARK!

Blue exploded into sound, charging toward a patch of grass behind them, growling low and fast.

Jake reacted first. "Stay back."

He moved fast, reaching for the shovel and stepping between Annie and the noise.

A sharp rattle answered Blue's warning.

Annie flinched hard as she spotted it. Coiled there just a few feet away, half-hidden in the grass, head raised, tongue flicking.

Jake didn't hesitate.

With one clean, brutal motion, he brought the shovel down. Hard.

The snake went still.

Blue backed away, tail wagging again like nothing had happened.

Annie's heart thundered in her chest. "That was… "

"Too close."

She nodded. "Yeah."

Jake looked at the rattler, then at her.

The moment was gone. Whatever had been rising between them had snapped like an old fence wire under too much strain.

He wiped the shovel clean on the ground and went back to the post like it was just another job.

Annie swallowed hard and turned to pick up the gloves she'd dropped.

"Well," she said, trying to sound breezy, "nothing like a deadly reptile to ruin the mood. At least you finally noticed my boots."

Jake didn't answer.

But his eyes lingered a second longer than they needed to before he turned back to work.

The ranch had gone quiet by nightfall.

Crickets chirped like they had something urgent to say, and the wind whispered through the porch beams, stirring the faded flag that hung beside the door. The moon was a pale ghost behind thin clouds, barely lighting the landscape beyond the barn.

Annie sat on the porch steps, her journal open on her knees, pen tapping softly against the paper. She had changed into one of the flannel shirts Meg had given her, sleeves too long, the fabric worn soft from time and love. It smelled like woodsmoke and laundry soap.

She flipped back through pages of scribbled thoughts and disconnected sentences. Half-formed poems. Grocery lists that never got bought. And then:

There's a space between who I was and who I might be.

And I think I'm living in it.

She stared at the line for a long time.

Today had thrown everything out of sync. Ricardo's message. That picture. That moment in the field that almost was... and then wasn't.

The truth was she didn't know who the "real her" was anymore. The girl in the photo? That wasn't her. Not really. But neither was the girl knee-deep in mud and barbed wire.

Somewhere in the middle was a woman trying to matter. Trying to be seen for more than who her father had groomed her to become.

She scribbled another line on the page:

Jake makes me feel like I'm standing on a cliff's edge. Not in a dangerous way. In an alive way.

She paused.

Then underlined *alive*.

Inside the barn, a single light still glowed.

Jake sat at the small workbench tucked between the tack shelves and the storage bins, sleeves rolled up, sweat clinging to his collar despite the evening chill. He held a thin strip of leather in one hand, a carving tool in the other, slowly etching a delicate pattern into a new bridle piece.

It was the kind of task that required patience. Focus. But tonight, his thoughts drifted, stubborn and circling.

Jake set the carving tool down and stared at the half-lit barn aisle. He could still taste the kiss from last night, the second one, the one that had nothing to do with gratitude or adrenaline. It had been quick, a spark struck in a storm, yet it burned brighter now in memory than anything he could put into words.

He brushed sawdust from his jeans, but the tremor in his

hands refused to settle. Wanting Annie was as natural as breathing; wanting her to stay felt reckless. Every beat of his heart counted the cost. The risk was simple: ask her to stay and still lose her. A man like him could lose land, cattle, even the roof over his head and start again. Lose her, though, and he feared there would be no starting over.

He lifted the bridle strap and tested the carved edge with his thumb. The vine pattern looped in tidy repetition, a safe design, predictable, nothing like Annie. She was lightning in an open sky, brilliant and dangerous, exactly what dry grass should avoid yet always hopes to meet in the rainstorm that followed.

He set the leather aside and leaned back on the stool, letting the dim bulb cast a cone of yellow over workbenches and shadowed tack. The hum of the single light mixed with night insects outside, and somewhere beyond the barn wall Blue shuffled, circled twice, and sighed.

"Why do I keep doing this to myself?" he whispered, though Blue could not answer.

He pictured Annie as he had first seen her: heels sinking in the corral dirt, perfume fighting the odor of manure, a thousand miles out of place. He had written her off in that first minute, figuring she would bolt within a week once the glamour wore thin. Instead, she had rolled up silk sleeves and dug in. She followed, she watched, she learned. She got kicked, clawed, and sunburned, and still she got back up. And yesterday, in the storm light, she had kissed him like she belonged nowhere else.

Jake scrubbed a hand over his jaw. The kiss should have settled something; instead, it stirred everything. If she stayed, what then? Would she regret trading ballroom chandeliers for a drafty ranch house and nights that smelled of diesel and cow hide? Would she resent the dust that never quite washed off? He had grown used to the ranch's hunger, the way it devoured time, money, and sometimes hope. Could she? Should he risk letting her try?

He reached for the old tin box on the shelf. Inside were photographs his mother had kept. He rarely opened it. Tonight, he eased the lid back and lifted a picture: his father and mother on their wedding day, standing in the very barn where he now sat. Her dress was plain cotton, but the way his father looked at her, like she was starlight made flesh, made the picture glow. His mother had lasted here because she had loved the land as fiercely as she had loved the man who tended it. It hit Jake then, he wanted someone who loved both, him and the acres under their boots. Wanted it more than he dared admit.

He set the picture down and let his gaze drift to the doorway, as if he might see Annie silhouetted there, hair dancing in a draft, eyes asking questions he still lacked the courage to answer.

She had said the only cost too high would be leaving. Maybe she meant it. Maybe she was already braver than he was.

Fear clawed up anyway. People like her had options. She could walk away tomorrow and board a plane to old stone villas and city lights that never flickered in a storm. He could not follow; his roots ran too deep in this soil.

He pinched the bridge of his nose, fighting the ache behind his eyes. A low bank balance was one thing. A broken heart felt like something the bank could never foreclose on, yet it threatened to take more.

Somewhere outside, an owl hooted, the notes drifting across damp night air. Jake straightened, wiped the leather strap clean, and set it beside three others he had carved this week. Four bridles for four horses that did not yet exist in the herd, an act of hope or madness, he could not say. He cleaned his blade, closed the toolbox, and doused the lamp.

On his way out, he paused by the door, hand resting on the latch. He pictured walking to the guesthouse porch, telling Annie everything. He wanted to say how he loved the way she mispronounced Angus when she was tired, how the little scar on her chin caught sunlight, how her determination scared him because it mirrored his own. He imagined saying all of it and wondered if the words would sound as sure spoken aloud as they did echoing in his skull.

He pushed the door open; the night greeted him with the scent of wet sage and the hush of wide land. A single lantern glowed on Annie's porch. He could just make out her figure curled on the steps; notebook pressed to her chest like a shield. Moonlight silvered her hair, and for one unguarded second, he let himself picture a lifetime of nights where he would walk out and find her exactly like that, home on this porch, under his sky.

His boot scuffed the threshold, and Annie lifted her head. Even at distance he saw the question in her posture; he felt it echo in his ribs. He raised a hand in greeting, a small unsure motion. She mirrored it. Neither crossed the yard.

Jake swallowed hard. Not tonight, then. He would gather the right words first, the ones that did not crumble when spoken. Tomorrow, maybe. Tomorrow, when feed orders balanced, and bank calls returned, and his courage outweighed his fear.

He shut the barn door and headed for the house. Each step away felt like stretching a taut rope between them. A rope could snap, or it could hold. He thought of the fence they fixed earlier, the way fresh wire could hum with tension yet stand strong. Maybe this thing between him and Annie was the same, just pulled tight, singing with electricity, but built to last once secured.

Behind him, Annie watched the barn light die, then the faint gleam of Jake's flashlight bob toward his porch. She exhaled, letting the night carry whispered hopes she was not ready to voice. In her lap the journal lay open, pages fluttering. She uncapped her pen and wrote a single line.

I am not afraid of the leaving anymore; I am afraid of the staying, and what it asks of my heart.

She closed the book, pressed her palm to its cover, and listened. Far off, a coyote yipped at the moon. Nearer, Blue settled with a satisfied huff. Between those two sounds lay the ranch's quiet heartbeat, steady and inviting.

Annie rose, stretched stiffness from her back, and brushed hay from her sleeves. She stepped to the edge of the porch and let the night wind run fingers through her hair. Somewhere beyond the dark, she sensed Jake watching the same sky. Their separate breaths mingled with the cool air, unseen threads drawing them closer, inch by fragile inch.

The space between still existed, but it felt fragile now. Tomorrow promised more work, more questions, more chances to close the distance.

Tomorrow, she thought, curling her fingers around the porch rail, I will help him believe I might be strong enough to stay.

CHAPTER SIXTEEN

THE STORM INSIDE

The morning air sat heavy on the ranch. It wasn't hot, not yet, but it was thick and wet, the kind of weight that settled into your skin and tightened your shoulders without warning. Somewhere behind the barn, a lone rooster crowed, uncertain. Even the animals seemed to know something was off.

The sky held a strange cast, not gray exactly, but bruised.

Maria stood near the steps with her hands on her hips, squinting toward the eastern ridge. Her apron twisted at her waist, forgotten.

"Something's coming," she said, flat and certain. No drama. Just fact.

Annie stepped onto the porch with a mug of coffee and stopped mid-sip. "Is that sky… green?"

Maria grunted. "Green means trouble."

Tommy jogged up the path, winded, his baseball cap turned backward. "Boss," he called, "just got a text from Carlos. The Miller brothers are headed into town. And the bank's already tightening up again."

Annie's gaze snapped to Jake. He was tightening a strap on the feed trailer, not looking up.

"They'll try to lowball us," Annie said. Her voice cut through the morning. "They'll use the storm, frame it like we're vulnerable."

Jake didn't stop working. "Aren't we?"

"No," Annie said, stepping closer. "Not if we hold the line."

Jake paused, one hand still on the leather strap. His jaw set, just a fraction.

Tommy shifted his weight, reading the air. "I'll go check the lower pens."

He disappeared around the barn as one of the old radios crackled to life from inside the tack room.

FLASH FLOOD WARNING IN EFFECT FOR GALLATIN AND SURROUNDING COUNTIES UNTIL 8 PM.

Jake finally looked up. "Perfect," he muttered. "Exactly what we needed."

The ranch snapped into motion.

Maria started calling orders without waiting for permission. Someone needed to move the animals out of the far paddock. Tarps over loose hay. Tools secured. Feed bins latched. Gutters checked.

Jake moved through it like a man who knew chaos and didn't waste time arguing with it. His voice stayed tight and efficient. People listened.

Annie watched him from the edge of the barn, then jogged after him.

"I want to help," she said. "I can handle myself."

"You'll stay by the barn," Jake said, not slowing.

"Jake."

"I said…"

"Let her," Maria cut in, appearing between them like she owned the ground. "You keep forgetting she's not glass."

Jake stopped. He looked at Maria, then at Annie. His expression stayed unreadable, but after a long beat he nodded once.

"Fine," he said. "With me. We check the back fence and clear the west pasture gate. Then you come back. No detours."

"Deal," Annie said, already pulling on gloves.

The wind picked up as they headed out, not the kind that cooled, but the kind that pressed harder.

The path to the back pasture was muddy before the first drop fell. Jake's boots cut clean lines through the soft earth. Annie slipped once, caught herself, and kept going without comment. She muttered something under her breath about Montana needing sidewalks. Jake ignored it.

He had that look again. Storm mode. Focused. Efficient. Closed off.

Annie matched his pace, canvas jacket pulled tight, hair shoved into a messy knot. She wasn't trying to impress him. Especially not when he walked a half step ahead like he didn't notice she was there.

"So," she said finally, "are we pretending that conversation with Tommy didn't happen?"

Jake didn't break stride. "Which part?"

"The part where the Millers are circling like buzzards."

He glanced at her, brief and unreadable. "You said it yourself. They smell blood. Let them circle. Doesn't mean they get a bite."

"Unless we hand it to them," Annie said. "They'll push for a discount, use storm damage as leverage. If we don't counter fast, they'll lock you into a lower price while the ranch is still recovering."

He stopped at the crest of a small rise and turned to face her. "And you've already got the counter lined up."

"I've been thinking about bundling a grazing lease with the barn restoration," she said. "Incentivize longevity. Build value."

Jake blinked. "You want to make a pitch during a flood warning."

"Yes," she said. "Before they get to us."

The silence stretched.

Then he turned back toward the fence line. "Let's fix the fence."

They reached the damaged stretch about fifteen minutes later. A corner post had snapped, and the wire sagged low over the grass. Water was already creeping toward the low ground, a sluggish trickle that would soon turn into a current.

Jake tossed her a second pair of gloves and the wire cutters. "Cut the top line first. We open it wide and funnel the herd toward the ridge."

"On it."

They worked without talking. The storm pressed closer with every gust. The air shifted cooler, sharper, meaner.

By the time they'd cleared a ten-foot stretch, a drizzle began to fall. Jake braced the last post while Annie unspooled fresh wire from the truck bed. Her hands burned. Her arms ached. She didn't stop. Not when the sky darkened. Not when thunder rolled across the hills like a warning shot.

Behind them the herd drifted nearer, unsettled by the chill and the smell of ozone.

Jake shouted over the wind and pointed toward a cluster of calves near the tree line. Annie turned just in time to see one break away, skittish and fast, heading for the low ground.

Jake moved without thinking.

He sprinted, boots slipping in mud. The calf jerked hard when he caught the lead rope. Jake yanked it back, the rope snapping tight, and his shoulder slammed into the post as he twisted. Pain flashed across his face. He went down on his side in the wet grass.

Annie dropped the wire and ran.

Jake was on one knee when she reached him, rain slicking his hair, his hand clamped to his shoulder like he could hold the joint together by force.

"You okay?" she asked.

"I'm fine." The word came out through his teeth. "Just a tweak."

Annie's eyes narrowed. "That's not a tweak."

He tried to stand and swayed. The arm throbbed violently at his side. He didn't lift it. He didn't even try.

"You hurt it before," she said.

"I said I'm fine."

She ignored him and got her hand under his good arm. "Come on. We're going back."

He resisted for half a second, pride pulling him one way and pain pulling harder the other. Then he let her steer him toward the truck.

The rain thickened as they pushed through the field, a full sheet now, loud and cold. By the time the barn came into view, the sky had turned a bruised green-gray.

They made it inside the tack room just as a gust slammed the barn door. Annie shoved it shut behind them and turned the latch.

The tack room was barely a room. A narrow shelf of supplies, a coil of rope, saddles hung on hooks. An overturned bucket sat near the wall. Everything smelled like leather and rain.

Jake leaned back against the boards, breathing hard, eyes fixed on a point over her shoulder as if looking anywhere else might hurt worse.

Annie stripped off her gloves and went straight to the first-aid bin. "Sit."

"I don't need…"

"Jake." Her voice lowered, steady and final. "Sit. Let me see that shoulder."

He dropped onto the bucket with a controlled wince.

The light from the small window was dull, gray, and thin, but enough. Annie pulled the wet flannel away from his shoulder. The skin was already swelling, angry red where he'd hit the post and twisted. "Looks like you did real damage," she said.

"It's just…"

"Don't." She shook her head once. "Don't try to be tough with me."

She touched the swollen area lightly. "Tell me where it hurts. Here? Or here?"

He swallowed. "Right there."

For a moment the storm noise faded behind the sound of their breathing. Jake's chest rose and fell under her hands, slow and deep. Annie became aware of how close she was, knee near his boot, her shoulder almost brushing his.

She looked up.

His eyes were already on her.

Neither of them spoke. The space between them felt charged, the way air felt right before lightning.

Annie lifted her hand and touched his cheek, more a question than a claim.

Jake stayed still for one heartbeat, maybe two. His breath hitched. His gaze dropped to her mouth, then back to her eyes.

Then he pulled away, just enough to break it.

"Don't," he said, low.

Annie froze.

Jake looked past her, jaw tight. "You think you want this," he said. "But you don't."

The words landed hard. Annie lowered her hand and stepped back as if she'd been burned.

Silence filled the small room. Even the rain seemed to hold its breath.

Outside, the downpour eased for a moment. Enough for Annie to hear her own heart.

"I'll check the ATV," she said, her voice too even.

Jake didn't stop her.

The door creaked, then shut. Her boots sounded on the barn boards, then faded.

Jake stared at the floor. He could let her go. He probably should.

But something inside him twisted, something that didn't care about pride or pain.

He pushed up from the bucket. His shoulder flared with the movement. He winced and kept going anyway, crossing to the door on stubborn legs.

Outside, the sky had gone that strange green-gray again, and the wind had started to shift.

The storm doubled down.

One second there was only a heavy hush in the air, a stillness that pressed against the ears. The next, the sky split open and dumped water in hard sheets, so violent it felt like the land itself was being punished.

Annie yanked the collar of her jacket up, blinking through the blur as wind slapped her face. "This is insane!" she shouted.

Jake didn't answer. He already knew what mattered. Get the herd up. Get them out of the low ground. Do it before the creek took the fence and everything with it.

He hauled himself onto the ATV and motioned for Annie. Rain stung his face. Mud grabbed at every step.

Annie jumped on behind him and wrapped her arms around his waist. It was practical, steadying, warm. It felt too good for a moment like this.

The engine growled. They tore back toward the pasture.

When they reached the fence line, the cattle were bunched tight, hooves slipping on the muddy slope. The low pasture, dry enough an hour ago, was drowning. The creek that had barely reached a child's knees was now a churning brown river.

Annie chased after Jake when he jumped off, boots sucking in thick muck. She could barely hear over the pounding rain and thunder, but she could feel panic working its way through the herd. They pressed against the sagging fence near the gully like they sensed the ground was about to give.

"Jake!" she shouted, slipping, catching herself.

He was already there, trying to cut a path around the mass, arms wide as he yelled and clapped to turn them back. They weren't listening. Lightning laced the sky, too close. A steer bellowed and shoved forward, wire bowing under the weight.

"Annie, the cutters!" Jake's voice went raw.

She snatched them from her belt loop and fought her wet fingers. The wire had tension, starting to warp. She found the weak point and clipped fast and low. The snap of release stung her hands, but the gap opened.

"Gate!" Jake shouted.

Annie threw her shoulder into the old metal gate and shoved. It swung wide with a scream of hinges. Water rushed around her boots, soaking her jeans. The nearest steer hesitated, snorting at the flood below.

"Move!" Annie yelled, smacking the post. "Go!"

Jake waved and shouted until the first few broke off and trotted through. Then the rest followed, charging the opening like a funnel.

Annie stepped back just in time as a second steer barreled past. Near the rear, one animal panicked, lost its footing, and swung wide.

She saw it in a slow, sick beat.

The steer clipped Jake sideways, its flank slamming into his left shoulder. Jake went down hard, disappearing into the mud with a grunt.

"Jake!" Annie ran, skidding to her knees beside him.

He didn't move right away. His face pinched tight with pain. His right hand clamped his left shoulder, eyes squeezed shut.

"Don't move," she said, breath coming hard.

"I wasn't planning to," he rasped.

The last few cattle pushed past them, spooked but unharmed. Water surged around Annie's knees now, tugging at her balance.

"We need high ground," she said, fighting panic.

Jake nodded once. "Help me up."

She got her arm under his good side and hauled. Together they staggered toward the nearest rise, mud-coated and shaking. Ten feet. Then twenty.

Behind them, the fence finally gave, posts ripping loose as the current took it.

Annie pointed through the rain. "There. The shed."

A squat wooden structure sat just beyond the corral, half-shadowed beneath a cluster of trees. Four walls. A door that latched. Dry enough to breathe.

Jake shoved it open with his shoulder and stumbled inside. Annie followed and slammed the door shut behind them.

The shed was tight, barely more than storage. The tin roof rattled under the downpour. The air smelled of wet leather, dust, and old hay. A bucket sat near the back wall. A shelf held a plastic bin of supplies, rope, and a few rusted tools.

Jake sank onto the bucket with a controlled wince, holding his arm against his chest.

He closed his eyes for a second and let his head hit the wall. Gritting his teeth in pain he said, "Now that's a proper Montana storm."

Annie's breath came fast. Her hair plastered to her cheeks. She stood there a beat, letting her pulse catch up, letting the thunder stay outside.

"You say 'proper' like you're proud of it," she said.

Then she crouched in front of him and pulled a bandana from her pocket. "Let me see that shoulder."

Jake didn't argue. That alone told her how bad it was.

He fumbled with soaked layers, jaw clenched as he eased his arm free. Annie helped without making a show of it, fingers quick and careful.

The swelling was already ugly, a deep, angry bruise darkening beneath the skin.

"You need a hospital," she said.

"I need you to stop fussing."

"You're hurt."

"I'm always hurt," he muttered.

Annie reached to the shelf, dug through the plastic bin, and found a roll of wrap. It smelled faintly of mildew, but it would hold.

"Hold still," she said.

He did.

The space was so small she couldn't work without getting close. Her shoulder brushed his knee as she wrapped, her hands steady now, the bandage pulling snug around muscle and heat.

Jake's hair dripped. Water ran down his jaw. His chest rose and fell like he'd sprinted uphill.

Annie tried to focus on the wrap. On pressure. On function. Not on the fact that the storm had shoved them into a room where there was nowhere to stand without touching.

"You're allowed to take care of yourself," she said quietly.

"Funny coming from you."

She looked up. "What's that supposed to mean?"

"You haven't stopped since you got here." His eyes held hers, storm-dark and sharp. "Trying to fix everything. The books. The cattle. The bank. Me."

The words landed hard.

"I'm not trying to fix you," she said, voice low.

"No?" Jake leaned back a fraction, watching her. "Then what is this, Annie? One minute you're kissing me like it means something. The next you're talking about pitches and packages and turning this place into some polished experience."

"That's not fair."

"Isn't it?"

She eased back just enough to break contact, not enough to break the tension.

"I kissed you," she said, soft but steady, "because I wanted to. Because for one second it felt like maybe you wanted it too."

Jake looked away. His jaw worked once.

Outside, the rain softened into a steady roar. Inside, the silence was worse.

"I thought…" Annie shook her head, swallowing. "I thought that night meant something to you. But you've barely looked at me since."

"It meant something." The words were so quiet she almost missed them.

Her heart jumped.

Jake shifted, cradling his arm against his chest. "But it doesn't change the fact that this… whatever this is, it can't go anywhere."

"Why?"

"Because you don't belong here."

Annie blinked. "Excuse me?"

He lifted his head, eyes hard with a kind of fear that wore anger like a coat. "You think you do, but you don't. This isn't your life. You'll go back to your world, meetings and boardrooms and five-star meals. I'll still be here trying to keep this place from falling apart."

"You don't get to decide where I belong," Annie said, her voice rising.

"You think this is what you want," he snapped. "But it's not. You're not built for this."

"Oh, really?" Her voice trembled now, not from cold. "Because I just helped you push cattle through a flood, and I wrapped your shoulder while you sat there acting like pain gives you permission to be rude."

Jake's mouth tightened. He looked away, then back. "You're trying to rescue something that doesn't want to be saved."

Annie stepped closer, eyes flashing. "I'm not here to save you. I'm here because I care about you."

Something raw rose in his expression, quick and gone. "And I'm telling you not to."

The rain rattled the tin roof. Water slid down the boards. The shed felt smaller with every heartbeat.

Annie reached up and brushed her fingers along his cheek, gentle and unsure, like she was testing the edge of him.

"I didn't come here looking for you," she said softly. "But I found you anyway."

Jake's eyes closed for a brief second. His face leaned toward her hand.

Then he pulled back, slow but firm, like a man stepping away from warmth before it burned him.

"I'm not someone you fix, Annie."

Her hand fell. "I never thought you were."

Silence filled the gap between them.

Then Annie exhaled and nodded once, as if deciding something inside herself. "You were right."

Jake cracked one eye open. "About what?"

"The storm. The Millers. All of it."

He gave a short, humorless laugh. "Don't sound so surprised."

"I'm not," Annie said. "Just admitting it out loud."

Thunder rolled in the distance, further off now. The worst of it had moved on.

Jake shifted, wincing as he tried to sit straighter. "You handled that well."

"Wasn't exactly my first emergency."

"No," he said, quieter. "But it was your first cattle flood."

She shrugged. "Seemed like a good time to learn."

He watched her for another beat, unreadable. Then his gaze dropped to his hands, flexing his fingers slowly as if he needed something to do besides feel.

"Annie…" he started.

"What?"

He swallowed. "Never mind."

She leaned in a little, stubborn. "No. Say it."

He met her gaze, something honest in his eyes at last. "I don't want you getting attached."

Annie blinked. "To what?"

"To all of this," he said. The words sounded like warning and confession at the same time.

Outside, a gate clanged in the wind. The shed creaked.

Annie sat back, the rush of adrenaline fading, leaving the ache underneath. "I'm not a child, Jake. I know what I'm doing."

He nodded once. "Okay."

But his face said he didn't believe it.

Annie stood and moved to the door, peering out. The rain had eased to a drizzle. The sky was still gray, but lighter.

"Storm's letting up," she said.

Jake pushed himself to his feet with a tight breath. "Let's get back."

As he left the shed he didn't look back at her. His shoulders stayed set, like turning around might break him.

Annie followed him into the mist.

After a minute, she called after him, forcing her voice to sound normal. "Let's get back before somebody sends out a search party."

Jake nodded without turning.

They slogged through the mud to the ATV and headed for the barn, the storm behind them but not forgotten.

By late afternoon the worst had passed, leaving a sky cracked open with weak streaks of sunlight. The air smelled like wet hay and overturned earth. Thunder still muttered in the distance, softer now.

Jake stood near the barn, stiff, his left arm hanging wrong at his side. The wrap Annie had put on him was soaked through. He refused to go inside. Watching the damage from a distance felt safer than admitting what it would take to repair.

The lower pasture was flooded. Tools were scattered or

buried in mud. Fence lines sagged. The ranch looked like it had taken a beating it hadn't earned.

Tommy jogged up, wide-eyed. "We lost at least a dozen feed bins. Some of the hay floated down into the creek. A couple calves need checking."

Jake gave a short nod and winced immediately. "I'll…"

"No," Annie cut in, stepping between them, voice firm. "You won't. You're done for the day. Sit down and let us work."

Jake blinked.

Annie had changed into a dry shirt, an old Henley from somewhere, sleeves pushed up. Her braid still dripped, but her shoulders were square and her jaw was set.

Tommy looked between them and nodded. "She's right, boss. I'll check on the calves."

As Tommy ran off, Jake looked at Annie. "You sure you want to take point on this?"

Annie didn't hesitate. "You said it yourself. We've got bigger problems. So I'm going to start fixing them."

She turned and strode toward the equipment shed, already calling orders. "Who's got the chain saws? We clear that downed oak first. Maria, can you head count the horses? And somebody shut that chicken coop before they end up in the neighbor's yard."

Jake leaned against a post and watched her go.

Trucks began arriving just after five. One by one, neighbors rolled in. Some carried tools. Others brought chains and gloves. More than a few carried casseroles under towels and wore damp jackets like badges.

Word traveled fast when a ranch took the brunt of a flood.

A rusted red truck kicked up gravel as it pulled into the drive. Two men climbed out with matching smirks and button-downs too clean for ranch work. The Miller brothers.

"Well, well," the taller one drawled. "Looks like y'all took a beating."

Jake straightened, ignoring the stab in his shoulder.

Annie beat him to it.

"We'll be standing again by morning," she said, light and calm. "If you're here to talk business, give us until the mud's cleared."

The shorter brother chuckled. "Still planning to meet?"

Annie nodded. "Tomorrow. Noon. I'll have coffee waiting."

The taller one lifted his brows, measuring her. "Tomorrow at noon," he said, smiling. "Storms have a way of changing numbers."

They climbed back into the truck and drove off without another word.

Maria appeared beside Jake. "You see that?" Pride warmed her voice. "She didn't blink."

Jake nodded slowly. "No. She didn't."

Maria smiled and moved away, rolling up her sleeves, headed straight toward the work.

Jake stayed where he was.

His shoulder throbbed. His pride ached worse.

Annie had taken hold of the disaster without breaking stride. People listened to her. Trusted her. Even the old-timers had stopped second-guessing her.

She was the one holding the place together right now.

That thought hit harder than the steer had.

Later, the kitchen light glowed warm against the dark. Annie stood alone at the sink, scrubbing mud from her hands. Her face was calm, but her eyes were somewhere else.

She stared through the window, past the porch, past the shadowed outline of the barn. Somewhere out there, Jake was probably sitting alone again, shoulder stiff, pretending solitude was strength.

She shut off the faucet and dried her hands slowly. The silence wrapped around her like a second skin.

If she had kissed him first, would it have changed anything?

CHAPTER SEVENTEEN

WHISKEY AND WILDFLOWERS

*L*ike so many things on the ranch, a new day brought new challenges. Annie hoped the stress of yesterday would shrink under fresh light and fresh work. Today felt different, encouraging. Cleanup had already begun. Maybe it was the bright sky, the clear weather, or the promise of the post-storm bonfire that had everyone in such a good mood. Annie even thought she saw a smile at the edge of Jake's lips. Or maybe she was just looking at his lips, remembering their kiss, hoping for another.

The pasture smelled like wet clover and sun-warmed mud. Men hauled limbs to a pile near the old cottonwood. Two of the hands pushed a broken panel toward the shop. Someone started a radio, soft at first, then louder. Above them the sky spread wide and rinsed clean, as if the storm had never happened. The creek still ran fast, but the water gleamed clear.

Annie breathed it in. The whole place felt sore and alive, the way a body felt when it was going to heal.

"Fence line next," Jake said. His voice carried that rough kindness she'd come to trust. "We brace the posts, then we check the north gate."

"I'll take the brace crew," Annie said. "Brett can start on the gate."

Jake tipped his chin, approval without a speech. He wore an old shirt and the same belt he always wore. The leather was scarred, the "SPIKE" buckle scratched, and it suited him. He worked beside her, not above her, and that had started to change how people looked at her. Not the heiress who'd shown up with city shoes, but a woman who rolled up her sleeves and got it done.

They walked the line. Annie pressed her palm against each post, feeling where the ground had given and where it had held. She sent Marisol for more gravel, then handed a level to Wes. They set a new anchor, knees in the mud, shoulders burning. It felt good and honest.

Her mind kept flicking to the bonfire stacked near the far corral. It would be lit at dusk if the wind stayed friendly. There would be music and stew, maybe a few bottles from Whiskey Creek for the adults. Someone had already braided wildflowers and draped them over a sawhorse. Kids would want crowns. She made a mental note to cut more twine.

"Careful," Jake said, steadying a post while she tightened the line. His hand brushed her wrist. It was nothing, and it was everything. It lit the memory she'd been trying to set aside, the kiss that had surprised them both, the gentleness that had followed, quiet and sure.

She wanted to ask if he was thinking about it too. She didn't. Work came first. Pride second. Questions last.

By late morning the crew hit a rhythm. Someone brought sweet tea in a cooler. Someone else passed around biscuits with honey butter. Laughter showed up easy and light. Annie tied her hair back, then knelt to show two teenagers how to set a brace wire tight without slicing fingers. She heard herself, crisp and patient, and wondered when this had become natural.

She liked it. She liked the ranch dirt on her knees. She liked the way she and Jake shifted around each other without speaking, each knowing where to stand.

At noon she took a quick call by the barn. "Gary, it's Annie. I want to talk about feed credit terms."

Gary ran a supply yard three towns over. He owed Jake a few favors. Annie was counting on that, and on the fact that people liked being part of a story that looked like resilience. She pitched clean and calm. The storm hit us, but we're moving. The bonfire tonight will show the town we're standing. I'd like to tell them we have your support. A two-week credit on the next two shipments will let us meet a tight window.

He whistled through his teeth. "You don't miss, do you?"

"I try not to," she said. "This helps the Millers trust our time-line. It helps us keep people on payroll. It helps me sleep."

He laughed. "You sound like a rancher."

"I'm learning," she said.

"You've got your credit," he said. "Two shipments, two weeks. Tell them Gary said the ranch is good for it."

She thanked him and hung up. For a moment she stood still, hand on the warm barn wall, and let herself feel proud. Not because she was owed it, but because she'd earned it.

Jake found her there. "That sounded promising."

"Two shipments on credit," she said.

"Good," he said, and his eyes softened. "You did that."

"We did that," she said, and she meant it.

The afternoon drifted forward on the hum of work. The sun climbed, then leaned west. Annie stole twenty minutes to cut wildflowers, purple lupine and Indian paintbrush, a few tough daisies that had survived the flood. She laid them across the tailgate and threaded twine through the stems. The first crown came out crooked. The second settled just right. She tried the third on a laughing girl with muddy boots, then made a fourth for the girl's brother. Their mother smiled the tired smile of a woman who needed one easy thing today and found two.

"Do I get one?" Jake asked from the shade of the truck.

"You're not brave enough," she said.

"Try me," he said.

She lifted a crown and stepped close. He dipped his head, not much, just enough for her to place it. It looked ridiculous on him. It might've been the best thing she'd seen all week. He reached up and touched it with two fingers, careful not to crush the stems, then set it on the tailgate like it was made of glass.

"Happy now?" he asked.

"Almost," she said.

Her gaze slid to his shoulder beneath the rolled sleeve. "How is it, truly?"

He rolled it once, careful. "Better."

She stepped in and laid her fingers where muscle met collarbone. Heat lived there, steady and human. "Here?"

"A little," he said.

Her thumb found a tight line and eased it. Her other hand hovered, then settled light against his chest. His breath deepened under her palm. The world narrowed to the low hush of wind and the small creak of leather.

"You're still tight," she said.

"I'm stubborn," he said.

"I noticed."

He smiled, then softened. "Last night helped. A good night of sleep fixes so many things, including this shoulder."

"You actually slept," she said.

"Enough," he said. "More than I expected."

"Good." She worked a slow circle with her thumb. "Tell me if I'm hurting you."

"You're not." He caught her wrist and guided her a fraction higher. "Right there."

She held the spot and felt the knot ease. His heartbeat tapped against her other hand. The rhythm steadied her in a way she wouldn't name.

"Better?" she asked.

"Getting there," he said. "Sleep took the edge off. You're finishing the job."

She looked up. "I can keep going."

"Dangerous offer," he said, but he didn't move away.

"Then call it a promise," she said.

His eyes warmed. "I'll hold you to it, after the fire."

They held each other's gaze for a breath too long. Footsteps approached. Tommy cleared his throat in the kindest way.

"Bonfire crew is asking about start time," he said. "Wind looks steady."

"Dusk," Jake said. "We'll keep it small and smart."

"I'll set up the food tables," Annie said. "We can pull the long boards from the shed."

"Already on it," Tommy said. "Maria made stew. The good kind."

"Then I'll handle the sign," Annie said.

"What sign?" Jake asked.

She grinned. "A simple one. Thank you for helping us rebuild. If you want to pledge work hours this week, add your name. If you want to donate, there's a jar. If you need help, write what you need."

He studied her a long second. "No pressure, just invitation."

"Exactly," she said.

By late afternoon the yard began to change. The work trucks eased away. Clean shirts appeared. A guitar leaned against a hay bale. Two neighbors carried in folding chairs. Someone strung lights between the porches and the old cottonwood.

The bonfire stack waited, ringed by a safe circle of gravel. A cooler of lemonade sat near. A smaller cooler, clearly marked, sat under the table for later. Whiskey Creek had sent a few bottles with a handwritten note: Glad you all are safe. Save us a dance some Saturday. The label showed a sprig of wildflowers tucked under the name. Annie set the bottles beside stacked paper cups and smiled at the way the night had already named itself, whiskey and wildflowers.

She wrote the sign in clear block letters and taped it to a salvaged board. Jake fixed the board to a post. He looked taller in the late light, less burdened. The almost-smile had turned into a real one, small and sure.

He pointed to the jar. "Think it'll work?"

"It will," she said. "People like to help when they can see the shape of it."

"Who taught you that?" he asked.

"My father," she said, then softened it. "And you."

He shifted, surprised. "Me?"

"You never ask with a speech," she said. "You hand someone a post and a purpose."

He took that in and didn't look away. "Annie?"

"Yes."

"Thank you," he said. Two words, steady and firm.

Dusk settled like a blessing. The first match touched the kindling. Fire woke, leaned, and grew. Heat kissed shins and faces. The crew gathered, then the neighbors, then a few more faces from town who'd heard there would be stew. Children chased the edges of the light. Someone tuned the guitar. Someone else started a soft beat on a turned bucket. Laughter threaded through the crackle of wood.

The jar collected folded bills and a few coins. The sign collected names in quick, honest handwriting. I can bring my chainsaw Monday. I can watch kids while you haul. I can bake bread. Annie felt her throat tighten and let it.

She moved through the crowd with a stack of paper bowls. She told stories about the storm and the creek and the stubborn calf that tried to climb into the back of a truck. People laughed and added their names. She kept the tone light, the message clear. They were standing. They were grateful. They weren't done.

Jake met her at the edge of the light. He held two cups and

offered one. "Not the barn fire whiskey," he said. "The kind that tastes like honey."

She took a small sip. Warmth bloomed slow and kind. Music rose.

The song ended. The crowd clapped. The fire cracked and hissed, lifting sparks into the dark. Annie tipped her chin up and watched them rise, little orange prayers drifting into the Montana night.

This bonfire wasn't just light on wood. It was a promise.

People said it started back in wagon days, when a flame on the ridge meant the same thing every time: we made it through. We're still here. Annie had heard it twice already tonight, from different mouths, like a line the valley remembered on its own. After a storm, the town gathered. Doors opened. Folks showed up, even families who didn't usually stand that close together. Old grudges got smaller beside heat, music, and the simple relief of seeing each other alive.

Someone near the front stepped up first, carrying a piece of broken wood, a porch rail maybe, or a shutter. Tommy had told her that part too. The first branch always came from someone who'd lost something that week. They laid it down without ceremony, and the rest of the town followed, as if the offering made it official.

Jake had insisted they all come.

"Goodwill matters," he'd said earlier. "Faces matter. Eating together. We go as one."

He'd walked the yard like a foreman calling roll, telling the ranch hands, "Rest can wait. Tonight, we stand with our neighbors."

Annie had borrowed boots from Maria. They were scuffed and a half-size too big, so she stuffed the toes with thick wool socks. Maria had added a plaid shirt that had once belonged to her brother. It hung wide and honest across Annie's shoulders.

Annie buttoned it, rolled the sleeves, and checked herself in the truck window.

She smiled. Not because she looked like she belonged, but because she'd decided to try.

When the music started again, Annie remembered Tommy rapping his knuckles against the bed of the truck earlier that day.

"Learn the steps before we get there," he'd told her, like it was as important as showing up at all.

"I plan to fake it," she said.

"Feet together. Small steps. Walk with rhythm." Tommy clapped a beat. Right, left, close, turn.

Annie tripped on the turn, then found it again.

"You've got it," he said.

"I've got nothing," she said, breathless and happy.

Annie had never seen anything like this back in Italy. Hay bales ringed the pit. Whiskey barrels held lanterns and cups. Strings of lights draped the cottonwood and porch rail. Fiddle and guitar slid out like honey. Dust turned gold in the firelight. Even the shy stepped closer when the first sparks rose. Country songs everyone knew spilled from the porch, easy and bold. Someone tuned a mandolin, the notes skipping like water over stone.

She was out of place and she loved it.

People who knew Jake called his name and tipped hats. A few studied her with open curiosity. She smiled and kept moving.

Tommy brought her water and pointed at the dirt patch where couples already danced. "Practice," he said.

He led her to the fringe. Light on his feet, patient with hers. She missed every other turn, then laughed and tried again. The beat quickened. Tommy caught her when she slipped.

"You're doing fine," he said.

She glanced toward the cottonwood tables. Jake was talking with the fire chief. She lifted her chin and gave him a grin that asked one simple thing: ask me.

His gaze found her, then slid away. He raked coals like they had offended him.

She kept her smile and kept dancing. A small voice wondered if she'd asked too much with her eyes. She chose joy anyway.

The fire settled into a steady heat. Children ran with marshmallow sticks. The crew guarded the ring of gravel. Lemonade passed to the kids. Stew and cornbread appeared in neat lines. Neighbors who'd lost shingles laughed with neighbors who'd lost a porch step. Hands that hauled debris that morning passed plates with the same steady care.

After a fast song, Tommy steered her to the water table. "You lived," he said.

"I did more than live," she said.

"Good. Don't let Jake vanish."

"He isn't vanishing," she said, but her eyes found him anyway.

Jake stood alone near the barrels, cup in hand. He watched the dancers, then the fire. Like he wanted to cross the space and take her into the next song, maybe the one after that too. He didn't move. Pride had reins. Fear did too. The town saw everything, and he called that patience.

During a water break he waited at the jug. Two hands talked behind him, low and careless.

"She's leaving Tuesday," one said.

"Back to Rome?" the other asked.

Jake's spine tightened. He didn't turn. He poured water and drank slow.

"Where'd you hear that?" the second asked.

"Courier stopped at the Gazette," the first said. "Call with a lovely accent. Said to watch the ranch. Said the lady misses home."

Jake set his cup down. Ricardo. He stared at the rim until his vision cleared.

Annie walked up with two bowls of stew. She read his face before he could fix it. "Hungry?" she asked.

"Always," he said.

They stood in the glow while a new song started up.

"Tommy says I didn't disgrace the ranch with my dancing," she said.

"You didn't," Jake said.

"He says I need work on the spin."

"You do," he said, trying for a smile.

She touched his arm. "What's wrong?"

He set the bowl on a barrel. "Nothing I can't handle."

She'd learned not to push until he pushed back. "Then handle it," she said. "After you eat."

They ate in quiet while the fire talked. Jake looked at her borrowed shirt and those too-big boots and felt the ache of what leaving would take from her. He didn't know what he was allowed to ask.

Across the green, the Gazette editor chatted with the fire chief. Jake could've crossed over and dragged the rumor into the light. He didn't feed it.

Annie finished and licked a thumb where stew had caught the edge. The small move undid him. She bumped his shoulder.

"Dance with me," she said. "I'll go slow." Then she winked.

He set the bowl aside and held out his hand. "Come on."

They stepped into the line. The music was a walk with rhythm. He set a pace she could keep. She laughed when she hit the turn, then laughed again when she missed it. The knot in his chest loosened.

Tommy swept past and tipped his hat. Maria waved from the bales. The fire sighed and threw up sparks. Tomorrow would bring work again, but tonight belonged to light and company.

More names filled the paper at the sign. More bills rested in the jar. People said yes to faces. People said yes to effort.

A song ended. Another began. Annie rested a hand on his chest and looked up. No words, just a steady look that said: I'm here.

He nodded back. I see you.

He'd ask her about Tuesday later, when the fire turned to coals. He'd trust her words over any call with a lovely accent.

For now, they danced. The old tradition held. The night did what it always did after storms, it took the pieces and made them warm again.

The line dance broke apart in laughter and boots. Annie pushed hair from her eyes.

A small hand tugged her sleeve. "You almost had it," the girl said. Pink boots. Escaped braid.

"Almost?" Annie grinned.

"You kept forgetting the slide," the girl said. "Two-step needs the slide. Like this." Heel, then toe. A soft shuffle.

Annie mirrored her, stepped on her own boot, and the girl giggled.

"What's your name?" Annie asked.

"June," she said.

"Will you teach me?" Annie asked.

June nodded, delighted. "Loose," she said. "Let the music work too."

Fiddle and guitar spilled from the porch. "Count with me," June said. "One, two; one, two."

They stepped together. Annie relaxed. Tommy's lesson returned. June added the missing piece.

"That's it," June said. "Now the slide."

Annie slid, push then glide, better when she stopped thinking. They moved between hay bales and whiskey barrels. People smiled as they passed. June beamed.

On the edge of the circle, Jake watched. Fire etched his jaw. His shoulders held tight.

He told himself he was only watching because Annie was learning. He told himself it was just a town thing.

June spun under Annie's arm. Annie laughed, sudden and bright. Jake felt it like a hand on his chest.

"You're good," June said. "You needed the slide."

"I needed June," Annie said.

"Everybody needs June," the girl said, then ran back to her mother.

Annie found Jake at the edge. She didn't wave him over. She met his eyes.

The band leader tapped the microphone. A slow song rose, close and easy. Couples drifted together.

Jake set his cup on a barrel. Enough watching. He moved through smoke and stopped in front of her.

"Will you dance with me?" he asked.

"Yes," she said.

He took her hand, rough and warm. Her other hand found his shoulder. His palm settled at her waist. The music wrapped them and they swayed.

They didn't speak at first. Her breath brushed his collar. His was smoke and mint. Sparks rose like jarred fireflies.

"I watched you," he said.

"I noticed," she said.

"You looked happy."

"I was." She lifted her chin. "I am."

Their bodies found a tiny circle, sway, pause. The world shrank to the space between their mouths.

He leaned in and stopped. She waited. He closed the last inch.

"Annie," he breathed.

"Jake," she answered.

Their lips met. A dancing kiss, warm and electric. Her hand tightened on his shoulder. His fingers flexed at her waist. It felt like the first clear breath after a storm.

For a heartbeat nothing else existed.

Then the world found them.

A whistle split the air. Then another. Someone whooped. "About time," a voice called. "Go on, Jake," another sang.

Jake heard the heat of eyes and tensed. He pulled back a fraction.

Annie aimed for light. "Looks like we won best show," she said.

His guard slammed up like a gate. "I'm not a sideshow," he muttered.

It hit like a punch. She kept her smile because pride was armor. "Of course not," she said. "Neither am I."

He stepped back. The space grew. The song kept going. Some pretended not to look. Others looked harder.

Maria hooked an arm through Annie's. "Help me steal a cookie," she said.

Annie let herself be guided out of the center. Faces turned friendly again. The slow song ended on a soft chord.

June returned with a fist of wildflowers. "For your hair," she said.

"Thank you," Annie said. "The slide saved me."

June tucked a stem behind Annie's ear. "There," she said. "Now you look like Mom's coffee mug."

Annie laughed. It didn't reach her eyes. Maria heard the thinness and squeezed her arm.

"Jake's a good man," Maria said, quiet. "He forgets the world isn't a cattle ranch. Folks look because they love a story."

"I know," Annie said. "I just wish he'd kept looking at me."

At the edge of the light, Jake stared into his cup. The kiss had felt right. The eyes had felt wrong. He hunted for a path between.

His pocket buzzed. Unknown number. A preview image of the kiss. Caption: That didn't take long.

He didn't open it. Another message landed, a link. His jaw tightened.

Across the fire, Annie's phone lit up. Ricardo.

Sweet, the text read. Montana suits you. Smile for the papers.

She locked the phone and slid it away.

"Everything alright?" Maria asked.

"Work," Annie said.

"Eat a cookie," Maria said. "Sugar helps."

Annie took one. Lemon and butter steadied the shake. The band lifted into something faster. Kids shrieked. Men lined up for coffee. The night kept doing what it did.

Jake pocketed his phone and crossed the distance. He stopped at the table and met Annie's eyes.

"I didn't mean it that way," he said.

"Which way did you mean it?" she asked.

He exhaled. "I'm still learning how to be seen."

"Me too," she said. "Tonight felt good. Then it felt like a spotlight."

"Me neither," he said. "I liked the first part."

Her mouth softened. "Me too."

They stood in the mild chaos, not touching. The pull between them stayed quiet and real.

"We don't have to be a show," he said.

"No," she said. "We can be a story."

A hint of a smile found him. "A slow one."

"Sometimes the slow ones last," she said.

Jake lifted a wildflower and turned it between his fingers, then tucked it behind her ear beside June's. "Better," he said.

"Better," she echoed.

The crowd shifted. The fire cracked. A gust carried wet earth. The storm was already turning into a story that would grow by morning. The kiss would grow too.

Annie decided something small and strong. She wouldn't chase him, and she wouldn't run. She'd keep her head high and her feet moving. She'd dance because she wanted to.

"Come on," she said. "June won't forgive us if we skip practice."

Jake huffed a laugh. "The slide," he said. "Yes, ma'am."

They stepped back into the circle, not center, not edge. Two people in a slow, stubborn story. They found the count. One, two; one, two. They didn't kiss again. Not here. They didn't tear apart either.

The song ended. The crowd clapped. The fire lifted sparks into the dark. Annie watched them float, warm little stars rising. She breathed and let the hurt find its place. Not gone, not running the show.

And for now, they danced.

Before long the bonfire died down and it was time for everyone to head home. The last song faded. Night settled on the pasture.

After a storm, one of the beautiful things was how people not only showed up, they stayed to put it back together. Hay bales slid onto trailers. Whiskey barrels rolled to the shed. Chairs stacked in towers. The fire sank to a red bed of coals, then to memory.

Annie tied off a bag and hauled it to the truck. June's mother waved goodnight. Tommy lifted the last cooler and tipped his hat. Maria counted serving spoons. The band snapped cases shut.

By the time the last taillights vanished, the pasture was quiet.

Jake waited at the gate, hands in his pockets, brim pulled low. He didn't look at her. Annie put the broom in the shed and closed the door. The click sounded louder than it should've.

They took the road toward the house. Gravel crunched under their boots. He didn't reach for her hand. She didn't ask why. Their shadows stretched, then vanished when a cloud swallowed the moon.

Silence grew between them.

Annie held on to the good parts, June's pink boots, the flower behind her ear, the slow dance, the way his palm had settled at her waist. She waited for him to speak. He didn't.

At the cottonwoods, she stopped. "What's wrong?" she asked.

He took two more steps, then turned. "What do you think is wrong?"

"I don't know. That's why I asked."

"All those looks," he said. "The way you threw them around like bait."

"Bait?" Her chest tightened. "I was dancing, Jake."

"Pretending," he said.

She heard the word and felt the sting. "June was teaching me. She's eight. It was sweet."

"It was a show," he said. "Your show. You had the whole town eating out of your hand. Then you had me."

She gave one sharp laugh. "You think I had you? You kissed me."

"You wanted it where everyone could see." His voice stayed low. "That's what those looks were. Come get me, Jake. Come put on the crowning act."

"I looked at the man I care about," she said. "I wanted him to dance with me. That's it."

"You'll be gone before the ground's dry," he said, gesturing at the field. "Just like everyone else who treats this place like a vacation stop."

"That's not fair."

"Fair has nothing to do with it," he said. "You'll fly off to Milan or Rome or wherever your family calls you. You'll remember a bonfire and a kiss. I'll still be here with busted posts and a note from the bank."

"Do you want me to leave?" she asked.

He flinched. "I want the truth."

"You're getting it," she said. "I'm here. I'm trying. I called Mr. Davidson. I pushed on the Millers. I didn't have to. I did it for the ranch. I did it for you."

"For me." He laughed without humor. "You don't know me."

"Because you won't let me," she said. "You hide behind the land like it's a wall. You push people away so they can't hurt you. You call it grit. I call it fear."

"Fear," he repeated.

"Yes," she said. "You think not needing anyone makes you strong. It just makes you lonely."

He stepped closer. "You don't get to come here for a handful of weeks and tell me what I am."

"Then tell me," she said. "What are you, Jake?"

He opened his mouth, then closed it.

"I know what I see," she said. "A good man who loves this place. A man who's been let down. A man who'd rather cut the rope than risk someone else dropping it."

"Stop," he said.

"No," she said. "Not this time. You say I'm playing a part. Look at you. You play the stoic rancher who doesn't feel. It's a costume."

His eyes sparked. "Don't talk to me about wanting."

"Then listen," she said. "I didn't pull you into that kiss. You came to me. You asked me to dance. You kissed me. You wanted it too. Be brave enough to say it."

Wind moved through the leaves.

"I wanted it," he said, low. "I wanted it until they started staring. Then it felt like I was twenty, and the whole county was waiting to see if I'd fail."

"No one was waiting for you to fail," she said. "They were happy for you. I was happy for you."

"They were happy for a show," he said. "I'm not a sideshow."

"You're not," she said. "So stop giving them power over you."

He stared at her, jaw working.

"You called me a coward," he said.

"Not yet," she said. "But I'm close."

Then she said it, steady and quiet. "You're a coward, Jake. Brave with bulls. Brave with barns at two in the morning. A coward with people. You tell yourself people leave and land stays, so you choose land. It's easier than being left."

He looked past her at the dark horizon.

"You don't get to decide I'm leaving," she said. "Not for me."

"I know your type," he said.

"You know your hurt," she said. "You don't know me."

They stood like two posts set too far apart to hold the same wire.

"I'm not your past," she said.

For a breath she saw the man from the dance. Then the shutter dropped.

"I can't do this," he said.

"You mean feel," she said.

"I mean this," he said, gesturing between them. "Goodnight, Annie."

He turned away and walked into the dark, boots sure, shoulders rigid.

Annie climbed the steps. The screen door sprung and snapped. She looked once at his back beyond the cottonwoods. She wanted to call him by name. She didn't.

Inside, she leaned both hands on the kitchen table and lowered her head. The flower June had tucked behind her ear slid loose and fell to the floor.

She didn't pick it up at first.

She breathed. The house smelled like lemon oil and pine.

She told herself she wouldn't cry. Tears came anyway, hot and real. She let them fall, then wiped her face with the back of her hand.

She straightened, picked up the fallen flower, and laid it on the sill.

"Alright," she whispered. "Alright."

She turned off the porch light. Darkness settled.

Annie went to bed alone.

Somewhere beyond the firelight, their kiss became a message on someone else's screen.

* * *

MANY MILES away in the city, in a tall modern hotel, the view of lights sat behind glass like a trophy. Ricardo turned his chair and watched car headlights stitch the highway. He preferred nights for decisions. After dark, people were slower to see the angles.

The suite hummed low, HVAC, distant elevators, the tiny whine of an espresso machine on the bar cart. He lifted the cup, sipped, and set it down with a careful clink.

On his screen, an unsent email waited.

Subject: Regarding Your Daughter's Future

To: Dante Contadelucci

The cursor blinked, patient.

Ricardo reread the first paragraph. Respectful. Warm. The second promised proof. The third offered a plan. He changed a single word and let it settle on his tongue.

He scrolled to the attachments. Photos from Montana. The bonfire. Wildflowers against blonde hair. Jake's hand at Annie's waist. A kiss that held a beat longer than friendly, town faces caught mid-cheer.

He tapped one image to full screen. Sparks hovered like stars. Her eyes were closed. Jake's weren't. The frame told the story better than any paragraph. Ricardo smiled, without warmth. Proof was a generous word, but it would do.

He clicked back to the draft. Dante liked efficiency. Clean lines, clear steps, exits you could defend in a boardroom. Ricardo wrote that way when he wrote to him. He thanked the Contadelucci family for their trust. He referenced the Milan portfolio and a timely opportunity in Naples.

Then he added the sentence he'd been sharpening since morning.

With your permission, I will bring your daughter home before her choices cause lasting damage to the Contadelucci name.

He let it sit. It looked reasonable. It felt like arithmetic.

He glanced at the second monitor. A map of travel bookings

glowed in soft blue, flights, cars, hotels. His assistant had flagged the next window. The storm had knocked Montana sideways. Emotions ran high. Timing mattered more than force, his mentor used to say.

The desktop pinged. A new message from the stringer in town.

Two lines.

Bar owner says the banker is sniffing around the ranch again. Miller family asking questions at the feed store.

Ricardo filed that under Useful. He already had a draft for Mr. Davidson that hinted at concern. He preferred pressure applied with fingertips, not fists. One nudge at the bank. One whisper near the Millers. One well-timed item in a business column about an heiress slumming it on a failing ranch. If the world supplied the wind, he only had to hold up a sail.

He opened his call log. Dante hadn't answered tonight. Not unusual. Dante liked to sleep on decisions and speak in the morning. The man had measured twice and cut once his whole life.

Ricardo checked the time. Past midnight. He thought of Annie laughing in the photos. She'd always been good with a room. He'd seen it in Rome. Put a camera near her and the world handed her light. He also knew what it did to men who thought they were made of stone.

He rolled closer and reread the final paragraph. Appreciation. Service. He didn't underline the word family, he didn't need to. Power hid inside courtesy.

The plan, as written, was tidy.

Step one: circulate the rumor that Annie was delaying a critical negotiation by chasing a romance.

Step two: leak photos to a gentle lifestyle site that specialized in heirs and their hobbies.

Step three: offer to escort her back for a scheduled event in Milan that only she could smooth.

No force. Pressure shaped like help.

His grin curved. The real plan had extra layers. He didn't type those. He would never type those. If Dante chose to read between the lines, that would be Dante's choice.

Behind the polish, Ricardo wanted two things. He wanted the ranch deal to fail on its own, far from his fingerprints, nudging a larger acquisition into range. And he wanted Annie under a light he controlled again. A man could hold two truths at once, useful and hungry, loyal and ambitious. He'd practiced that skill for years.

He clicked **Send**.

The email flashed, then disappeared into the system. Somewhere in Italy, a server wrote his promise into memory. Somewhere in Montana, Annie was laughing in firelight, and he was taking it from her one clean inch at a time.

He stood and walked to the window. The city was beautiful in the way a knife could be beautiful. An old truck moved below, slow and patient. Ricardo appreciated patience. It made arrival feel inevitable.

His phone buzzed. A reply from the stringer. One more line, then a picture.

Headline idea: Heiress Trades Boardroom for Barn Boots, Kiss at Town Bonfire Confirms New Romance.

Ricardo studied the frame. It would play.

He typed back: Make the tone respectful. No insults. Salt it with concern. People loved concern.

He rinsed the cup. He believed in clean endings. In a city like this, residue built up fast if you weren't careful. Habits saved reputations.

He opened a new tab and skimmed a brief on cattle futures and a local water rights dispute that hadn't hit national feeds yet. If the ranch felt a dry summer worse than expected, the banker would press. If the banker pressed, the Millers would revisit their numbers. Ricardo didn't need to touch the scale. He only needed to watch it tilt.

The phone buzzed again. His assistant, insomniac and precise.

Flights to Bozeman on hold for Wednesday morning. Shall I confirm.

He typed: Wait for Dante's answer. Prepare a cover story for Naples if he declines.

A delivery receipt chimed on his laptop. He let it fade. He didn't need dopamine. He needed follow-through.

He unlocked a drawer and took out a leather notebook. He wrote a short list.

Pressure bank.

Feed Miller doubt.

Keep Annie busy.

Make return easy.

He capped the pen. He liked lists that fit on one line. They were honest.

He killed the lights. The city sharpened, all teeth and promise. In the dark, the analog clock ticked. Minutes were loud if you paid attention. He let three pass, then switched the lights back on and sat again.

He opened a secure thread, a name that didn't exist in any directory.

The window is open. Keep the banker cautious and the Millers careful. No one gets their hands dirty.

He hit send and closed it.

His grin arrived, small and sharp. Ulterior motives, he thought. Such a moral phrase for something as simple as desire.

He finished the last swallow of espresso, cold now and bitter, and smiled again.

CHAPTER EIGHTEEN

OLD GHOSTS, NEW FENCES

Jake rode out before the sun crested the ridge, the cool air sharp in his lungs as he guided his horse along the narrow path that climbed toward the family plot near the Ridge. Frost glazed the tips of the bunchgrass even though the season had already turned, and each hoof step made a soft whisper as if the ground were trying to keep his presence quiet. The world still belonged to night up there, a thin blue edge all that marked the coming morning. He let the gelding choose his pace. No one waited for him at the top except the names carved into stone and the woman who had made him. He did not rush toward that kind of company.

The cemetery lay inside a rough rectangle of split rails, posts leaned by years of wind, set on a rise that looked out over the valley like it was keeping watch. Cottonwoods bracketed the place like tall guardians. Their leaves held steady in the cold, then muttered as a thin breeze slipped through the branches. Old markers stood nearest the gate; their letters rubbed soft by time. Those were the first ones. Clem. Millie. A small stone didn't match the rest, because it had never had time to. John, gone before he could grow into his name. A little beyond that sat William "Spike" Spyker's marker. The pain of not knowing him stayed sharp, even as the stone itself had dulled under years of wind and rain.

Jake dismounted and looped his reins over the same rail he always used. The horse turned an ear toward him and blew a stream of white breath into the air, patient and warm, the way good horses are when they know a man needs time.

He walked to his mother's grave and stood with his hat pressed against his chest. The grass felt wet through his boots. He read her name, then the dates, and the short line his grandmother had chosen, a simple truth that fit Beth better than any poem. He had come here on other hard mornings, after storms, after calving nights that broke him, after the last time the bank had called with a voice that did not know him. Today felt different. Today was mixed with fear. He swallowed hard, but the fear lingered.

"I am trying, Ma," he said, keeping his voice low so he did not startle the quiet. "I swear I am." His breath wavered in the air and the sound of it made him feel like a boy again, caught with a broken thing in his hands. He stared at the stone and let the first admission out, the one that had been pressing hard in his ribs. "I am scared I am going to lose it. The pasture, the house, the water right. All of it. I count and plan and call in favors and it never adds up in a way that helps me sleep." He rubbed the brim of his hat with his thumb as if he could smooth a crease no one else could see. "I don't know how to fail this place without failing you."

He let the words hang. Wind moved, then settled. He pictured her hands, a bit rough from rope and winter air, that soft tapping she did on his back when he was small and had taken a spill. She used to say that a bruise blooms before it fades, that pain shows itself before it leaves. Maybe fear did the same. He found himself talking about ranch life and winter feed, about a pump that needed a new seal and a heifer that had turned out meaner than she looked. He talked about bills without saying numbers, because numbers made him feel small. He talked about the kind of tired that was not in the bones but behind the eyes, the kind that made thoughts heavy.

He spoke of legacy without using the word. He told her he still checked the fence the way she taught him, not by glancing but by walking the line, by putting a hand on each post, by listening for the faint song of wire pulled too tight. He told her he counted calves by pairs, calf to cow, not by a number on a page. He told her he still kept a ledger, written clean, because she liked to see inked lines and not just the glow of a screen. He told her the land still held the shape of her work and that he wanted to move inside that shape forever.

The truth had more edges. He bent to it. "I am scared of letting them down," he said, and the faces came easy. Tommy with his quick jokes and quicker temper. Maria with her kind eyes and hard hands. The neighbors who had stood hip deep in the flooded pasture last spring, their boots heavy with mud and their mouths set tight because they did not give up. "I am scared of being the one who lost what you held together." He looked out over the slope that rolled into the valley, and the whole spread seemed to breathe in the cold. He had never wanted anything beyond it.

He could have stopped there. He could have let the cold do its slow work on his cheeks and then ridden back down and called it good. The other truth waited, stubborn and alive, and he knew if he left it unsaid it would keep rising. He drew in another breath and spoke her name like a confession. "Annie." He paused. "She complicates everything." He tried to smile and could not quite get there. "Not because she's trouble. Because she makes me hope again."

He had not planned to say that. It kept coming. "Hope feels dangerous, Ma. Drought is simple. A broken bearing is simple. A man can put his back into simple things. Hope is different. Hope makes your hands light. Hope makes you plan for cabins and clear nights and music under string lights, and then the bank reminds you what you actually have. Hope feels like riding a colt that looks gentle, right until he swaps ends and throws you hard." He huffed a weak laugh and shook his head. "You would have liked her. She does not scare easy. She works until her knuckles go white. She is softer than she wants people to think, and harder than I first believed."

He told his mother small things he had noticed because small things reveal the big ones. Annie taking her hat off in the house, that respect learned somewhere old. The way she watched a gate chain as if a chain could tell a story. The way she bit her lower lip when she read contracts. The way she made a mess when she learned something, then cleaned it up with a care that felt like apology and pride at the same time. He told her Annie tried to carry more than any one person should carry, and that he knew that weight, and that perhaps knowing it in someone else made it heavier in himself.

He let himself speak of his jealousy and felt the heat rise in his face even though no one watched. He said he didn't care about Milan, but he cared about the part of Annie that stood straighter when that city called. He said he wanted to be big enough for her to choose him without regret. He said he did not know what he would do if she left, if a jet took her away the way a hard gust steals a hat off a head, quick and final. He said he should be old enough not to speak like that and that the words did not care. They came anyway.

He went quiet again and let the cottonwoods talk. He took the small bunch of wildflowers he had cut near the creek and set them at the base of the stone. A bit of dirt clung to the stems. He brushed it clean and tightened the ribbon Maria had found for him last year. He bowed his head and finished with the only promise he could make that did not feel like a lie. "I will not lose this land. Not for anything."

It felt too easy to stop on a line like that, as if words by themselves could hold off a foreclosure or a bad winter. He tried again, speaking more plainly. "I will work until my hands do not open at night. I will sell a horse that I should keep. I will ask for help if I have to. I will not pretend I do not need it. I will make the cuts that hurt and not look back. I will stop telling myself that pride is the same as grit." He swallowed, looked at the stone, and forced the last part out because it mattered more than anything that had come before it. "I will try not to push her away because I am scared. I will try to be the man you raised and not the man who hides."

He pressed his fingers to the cold top of the marker, the way he had when he was twelve and their first border collie had died, the way he had when he'd slipped off the barn roof and cracked a rib, and his mother had told him that men break and heal and keep going. The stone did not answer, but the steadiness of it worked on him, the way a post set true makes the line hold. He felt a little taller when he straightened. Not lighter, exactly, just more even inside his skin.

He set his hat on and turned for the horse. The gelding had shifted one hind foot, rested a hip, and watched a jackrabbit that had frozen in the grass ten yards away. The world beyond the fence had started to take on color, pearly at first, then faint gold along the far ridge. He swung into the saddle and sat there for a breath, letting the chill bite his cheeks, letting the quiet take a last pass through his mind. He looked once more at his mother's name, then at the sweep of the valley that waited below.

On the way down, the light caught on the river and made it shine, thin and bright. Cows moved in the distance, slow as spilled molasses. A pickup rolled along the road toward the house, a tiny box with a dust tail behind it. Morning would thicken and the chores would stack and the day would ask for his back and his judgment. He nudged the gelding into a walk and felt the familiar swing of the stride settle into his hips. He did not know if the vow would be enough, but he had made it. He would make it again if he had to. He guided the horse off the hill and toward work and toward whatever waited for him in the kitchen, where the last of the peaches might still be holding on from yesterday and where a woman with complicated eyes might look up and change the shape of his day with a single word.

Back at the house, steam curled from the big pot and fogged the lower panes of the kitchen window. Annie stood at the counter with her hands sticky, peach juice running into the crease of her wrist and dripping from her elbow. The cutting board gleamed with halves and pits piled in a little mountain. Maria moved like a quiet clock, steady and exact. She lifted a jar with the tongs, tipped out the hot water, and set the glass upright on a towel. The jar clicked against the wood and settled. Another small sound a person could come to love.

"Score the skin like this," Maria said. She drew the tip of her knife across the curve of a peach, a clean X that barely broke the velvet. "Gentle. You do not need to fight it."

"I'm not," Annie said. The peach in her hand slipped and she chased it with a laugh that sounded a little thin. "It's fighting me."

"We'll teach it manners," Maria said. She dunked the scored fruit into the simmering pot and counted under her breath. "One, two, three." She lifted it into a bowl of cold water. "Peel. See. Easy."

Annie tried again. The skin came off in long strips that felt like satin. The flesh shone. She felt a small bloom of pride, quick and quiet. She set the peeled half beside the others and reached for another peach. The room smelled like summer and sugar. The air pressed sweet on her tongue.

They worked in rhythm. Score. Dip. Chill. Peel. Halve and twist. Pit out the stone. Slice into even moons. The pile of fruit grew. So did the bowl of bright segments. Maria scooped sugar with a dented cup and shook it into a pot with lemon juice. She stirred until the grains dissolved and the liquid went clear. She hummed while she stirred, the same tune she always hummed when the work asked for patience. Annie didn't know the words. She did not need the words to feel the shape of the song. It grounded the room.

On the stove, a second kettle rattled. Lids warmed in a small pan of water. The jar lifter sat within reach. The towels on the counter were already damp from jar after jar. Annie wiped her hands and looked around as if she could memorize this exact frame. The light through the window. The nick in the cutting board. The way the steam faded and came back. There were so many kinds of rooms in her life. Meeting rooms with the shine of glass and the chill of air conditioning. Hotel rooms with carpet that tried too hard. Kitchens that belonged to other people where she was a guest with perfect manners. This kitchen did not care about manners. It cared about method. It cared about care itself.

Maria tipped the sugared syrup over the slices and the peaches sighed as they sank. She stirred. They turned the color of sunset. Annie reached out to steady the pot as Maria poured the hot fruit into the waiting jars. The funnel clinked against glass, then settled. The first jar filled, the second, the third. Annie used a wooden skewer to chase bubbles to the top. She wiped the rims with vinegar and a strip of clean cloth until they shone. She set a lid, then a ring, turning the metal only until it was snug. Not too tight. Not too loose. Just right, Maria had said.

"You learn fast," Maria said.

"I make a mess while I learn," Annie said. She lifted her hands. Syrup shined in the lines of her palms. "You should see a board-room table after I have used too many sticky notes."

Maria smiled without looking up from the pot. "Learning makes a mess. Cleaning up is part of the lesson."

The canner burbled. Maria lowered a rack of jars into the hot bath until water covered the lids by an inch. She set a timer with a chipped thumbnail and leaned back against the counter for a moment. The humming returned, soft as breath. Annie wiped the board and stacked the knives, then leaned beside her, shoulder to shoulder, the kind of closeness that grows from work and not from talk.

"Do you ever get used to this?" Annie asked. "The way a job fills the whole day and then you go to bed and the next day asks for you again."

"Yes," Maria said. "But also no. Some days are heavier. You feel them when you lie down. Other days slide right past. That is true in the kitchen. It is true outside. It is true in the heart." She rubbed her forearm with the heel of her hand as if the ache there could be invited to leave. "You learn where to put your weight. The day stops feeling like it is pushing you."

Annie nodded. She watched the swirl in the canner and thought about weight. She thought about the way the ranch asked for her back and her hands and her judgment, the same way a board asked for her slides and her voice and the cool set of her mouth. She thought about Jake's laugh when she teased him about his straight fence lines. She thought about the way his laugh died when the phone rang. She thought about the room that waited for her in Milan and the way the windows there turned every sky to a reflection of glass.

"Maria," she said. "Do you think some people just do not fit?" She tried again. "Do you think some people are a size that no life can hold?"

"I think people change shape," Maria said. She lifted the lid for a second and let the steam roll. "Sometimes you do it on purpose. Sometimes the day does it to you."

Annie nodded again, then shook her head. The two motions canceled each other and left her with the same knot. She turned so she faced the window. The yard looked simple from here. A gravel drive. A stack of old wagon wheels. A jacket thrown over the back of a chair on the porch. She pressed her thumbs into the edge of the counter until the wood marked her skin.

"I do not know if I belong here," she said. The words surprised her with how clear they sounded. "Or with him." The last two words were quiet, but they did not break. "Or with anyone. If I am honest."

Maria did not answer right away. She let the timer tick. She watched the space where the steam faded, then looked at Annie the way a mother looks at a child who has fallen and stands up pretending not to hurt. "Who told you that belonging is a place you find once," Maria said. "Sometimes belonging is a habit you practice."

Annie breathed in. The kitchen smelled of fruit and hot metal and a thread of vinegar where the cloth sat in a cup. She could feel a strand of hair stuck to her cheek. She did not reach up to move it. "What if I am never enough," she said. "Not enough for this land. Not enough for Jake. Not enough for my father's boardroom." She thought of the jet and the suits and the way a man could fill a doorway with his plans for you. "What if there is not a version of me that fits all the pieces I have to carry."

Maria's mouth softened at the corners. "You are a woman," she said. "Not a suitcase." She reached for the dial and turned off the flame beneath the canner. The water stilled from a boil to a tremble. "Being enough does not mean doing it alone."

The words landed and stayed. They did not rush. They did not demand. They rested in the middle of the kitchen. Annie looked at Maria to see if she would add a list or a rule. Maria didn't. She lifted the rack and the jars rose from the bath shining and hot. She set each one on the towel, careful to leave space between them for air to move. They sat and ticked and then one by one their lids pulled down with a soft ping.

Annie flinched at the first ping, then smiled at herself. "That sound," she said. "It feels like proof."

"It is," Maria said. She touched the top of a jar with a fingertip and drew back quick from the heat. "You put good things in, you apply the right amount of pressure, then you let them cool. The seal happens while you are not touching. You trust it. Tomorrow you press the lid and it does not give. That is how you know the jar will hold."

Annie watched the jars and thought about pressure and heat and the part where you have to stop touching. That last part felt hardest. She liked to keep her hands-on things until they behaved. Projects. People. Her own thoughts.

"Let me ask you a question," Maria said. She took off her apron and shook out a crumb of sugar that had found the hem. "If you could only pick one thing to be good at this week, what would you pick."

"Only one," Annie said. The idea made her mouth twist. "That sounds like a trick."

"It is a practice," Maria said. "One thing you can be good at without stealing from the rest."

Annie looked past the window again, then watched the steam fade from the glass. "Listening," she said. "I could be good at listening."

Maria nodded. "Good." She began to wipe the counter, small circles that cleaned syrup the way worry beads wear down sharp thoughts. "Start with listening to yourself. When you hear the old fear voice say never or always, tell it to sit in the corner and be quiet until you are done."

Annie laughed, and the sound this time had some weight to it. "I like that." She picked up a jar and set it back down when the heat surprised her. "I want to be good at staying too."

"You already stayed," Maria said. She nodded toward the window, toward the ridge where the world opened in a wide V. "You chose once. You will choose again tomorrow. That is how staying works."

They cleaned the last sticky spot and put the knives to dry. Maria set a slice of peach on a saucer and pushed it across the counter. "Taste," she said. Annie lifted it to her mouth and bit. The flesh gave, the syrup ran, and for a second the whole world stopped.

"Do you know what I like best about canning?" Maria said. "It is a way to keep the sweet for a day when you need it." She tapped the jar nearest her knuckle. "We put this on a shelf. Winter will come. We will take it down. We will open it, and that first breath will be this kitchen again. It reminds us that seasons turn both ways. Not just toward cold."

Annie let that sink in. She looked at the row of jars. Simple light slid through gold and orange and made small suns on the towel. She imagined a gray morning in January and the sound of a lid breaking its seal. She imagined the scent rising, bright and stubborn. She imagined her own shoulders, lower by an inch because she would have proof that sweetness returns.

Maria lifted one jar and held it toward her. "For your shelf," she said. "Not his. Yours."

Annie wrapped both hands around the glass and felt the heat press into her palms. "Thank you," she said. She meant it for the jar. She meant it for the morning. She meant it for the way Maria had not tried to rearrange her into a person who knew all the moves before she learned them.

Another ping sounded. Then another. The kitchen fell quiet except for those small declarations and the faint tap of the timer cooling on the stove. Outside, a truck door shut and a laugh floated across the yard. The day waited with its list. The jars waited with their proof. Annie stood with her hands warm and sticky and thought, maybe belonging was not a place or a role. Maybe it was the act of being here, doing the next needed thing, letting someone stand beside you while you learned. She could practice that. She could practice it again tomorrow.

Later that day, she and Jake found themselves working side by side on the fence line, again. They parked the truck where the grass turned to a narrow strip of bare ground. The fence ran toward the ridge in a straight line that was not quite straight when you looked long enough. Sun pressed warm on their backs. Wind kept the flies honest. They unloaded in a quiet that made every tool sound louder than it should. The post hole digger clacked when Jake set it down. The bucket with staples rattled. The roll of wire thunked into the dirt and tried to roll away until Annie caught it with her boot. Spike grazed in the near pasture and lifted his head now and then to watch them with the bored interest of a horse who approves of other people working.

At first, they kept to the business of work. Jake tested posts along a fifty-yard stretch, hand on each top to check for sway. Annie followed with a tape and a level. He would point. She would measure. He would nod. She would mark the ground with the heel of her glove. They did not meet each other's eyes for more than a second at a time. The air felt full of words that had not been said, so the two of them used numbers instead. Two feet off. Six inches to the south. Three staples per stay. They said these things as if they were prayers.

They started on the worst leaner. Jake set the digger and Annie took the other handle. The first bite of earth fought them, then gave. They pulled and pressed, a clumsy dance that found its rhythm by the third bite. Dirt lifted in neat jaws and dropped in a dark pile. When the hole hit the right depth, he eased the new cedar post in and stood back while she checked the bubble in the level. She squinted, moved the pole a hair, and nodded. He tamped gravel around the base with a steel bar, slow and steady, the way his grandmother had shown him when his head still barely reached the top wire.

Conversation loosened in half steps. Annie asked how deep he liked the corner posts. He asked how long a deck presentation usually ran when the people in suits looked bored. She wanted to know if he preferred cedar to pressure treated pine. He wanted to know if the right coffee in a boardroom could bribe a yes. The questions did not carry much weight. They kept the air moving.

She held the post while he ran the new strand through a tensioner, and the wire sang a low note as it pulled tight. He liked that sound and, without thinking, said so. She smiled at that and said she liked the sound the jar lids made when they sealed. He said he did not know jar lids had a sound. She said they did, and that he would hear it later.

They moved down the line. The fence began to look like it belonged to people who cared. Annie brushed dirt from her palms and blew hair out of her face. A smear of dust crossed her cheek where she had scratched an itch with the back of her glove. She did not bother to wipe it. She watched Jake set a staple with a calm she envied. His hands looked certain even when the day was not. She thought about how many days of practice it took to make that certainty. She thought about her own hands and the way they looked in a boardroom when the clicker misfired and a slide stalled and twenty eyes waited for her to make it seamless again.

She told that story because silence had started to itch. A pitch in Milan, a long glass table, a view that tried to steal the room. She said she had stacked her note cards in the order that matched the slides, only she had flipped two when she reached in her bag. She said a pair of new investors watched her mouth while she spoke and nodded like polite statues, and she kept right on speaking even when she knew she had read the revenue forecast from the wrong year. She said her heel snapped when she stood to hand out the printed summary, and that she limped back to her seat. She said she kept her chin up the whole time and that when the meeting ended, she smiled at the glass.

Jake's laugh came out before he could stop it. It was a good laugh, low and surprised, as if the sound had been sitting on his tongue waiting for permission. It made her laugh too, because laughter is a thing that collects quick and spills once someone tips the bowl. He shook his head and said he could see it, the glass, the heels, the wrong year read like it was the right one, and she said he was not allowed to enjoy it that much. He said any person who had never pitched the wrong number had never pitched for real, and she said he would not survive five minutes in that room, and he said he would bring a hat and see how they liked that.

The laughter ran out and left a warm place behind. They stood there in it for a second, then reached for work again. He passed her the fencing pliers and she clipped an old twist clean. He threaded new wire through the last cedar stay while she held the gap with her knee. Their shoulders brushed once and neither of them stepped away. A horned lark sang towards the sky as if it had been waiting for the mood to turn.

They settled into silence that did not feel hostile. It felt like a field that has been harrowed smooth. Hammer and shovel took the role of talk. The shovel bit. The hammer set. Wire ran true. Heat lifted from the dirt in small wavers that made the far hill look like it was breathing. Annie rolled her shoulders, found a groove for the weight of the driver, and swung in clean arcs that landed square. Jake watched the top of each post as it accepted the hit and said nothing, which was his way of approving.

A pair of calves nosed up to watch. One pushed its nose through the bottom gap and licked the new wood with a long pink tongue. Annie laughed again, a softer sound now, and used the back of her glove to shoo it without much effect. The calf licked her glove instead. Jake said they were like children and that you had to pretend you did not notice or they would demand attention until the gate fell off. She said that sounded like investors. He said investors sounded worse. She said calves at least improve on hay. He said investors improved on whiskey. She laughed and said she would bring a bottle to the next meeting and tell them Jake Spyker said it would help.

They finished a run and stepped back. The line looked right. The new wood glowed against the older gray as if the fence itself were telling the truth that time moves and that care can keep up.

Annie set the level on the truck bed and flexed her fingers. The ache felt honest. She liked that honesty. You did a thing, your hands told you about it, and the proof stood in the ground across from you. She could live inside that loop. She remembered the meetings. Last-minute changes on slide nineteen. Then another. Soon the promise did not feel true. She was glad to be here.

Jake checked the spool and counted how much wire they had left. Enough to finish the last twenty yards if they did not waste staples. He opened the cooler and handed her a bottle of water. She took it and tilted her head back, and for a second he looked at her without the armor he wore when the day felt hard. She looked strong and tired and not careful about being pretty. He liked that more than he should admit.

The sun slid west enough to cast long shadows. They took up the tools again and worked the last stretch. Hands found a shared pace. She anticipated when he needed the pliers. He guessed when she needed the post held a hair to the left. The space between them stopped feeling like a place where a plane might land. It felt like room for air. The fragile peace arrived without asking permission. They did not speak to acknowledge it. They did not want to scare it off.

By the time they cleared the tools, a light wind had come up and the heat of the day softened at the edges. They stood at the end of the line and looked back toward the truck. New posts stepped away from them in an even rhythm. The wire held a steady shine. Somewhere a dog barked. Somewhere a gate creaked and then closed. Annie rested her palm on the top board and felt the faint vibration of the wire. Jake put the driver in the bed and closed the tailgate with a gentle hand. They glanced at each other, quick and small.

They did not talk on the short ride back to the yard. The quiet did not pinch. Tires hissed on dust. The pasture opened and then gave way to the outbuildings and the porch where a jacket still hung from the morning. Spike trotted along the fence as if to inspect their work and then lost interest when a grass tuft looked more promising. Jake pulled the truck next to the barn and cut the engine. The world kept its hum. The fragile peace stayed where it was. For the moment, that felt like enough.

The phone buzzed in the console, a tiny rattle against loose coins. Jake glanced at the screen. The bank. Of course it was. He let it ring once more, then tapped accept and brought it to his ear without taking his eyes off the horizon.

"Spyker," he said.

The banker's voice came brisk, clipped, a tone trained in climate control and carpet. "Good afternoon, Mr. Spyker. Small schedule update for you." Papers shuffled on the other end. He could hear the shrug in it. "Loan review has been moved up by two weeks. You will receive the new date by email. Thank you for your flexibility."

Jake kept his eyes straight. "Two weeks," he said. He made the words flat. "We had a date on the calendar."

"I know this is inconvenient," the voice said, still even. "Unfortunately, we have internal deadlines to meet."

Jake watched a hawk tilt above the pasture. Annie sat beside him with her hand on the seat near the shifter. She did not look over. She could read a mood without seeing a face. Spike flicked an ear across the field, a moving dot among other moving dots, and lifted his head toward the truck like he knew more than Jake wanted to admit.

"I'll need to resubmit any new receipts," the banker continued. "If you have additional documentation, please bring it. Current cash flow, any signed contracts, insurance updates. You know the drill."

Jake swallowed hard. "Two weeks," he said again, because the body sometimes repeats what the mind refuses to understand. "That's tight."

"Think of it as a head start," the man said.

The words bumped against Jake's ribs. He pictured the ledger drawer, the thin letter he had not shown anyone. He pictured the stack of notes with corners worn from too much handling. He pictured the fence they had just set straight and the jars cooling on a towel that he had not seen but could imagine, lids pinging down as if the kitchen were agreeing with itself. None of that would convince a man who measured only by columns.

"I appreciate the notice," Jake said. He did not appreciate it. The wheel felt small in his hands. "We will be there."

"Excellent," the banker said. "Please confirm receipt of the email. Enjoy the rest of your day."

The line clicked. The phone screen went dark and stared up at him. Jake set it face down and breathed out through his nose. His jaw had found that locked place again. He loosened it with effort and felt the ache that came when you made a muscle pretend to relax.

Annie said nothing. She watched the horizon with a steady gaze, the kind you use on a skittish colt. Blue was a flash of movement between brush and wire, tail wagging back and forth for the land.

"What did he want?" she asked at last. Her voice kept the edges kind.

Jake reached for the bottle in the holder, changed his mind, put his hand back on the wheel. "Schedule," he said. "Shifting things around."

She waited. He could feel the wait more than hear it. He had learned that silence could be as loud as a slammed door. He kept his eyes forward and let the horizon give him something to focus on. A killdeer hopped sideways ahead of them, then flitted off at the last second, its call scolding and small.

"How bad?" she said.

"Manageable," he said. He made the word smooth. He had a talent for smooth when a day required it. He hated that talent and needed it in the same breath.

Wind found a crack in the window and sang a thin note that

rose and fell. Annie shifted, rested her forearm against the open triangle of air, then brought it back. She almost touched his arm, then didn't. The almost felt good.

Two weeks. He counted without trying. Feed. Fuel. A bill to the mechanic for a leaky hose that had turned out to be two. The vet. The insurance premium. The small things that were not small. He could feel the ledger settle on his chest. He imagined lifting it and setting it down and could not find where to put it that did not crack the floor.

He pictured the meeting. The same small conference room with the painting of a lake that no one had seen. The man with the brisk voice and a legal pad, pen uncapped. Another man who never spoke, who read the numbers as if they were a weather map only he could see. Maybe a third who had come to learn how to say no in a way that sounded professional. He pictured his hat in his hands and his back too straight for comfort. He pictured the part where you explained your life to a person who had never opened a gate or hauled a calf out of a mud hole before dawn.

Don't go there, he told himself. The gate first. Then the hose you promised to replace before it split. Then the list on the fridge. The day always gives you the next thing if you let it. One problem at a time.

He said it under his breath. "One problem at a time."

"What?" Annie asked.

"Nothing," he said. "Talking to myself."

He could tell her now. He could say the words and let them sit between. He could admit that two weeks was a blade, and that he didn't know how to make the cut land soft. He could ask for her help with the numbers the way he took her help with the wire. His hands tightened on the wheel instead. Pride climbed his throat and settled behind his teeth. Only silence came out.

"After lunch," he said, as if they had been talking about something else. "I need to check the east trough. The float stuck yesterday." He heard the falseness as it left his mouth. He hated it in the moment and said it anyway.

"I will come," she said. Simple as that. No push. No lecture. He felt the generosity of it and did not know what to do with the gift.

Jake rolled to a stop near the yard and killed the engine. For a moment they stayed in the cab, listening to the tick of cooling metal and the soft hiss of wind through the grass. Annie's hand hovered near the door handle. She didn't pull it yet. She studied him, like she was weighing a question against the cost of asking it. Jake kept his eyes forward, jaw set, both hands resting on the wheel as if it gave him something solid to hold. Annie exhaled, then pushed the door open and stepped down into the dust. The door closed with a small, final thud. Jake followed a beat later, slower, his shoulder still stiff. Together they started walking toward the yard.

Blue cut across the drive and shot under the fence, a streak of joy that did not understand banks or dates. A fly tapped a window. Somewhere a hen announced an egg with the confidence of a leader.

"You sure you are alright," she asked.

He nodded. The lie tasted flat. "Fine."

She studied him a beat longer. Then she moved toward the porch, turned back, and offered a half-smile that didn't quite land. He lifted a hand. It felt like holding up a sign that said keep out.

He could still feel the phone's buzz in the bones of his hand. He looked at the house, at the sky that had made itself a hard blue, and he made a decision that solved nothing and kept the day standing. He would not tell her yet. Not until he had looked again at the numbers. Not until he had called Davidson and tried to argue a week back. Not until he had checked the trough. Not until he had tried to be the man who does not hand off weight at the first lift.

The bank would send an email with a date written in black. The date would sit there and wait. The ranch did not wait. The valve on the trough did not care about calendars.

"One problem at a time," he said again, so quiet only he could hear it.

CHAPTER NINETEEN

THE BUSINESS OF BREAKING HEARTS

Annie worked in the quiet of the office, the screen filling with clean lines and soft earth tones, a grit-meets-silk ranch look that felt both honest and bold. She built tiers and timelines, margins and add-ons, a future sketched in cabins and stargazing, a complete package designed to turn interest into cash.

Tommy paused in the doorway, took in the mockups, and grinned. "That's some real fancy cowgirl magic." Annie smiled, but her stomach flipped. Magic only mattered if it saved the place she was starting to love.

"Tell me you've got a plan that isn't just pretty," Tommy said, stepping in. "Jake's not sleeping. Maria's pacing. We need something real."

"We do," she said. "This isn't fluff. I'm carving out products we can sell now. Weekend tiers. Keep it exclusive. Ranch Hand for a Day, Starlight Supper, Sky Cabin nights. Pricing here, margins here. Deposits up front so cash lands before costs."

Tommy whistled. "Sky Cabin, huh? Something folks brag about at church."

"They will if we make it rare," Annie said. "Two new moon

weekends a month. Quilts, a heater, a simple menu. Local honey, Maria's biscuits, coffee that doesn't taste like regret. People want simple they can trust."

Blue nosed the door open, dropped a chewed ball at Tommy's boots, and sat, waiting.

"So. What do you need from me?" Tommy asked.

"Names," Annie said. "Ten locals who'll book first and talk loud. Give them Founders' Night with a free add-on if they bring paying friends. We seed the market."

Tommy nodded. "Maria's got numbers. I'll pull mine too."

Annie clicked to a slide. "Timeline. Pilot Saturday. Small, controlled. Ten guests. We get photos, testimonials, and cash in the drawer."

"I know it's soon," she said. "Waiting burns money."

"Costs?" Tommy asked. "I know you've got numbers."

"Basic tier hits sixty percent," she said. "Upsells can push seventy. We can pre-sell three Sky Cabins nights as a pop-up using the bunkhouse with a quick makeover. Fresh paint, string lights, clean quilts, an outdoor fire pit. It doesn't need perfect. It needs good, clean, and a little romantic."

"That last part's your specialty," he said.

"I'm just practical."

"You're also a Contadelucci," he said. "People listen when you talk money."

She looked at the window. Clouds were stacking over the ridge. "My last name helps if I act like it doesn't," she said. "What sells is trust."

The door pushed open. Jake stepped in, dust on his sleeves. He took in the mockups without a word.

"Hey," Annie said. "Got two minutes?"

"One," he said. He leaned on the frame.

She clicked to the first slide. "We start small on Saturday. Founders' Night. Ten people. Maria's menu. A sunset ride on Spike, one photo per couple, if you're up for it. We'll price it fair and take deposits now. Then a Sky Cabin pop-up for the next two weekends. That pulls cash forward and proves the concept before we spend on upgrades."

Jake's eyes moved slow and careful. "What's the risk?"

"Food costs and time. If no one books, I'll eat the biscuits and we'll call it a lesson. But I think they'll book."

Tommy lifted a hand. "I've got names. The sort who turn a whisper into a crowd."

"Permits?" Jake asked.

"Covered," she said. "County site says events under twenty on private land are fine. We need a food handler, which Maria already is. Insurance is current. I called. We're just being organized about what folks already do here."

His jaw settled a little. "You checked all that today?"

"At dawn," she said. "Couldn't sleep."

Something flickered in his eyes. He hadn't either. "It's a lot to pull off by Saturday."

"I'll need your help for two hours and you're okay on the rest," she said. "I'll beg Maria, bribe Tommy, and call Mr. Davidson about the Millers after lunch. If we can move that meeting, we should. Pressure helps."

Jake rubbed his neck. "One problem at a time."

"I know," she said softly. "I'm solving the ones I can touch."

He looked at her. Blue's ball bumped his boot. He bent and picked it up, then didn't throw it.

Jake said he'd think about it for a few hours. He turned and left. Annie and Tommy followed him out, all of them drifting toward the barn like habit pulled them on a string. At the last second, Jake doubled back. He muttered something about invoices, cut down the hall, and found the laptop open on the office table. The proposal sat there, glowing. Page after page of polished cabins, curated experiences, smiling strangers under a sky cleaner than any he knew. To him, it read as a life scrubbed of mud and sweat, a future that didn't need him.

He stood, shoulders tight, and scrolled. Price tiers. Add-ons. Words that turned the ranch he loved into a product with a truck. He knew why she'd built it. He knew the bank's clock. Still, knowing didn't make the swallow any easier.

Annie noticed he hadn't come to the barn. She doubled back with a quick, uneasy step, pushed the door, and found him holding the laptop like it might bite.

"It's a plan to save the ranch," she said before he could speak. "To bring in cash fast. To keep us standing."

He didn't look up. He heard different words. He heard takeover. He heard goodbye. He set the laptop down with care he didn't feel. "You're not saving the ranch," he said, voice rough. "You're replacing it."

The room felt smaller. So did they. Annie took a breath that didn't go anywhere. "I'm not trying to erase what you built. I'm trying to keep it alive."

"With glossy pictures and strangers in hats they bought yesterday," he said. "You turn it into a theme park. Folks play cowboy, go home, and nothing here is the same."

"Everything's already not the same," she said. "The storm cut fences. The herd's light. The banker moved the review up. We can't pretend we've got months. We don't. We have days. Cash now keeps the lights on so you can keep doing the work that's real."

He stared at the corner of the screen where her slides lined up like soldiers. "And me in this plan?"

"You ride Spike for ten minutes at sunset," she said, trying for light and missing. "You drink coffee with a couple from Dallas. You wave. Then you go fix the real fence because you're still the ranch. This isn't a replacement. It's a bridge."

Her phone lit with a vibrating buzz that felt too loud. A video call bloomed across the screen, her father's name in hard type. She didn't want to take it. She knew what it would be. But the timing, the timing came like a tide. She swiped, and Dante

Contadelucci filled the glass, Milan behind him, clean lines and a shard of sky trapped between towers.

"Antonietta," he said. He didn't ask how she was. He didn't say he missed her. "The board convenes Thursday. Your presence is expected. If you're not here, your proxy dissolves. Your trust protections will be reassigned until the next cycle. This is not personal. It's a vote."

Annie kept her chin up, but she felt the old gravity tug at her bones. Light years of expectations pressed into one polite voice. "I'm working," she said. "I'm in the middle of something that matters."

"You're in the middle of a phase," he said. "You'll come home for forty-eight hours. You'll sit. You'll vote. You'll learn. Then you can return to your, what is it, cows or cattle or whatever you call it."

He made her life now sound like a toy. Jake didn't move, but she felt him go very still. He didn't mean to eavesdrop. He couldn't help it. The date landed. The threat landed. Her father's certainty slid into place like a key in a lock.

"I'm not a girl," she said, quiet and steady. "I'm not a phase."

"You're my daughter," he said. "And you're an officer of the company. Thursday, Antonietta. Noon. I'll have a car. Decide you don't want to accept your obligations, and I'll accept that decision. With consequences."

The call ended with the neat click of power. Annie stared at her reflection on the black phone glass. Behind her, Jake set the laptop down. Then he walked out without a word. His worst fear had just stood up, smoothed its suit, and smiled at him.

"Jake," she said, moving after him, but the hall was already empty. Blue wasn't there either. Blue had gone with him.

Annie stood at the doorway and listened to the house. It creaked like old ships do, tired yet holding. Tommy filled the door from the yard, eyes searching her face. "You alright?"

"Not yet," she said. "Give me a minute."

He dipped his head. "I'll go check the string lights."

"That's good," she said. "Keep the ranch looking nice."

He left, light on his feet. Annie leaned on the table with both hands. The wood was warm. She watched quiet things; dust in the sun, a fly bumping glass, a ribbon of cloud climbing the slope of the window. Then she pushed to standing. If the house could hold, so could she.

Maria stood by the porch table with a stack of paper cups and a pen behind her ear. She looked Annie over and said nothing, which said plenty. She handed her a cup. "Drink. Then fix whatever man mess you just walked into."

"I will," Annie said. "Did you know about the bank review moving up?"

"Jake told me after he came in from the east fence this morning," Maria said. "He pretended like it was a weather report. He's like that. Quiet until quiet cuts."

Annie nodded. "I've built a plan. It's not pretty to him. It looks like I'm selling his life in pieces."

Maria's mouth went soft. "Maybe you are, a little, for a minute. Maybe that's what we do when we need to eat. We cut the stew small. He'll come around if he can see himself in it."

"He needs to see he's still the center," Annie said.

"He is," Maria said. "But you've got to tell him that in a language he believes."

Annie walked past the barn, past the back lot, toward the north pasture. The ground gave under her boots. A fence line cut the field in long stripes, silvered wire humming softly where it caught the breeze. She saw him before he saw her, shoulders bent over a corner post, tamping the dirt slow and even. Spike stood a few feet away, reins loose on a low branch, one ear toward Jake, one ear toward her. Blue lay in the grass between them, eyes narrowed to slits.

"Can we talk?" she asked.

"Talking's free," he said without looking up.

She stopped a yard off. "What you heard wasn't what I meant. Not with the plan. Not with my father."

"What I heard," he said, tamping again, "was that Thursday you go to Milan to vote with the people who own you, and then you fly back to finish turning my place into a postcard."

"That's not fair," she said, heat rising. "No one owns me. Not him. Not the board."

"You sure?" he asked. He straightened and looked at her. His eyes were steady and tired. "Because it sounded like a man who pays the bills telling you where to sit, and when. You said yes with your face. I saw it."

"I didn't say yes," she said. "I didn't say anything."

"You didn't have to," he said. "You've got a ticket in your head already."

She bit back a rush of words that would only burn them both. "Thursday is a threat. That's all. He wants me to come home and be what fits. I won't. But I can't pretend his power isn't real. I lived under it most of my life. You don't walk out from a gravity like that in a day."

He looked at the post, at Spike, at the hills that cupped the pasture like a hand. "You can walk out if you want to."

"I am walking out," she said. "Every minute I stay here, I'm walking out. You think I don't see how different I am when I'm here? I do. It scares me and it saves me at the same time."

He softened, only a notch. "Then why did that plan read like I'm a prop for your brochure?"

"Because what I wrote, what you saw, is wrong for you," she said. "I wrote it for the banker and the first ten customers. It's a proposal to them, not to you. I forgot to write it for the man who has to live under it. Let me try again, with you in the center."

"How?" he asked. "Talk plain."

"Okay," she said, palms open. "Cards on the table. What you know, what you do here, doesn't change. You keep doing all that you do. But, in the background, we run things like Founders'

Night. Ten people, not twenty. We keep the food simple. Your beef. Maria's biscuits. No silly names. No brand story that sounds like perfume. I'll shoot the photos, not a stranger. You choose which parts of the ranch we show and which parts we don't. You say no to any shot that feels like a lie. You ride Spike if you want to, or you don't, and no one gets a refund because of it. The Sky Cabin pop-up isn't a new build. It's the bunkhouse cleaned to the bone, quilts washed, a star map, a kettle, and a promise of quiet. That's it. No gilt. No fake. We charge what's fair, we take deposits, and we tell the truth. If it doesn't feel like truth, we don't sell it."

He listened, jaw easing. Blue's ears tipped forward. A hawk made a curve above the far line of cottonwoods, then slid out of sight.

"What about the bank?" he said. "What about the Millers?"

"I call Mr. Davidson this afternoon," she said. "I tell him we've got a plan on the books and I explain it all to him in detail. I ask him to keep the review where it is and not move it up again. Then I call the Millers and get clarity on that contract, because I know they'll try to squeeze. I'll speak the language they speak. I'm good at it."

"You are," he said. The ghost of a smile touched his mouth. "You get scary good when you want something."

"I want this place standing," she said. "And I want you standing in it."

He looked at her a long second that felt like a whole day. Then he huffed a breath that wasn't quite a laugh. "You're still a Contadelucci."

"And you're still Jake Spyker," she said. "Which means we're both stubborn. We can either point that at each other or point it at the problem."

"One problem at a time," he said, softer than before.

"Start with this fence," she said. "Then my father. In that order."

He nodded. "I can live with that order."

"Can you live with me flying out for a day if I decide the vote matters in a way that protects us?" she asked, risking it. "I'm not saying I will. I'm saying if that's the move that keeps him off us long enough to breathe, can you live with it?"

He took off his hat, dragged a hand through his hair, and put the hat back on. "I don't like it. I won't pretend I do. But I won't tell you where you can be. I hate it when a man thinks he owns that right. If you go, you go. If you don't come back, say it before you leave."

"I'll come back," she said. She felt the words settle inside. "And if I change, I'll say it to your face. No ghosts."

Blue thumped his tail. Spike shook his head once, as if he'd heard enough promises and would prefer lunch.

"Help me with the post," Jake said, holding out the tamp. She took it, feet set, arms working. Dirt gave and then held. They reset wire. They tightened it to a clean note. Work filled the space between them and made its own kind of peace.

By the time they walked back, the light had shifted to the thick gold that told you afternoon knew where it was going. Maria had the porch table looking like a small fair. Chili simmered in a big pot. Biscuits rose in neat rows. Tommy had strung the lights from tree to eave to gate, a soft roof for night coming on.

"Bosses," Tommy said, mock salute. "We're here for you. We are here to help. And iff'n you don't mind me saying so, I think Ms. Annie is a really good fit 'round here."

Jake raised an eyebrow. Tommy held his gaze and Jake said, "Yep, I have to agree with you."

Annie's phone buzzed again. A number she didn't know. She let it go. A text landed. New message, crisp and smug. Thought you'd be back in Milan by now. Dante says hello. Tell him you're playing cowgirl on a sinking ship. Coffee soon. R.

Her chest tightened. She didn't say Ricardo's name. She didn't have to. The old life had a way of slipping through any open crack.

Jake saw the way her jaw set. "Problem?"

"Spam," she said, too fast. Then she caught herself. "No. Not spam. A person who loves to feel important and isn't. He can't touch us unless we let him."

"Then don't let him," Jake said. He didn't push. He didn't ask. He trusted her to decide what came in and what stayed out. That trust was a gift she didn't plan to waste.

She took a breath and made two calls. Mr. Davidson picked up on the third ring. She laid out the plan, the pilot, the timeline, the ideas. She spoke clearly, no fluff, no panic. He listened, asked two questions, and told her the review would hold steady for now. "Show me more when the plan goes into action," he said. "Then we'll talk."

She thanked him and hung up. Then she called the Millers. She asked for their latest draft. She used three quiet words that meant lawyer. She mentioned delivery windows and penalties that would hurt them worse than they would hurt the ranch. The Miller voice on the line softened, then hedged, then promised a revised file by morning. She smiled without warmth and said she'd expect it by ten.

When she looked up, Jake had been watching; not the way a man watches a show, but the way a man watches a woman he cares about. "You're good at that," he said.

"I told you."

"You did," he said. "I'm still impressed."

They ate standing up, bowls in hand, spoons clinking against enamel. Maria slid a biscuit and bacon into Annie's palm. "Food before fight," she said. "Always."

"Always," Annie said. She took two bites and felt the world lift a little.

The sun dropped. The first stars showed. Tommy's grin went wide. Blue's tongue lolled. Spike flicked an ear and snorted.

Annie kept working and forgot to be afraid. Work did that for her when it was the right kind. It built a fence around panic and kept it where it belonged, outside the yard.

"You ever going to tell me what that text said?" Jake asked at last, soft.

"Soon," she said. "But not tonight."

He nodded. "One problem at a time," he said again, not as defense this time, but as a prayer that knew its place.

She held his gaze. "Thursday isn't going to decide us," she said. "We are."

He took off his hat, then put it back on, a habit when he didn't know where to put his hands. "I'll hold you to that."

"Good," she said. "Hold me to it."

Back at her cabin, Annie stood a minute longer, hand on the laptop, and let herself feel every part of the day, the fear, the fight, the quiet, the good. Then, a message icon pulsed at the corner of her phone, patient and persistent. She opened it because hiding never worked for long. Ricardo again. A photo of the Milan boardroom at dusk. Caption: Thursday will be quick. Bring heels.

She didn't answer. She blocked him a second time, because the first had been from one of his many numbers. She set the phone face down and went to bed.

Out in the dark, wind pulled at the eaves and then let go. A coyote called once, a single long note. Jake lay awake in his house and listened to the same night. He thought about a girl in Milan who wasn't a girl, about a boardroom he'd never seen, about a ranch that had never been a theme park and would not become one on his watch. He thought about a plan that might be a bridge if he had the nerve to walk across it beside her.

He closed his eyes on a picture he didn't hate. Spike at the gate. Blue at his heel.

Morning would bring bills and choices. He didn't have to solve them now. He reached for the phrase that had carried him through worse. Tonight it wasn't a cage. It was a tool.

One problem at a time.

It was pretty late at night in the yard when a luxury SUV rolled up, quiet and stealth. Nobody, not even Blue, knew it was there. The porch lights were out, the lantern wicks cold. A thin skin of frost made the old trough sparkle. The wind had taken a break for once, so sound carried in gentle ways; a hinge clicked somewhere, a cord tapped wood, a night bird said one word and then decided the rest could wait till morning.

Ricardo climbed out with an easy smile and eyes that measured everything. His shoes were city dark, not a scuff on them, the kind of leather that you only see in city stores. He tucked his keys in his pocket the way a man hides a queen in a card trick. He praised himself in a whisper, a little show for the dark. He called his idea chaos, but charming. He let out a few insults, then tucked them under compliments so they passed as jokes. He looked at the barn and the porch, looked at the neat path of lantern hooks waiting for their next job, and smiled like a cat.

"She's wasted here. Milan needs her," he said. He said it lightly, like a joke told at a funeral, the kind where people laugh so they don't cry, and then they feel worse for having laughed at all.

He strolled farther into the yard, hands in his coat pockets, head tilted like a man listening to a song only he could hear. If Blue had been loose, he would have been a soft shadow circling, reading the air. But Blue was in the mudroom, sleeping off chili dreams, paws twitching, tail thumping once, then still. Maria had shut him in earlier that night, said coyotes were talkative tonight, said she didn't want to wake the world over a rabbit.

Ricardo stopped at the gate that led to the north pasture and smiled at his reflection in the dark pane of the kitchen window. He practiced a face, the sympathetic one, the I understand your struggle, I too am human face, and then practiced the one that says the elevator simply opens for me because I am me. He slipped a white envelope from his coat and weighed it, tapping the edge against his palm. He looked at the porch like he might climb the steps, then thought better of it. He didn't come to knock. He came to haunt.

"Charming," he told the night. "Chaotic, but charming."

Something woke Jake up. It wasn't a noise, not really. Some nights wake a man because the night itself has a seam in it that needs looking at. He stirred and hurried to the window, bare feet quiet on old wood. He eased the curtain with two fingers and saw the glow first, a white curve sliding slow along the cottonwoods. He set his jaw as the luxury SUV rolled away. He stayed there a breath longer, watching the tail lights thread the drive, and every part of him that could clench did. He thought about boots on gravel, about stepping into the cold and letting words turn into something you can't pull back into your mouth once you throw them.

He turned and went back to bed before he did something he couldn't take back. The mattress was warm from where he'd been. Blue gave a sleepy huff from the mudroom, a dream sound, a nothing. Jake laid on his back and stared at the ceiling where the streetlight shimmer pushed a faint grid through the blinds. He told himself this was a ranch and not a stage. He told himself the ground would still be the ground in the morning. He told himself to sleep. The night nodded and then stretched on for hours anyway.

In her cabin, as all of this was happening unknown to Annie, she was curled on her bed, the laptop's glow washing the ceiling in pale blue. Slides slid by. Cabins, numbers, hope in bullet points. She had written in her clean voice, the one that cut through boardrooms, and now the words floated above her like prayer flags. She thought of peaches in glass jars that caught the afternoon light like little suns. She thought of fence posts set straight so a line runs true for years. She thought of a man who she hoped was laughing at her bad pitch, a soft, real laugh that starts in the chest and hits the eyes before it gets to the mouth.

She pressed her palms to her eyes and breathed. "What if I don't belong anywhere?" she whispered, and the room didn't answer. Rooms rarely do. They hold things. They don't fix them.

She lowered her hands and tried again with the kind of thinking that had gotten her through planes that landed in blizzards and meetings that started with a smile and ended with a knife. What belongs is what you decide to keep, she told herself. You decide to keep the quiet and the coffee and the way Maria hums when the biscuits rise. You decide to keep the way Jake checks Spike's hooves like a father checks a sleeping child, gentle, sure, grateful. You decide to keep Blue's look right before he drops a ball, that trust that says you'll throw it, because of course you will. You decide to keep your name, both of them, the one that sounds good on a board agenda and the one that smells like cedar.

The laptop screen timed out and went black. She watched her reflection in the glass. She looked like a girl and a woman layered in the same face, which is to say she looked like a person who had lived enough to know better and needed to learn more anyway. She tapped the spacebar, the slides returned, and her breath steadied.

The yard had a different dark now, the kind right before dawn yawns and thinks about getting up. Ricardo parked at the mouth of the drive and sat quiet for a long minute, hands still on the wheel. He liked the way silence sounded when he controlled it. He liked the way choices arranged themselves when he was the one making them. He slid the envelope back into his coat and smoothed the edge again, then smiled at his own discipline. He was good at not rushing. He was very good at arriving an hour before anyone knew they had invited him.

He pulled out a phone and snapped a photo of the house from the road. No flash. He checked the frame and liked the way the porch light made a halo on the step, even though the porch light was off. It was the kind of trick a lens does on a long exposure. He wrote a caption he wouldn't send, because he liked to write things he wouldn't send, it gave him a private power. Home is a word for children, he typed, then deleted it, then typed something worse, then deleted that too. He was careful, after all. Careful men live long enough to ruin a few afternoons.

He turned the wheel and faded back to the highway, the engine so quiet it felt like a thought more than a machine. Gravel settled. Owls said goodnight. The ranch exhaled.

Jake drifted and woke and drifted again, the way men do when a decision waits, patient and heavy. He saw the SUV in his mind. He let the picture empty. He filled it with something else. The goal. The plan. The order of it. Fence. Founders' Night. Bank. Her father. Not an easy list, but a clean one. He told himself he could do clean lists. He had built a life on them.

In her cabin, Annie sat up and tucked her legs under the quilt. She made a tiny list on the pad she kept by the bed. It wasn't a to do so much as a to feel. Be kind to Maria first thing. Tell Tommy thank you twice. Show Jake the numbers without dressing them like a parade. Ask Blue for a blessing, which is another way of saying rub his head until you both feel better. She wrote, Call Mr. Davidson again if the Millers drag their feet, and then she added, DO NOT say please, which made her smile because she rarely said please to men like the Millers. She did not give them that word for free.

She thought of her father's face and how it had taken up the whole screen, like the way a building blocks the sky. She pictured him as a young man standing in an old factory, the one with windows so tall a choir could stand in the light and sing to the nails. She pictured the way he had learned to love control because he had started with none. It didn't make what he did right. It made it understandable in the way a storm is understandable if you grew up in a house with a leaky roof. She closed her eyes and chose what to carry into morning. She would carry respect for the roof that kept her dry. She would not carry the part of the roof that dripped or that was broken.

She put the laptop on the chair and turned the screen face down. The cabin breathed its good small breath around her. The clock ticked. The cold at the window had teeth but not sharp ones. She thought about the line she had fed Jake earlier, the one about a bridge. She believed it more now in the thin hours than she had believed it when she said it. You build a bridge from what you have to what you need. You keep the river honest by not pretending it isn't there.

At the edge of morning, the ranch made the first shy sounds of waking. Frost softened. A truck coughed in the far distance. A few starlings fussed. Out by the barn, Spike shifted his weight, hip to hip, then blew a soft breath that came out in a cloud. Blue woke himself snoring and looked offended about it. He stretched in a long curve, shook hard enough to rattle his collar, and trotted to the back door to check on the yard and claim it again.

Ricardo parked at a gas station two towns over and went inside for a coffee he wouldn't drink. He bought a lottery ticket because he wanted it. He told the clerk the weather was perfect for business and the clerk nodded like men nod when they want the line to move along. He sat in his car, scrolled through messages, and sent one to a number labeled D.C. It said, All quiet. The brand is ready to pivot with the right pressure. He put the phone away, turned on the radio, found a station playing something that made a lot of noise and not much sense, and smiled like a man who had all the time in the world. He didn't. But men like him often pretend, and sometimes pretending feels a lot like having.

Back at the ranch, Jake made coffee in the dark because it felt right to light the day from the inside out. He didn't bother with the overhead. He used the little lamp by the sink that turned the steam into a ghost for a second before it vanished. He poured two mugs out of habit and put one on the table for a person who wasn't there yet. He waited and then laughed at himself. He picked up both mugs and stepped onto the porch. Cold air rubbed his face and reminded him he was alive.

Annie's porch light flicked on like a wink. He thought of walking down with a mug. He thought of knocking, the soft kind of knock that means I know it's early, I know you don't owe me your face at this hour, but I made coffee and I want to hand it to you, warm into warm. He stood there a full minute and let the picture play all the way through to the part where she opens the door and says good morning in that voice that has a smile inside it. Then he decided to wait. Not because he was scared. Because timing matters. Because words have better luck finding their target when morning is fully awake.

Annie dressed in layers and braided her hair because work and wind both appreciate order. She laced her boots, not the city ones, the ranch ones that had learned her feet already. She checked her phone out of habit and found nothing new except silence, which felt like a gift she didn't trust yet. She slipped the phone in her pocket and picked up the laptop, then set it down again and left it. Today needed her eyes up. Today was going to be real ranch work. Today the calves needed vaccinations.

She stepped outside and the cold kissed her. It was still dark. Steam rose from the coffee in her hand and wrote her name in the air for a half second, then didn't. She laughed a little and shook her head at herself, then walked the path to the house.

"Morning," Jake said, which is one of those words that does more work than folks give it credit for.

"Morning," she said, and held up her mug like a toast. "You beat me to it."

"I woke up a few times," he said.

"Me too," she said. "The ranch felt busy even when it wasn't."

They stood there a breath, not saying anything. Frost sighed and let go of grass.

Blue bounded out, said everything with his whole body, then settled between them like a thread sewing two pieces of cloth together. He leaned into Jake's leg and bumped Annie's knee with his head.

"I made a small list," she said. "It's not a bossy list. More of a polite suggestion list."

"I like polite suggestions," he said. "They feel like options even when they aren't."

They smiled at the same time. She told him her three points, no theater. He told her his three, same rule.

"Alright," she said. "Then we'll do what we said we'd do."

"Alright," he said. "We'll do it that way."

Today was going to be tough. She was going to be doing things she had never done before. Jake called it "Real ranch work."

Maria stepped onto the porch and waved her spoon like a conductor. Tommy arrived with a grin and a joke about how the string lights look even better in the morning if you squint right. Spike flicked flies that weren't there yet and pretended he didn't care who was watching.

Night had seemed to stretch on for hours, and maybe it had, but morning made a fair trade. It brought clarity in small, steady cups. It brought ordinary courage. It brought a long to do that looked less like a mountain and more like a path. They could walk a path. They had boots. They had hands. They had a dog who believed in them like it was his paying job.

Annie took the polite suggestion list and added one more line at the bottom with a star next to it. Laugh somewhere on purpose. She held it up for Jake to see. He read it and nodded like a man who already knew how to do that. He looked at her and said, "I can try," and then he did, and the sound made the kitchen warmer without the stove lifting a finger.

Annie thought again of the question she had whispered in the dark, the one about belonging. The morning didn't answer either, not in words. It answered the way mornings do. It handed her a mug and a task and a pair of eyes that met hers without flinching. It handed her a dog who would find her even if she hid. It handed her a man who said alright and meant it.

She laughed, there on purpose, checked the door latch with a quick tug, and stepped into the yard.

"It's got to work," she whispered under her breath.

CHAPTER TWENTY

LINES IN THE DIRT

They started before the sun, vaccination day for the calves. You could see their breath clouding in the cold. Calves bawled, the pens clanged, the air clean. Annie would not sit out, even though both Jake and Tommy offered her a way out of this kind of work. She held the vial steady, counted beats, pushed the plunger. Her hands shook. The world tilted. Jake caught her by the elbows before she dropped.

"You don't have to prove anything," he muttered, steadying her.

She drew a breath, met his eyes. "I'm not proving anything. I'm choosing it. I choose this."

Tommy swung the alley gate and Blue flowed at his heel, pressing the calves forward with quick, silent moves. "Keep them tight," Tommy called. "Low voice, slow hands."

A red calf balked, slid backward, then surged. Spike shifted at the rail, ears flicking. Jake nodded toward the head gate. "Next one," he said. "We'll make it smooth."

Maria came with thermoses and a crate of biscuits. "Eat or fall down," she said. Annie took a biscuit and a swallow of coffee that tasted like courage. Warmth found her fingers. The tremble eased.

They found a rhythm. Tommy set the gate. Jake worked the head. Annie cleaned the shoulder, quick swipe, clean, inject. Record in the book. Tag matched the number. Blue watched for gaps and filled them. Frost broke into glitter along the top wire.

"Breathe between calves," Jake said. "You're fine."

"I am," she said, and the ground agreed.

A small black heifer shook her head at the needle and tried to take the whole alley with her. Jake set a palm to her shoulder and murmured. Annie felt the wild ease under that voice. She slid the needle in and out clean. The heifer blinked, offended, then trotted on.

"That's right," Tommy said. "Act like you invented calm."

"Fake it till it sticks," Annie said.

"On this place, it sticks," Jake said.

They worked the first pen, then the second. Morning lifted from blue to pale gold. Annie's shoulders burned and her back hummed. Pain meant use. Use meant she belonged.

Between pens Maria handed out muffins. "Eat, drink, brag a little," she said.

Annie leaned on the rail and wrote tag numbers with neat strokes. She thought of lines in the dirt. Sorting lines. Property lines. The kind a banker draws in a ledger. The kind a father draws when he tries to decide who you are for you. Dust traced its own map across her boots.

"Ready?" Jake asked.

"Ready," she said.

They started the third pen, smaller calves, more noise, less sense. Blue danced them forward. One little bull calf fell over his own feet. Annie laughed and caught him by the chest with both hands, surprised by the soft heat of him. He snorted, scrambled, and found forward again.

"You and me both," she whispered.

By midmorning the sun finally committed. Fear gave way to focus. The work set its own steady, merciful pace.

They hit a snag at pen four. The headgate stuck. A latch had bent in the storm. Jake crouched with a wrench. Annie looked for what she could touch that would matter. The path between pens was slick.

She found a shovel and cut a trench to carry water away from the alley. She laid a path with broken pallets and old mats. She moved without asking. When she finished, the way held. Calves trotted instead of skidding.

"Look at that," Tommy said. "The city girl built a trail."

"I like dry feet," she said.

Jake tested the latch. It clicked. He looked at the path, at her, and gave a short nod.

They pushed on. Annie missed once and nicked her glove. She swore, changed gloves, cleaned again. Slower now. Cleaner now. Jake didn't comment. She had already corrected.

A wind came up from the west and ran through the cottonwoods. Clouds wandered the far horizon. Spike dozed and woke when Blue trotted past.

At the last pen, a calf with a white splash face planted his forehead into the rail and refused philosophy. Annie set down the syringe, rolled her shoulders, and looked at the sky until the blue rinsed the heat from her. She picked up the syringe and tried a different angle, lower, softer, not at the shoulder that had learned to flinch. In and out. Clean.

"You're learning," Jake said.

"I am," she said.

They finished before 10am. The corrals hummed. Maria clapped once and declared the day survivable. Tommy whooped to hear it bounce off the barn.

Annie sank onto an upside-down bucket and stretched her legs. Her hands smelled like iodine, leather, and biscuit. She closed her eyes and saw slides, then saw the calves instead, and the calves won.

Jake sat on the rail near her. "You did it," he said.

"We did it," she said.

He tipped his chin at the trench she had cut. "You saw a line and moved it."

"Lines belong to whoever picks up the shovel," she said.

He laughed, low. "Sometimes."

Maria handed around more biscuits, the solution to all hunger problems. "Eat, then talk," she said. "Talking with hunger pains should be criminal."

They ate. Blue curled under the table and sighed. Spike found a patch of sun and took credit for it.

Tommy tapped the book. "Numbers look clean," he said. "We can send the report. Miller folks can wait their turn."

Annie swallowed. "After lunch I'll call Mr. Davidson. I'll send photos and brochure samples. I'll also send projected numbers. But, he's going to want proof of life. We've got to actually put this project into action. Real number. Real proof."

Jake glanced at her. "OK, let's see how today goes. Then we'll work on your project, maybe."

"OK, no theater," she said. "Only what's true."

The talk drifted to small things. A hinge. A tire that looked suspect. A neighbor who had returned a tool with a note and cookies. The small things stacked into a morning that made sense.

When the biscuits were gone, Annie stood. Her legs wobbled and then remembered their job. She took the cooler by the handle and headed for the house to clean and restock. Jake fell in beside her. They walked the path she had built, boards thumping softly. At the edge of the yard she stopped.

"What?" he asked.

She drew a line in the dirt with the heel of her boot. Straight, clean, simple. Then she scuffed half of it away. "That's mine," she said. "Not Milan's. Not your bank. Not even your fear."

He studied her. "You sure?"

"I am," she said. "I can feel it."

He nodded. "Alright."

They kept walking. Blue bounded ahead and then came back. The house waited, ordinary and kind. The day didn't feel lighter. It felt honest, which was better.

By the sink, Annie scrubbed the trays and set them to dry. Jake rinsed syringes and stood them in a rack. Their elbows bumped once, then didn't.

"How about a real breakfast, now that the work's done?" Jake asked.

"Alright," she said. "Let me make it."

Jakes eyes got wider. "You?"

"Yes," she said. "I know how to cook you know."

"OK," Jake said. "Impress me then. Let's see what you got."

Annie smiled. "One problem at a time."

"One at a time," he said.

The vaccinations were done. The corrals had gone quiet in that satisfied way a place gets after hard work. Boots were by the door. A strip of sun laid itself across the kitchen floor. Annie was killing it at the stove, sleeves pushed up, hair twisted into a quick knot that kept falling and getting pushed back again. Butter hissed. A skillet of potatoes crisped at the edges. She stirred eggs that had waited a beat too long while she grabbed plates, then remembered the biscuits, then laughed at herself and spun back to the pan.

Jake had to admit, someone other than Maria in the kitchen was nice. Maria's cooking was like love. Annie's cooking like a novice trying hard to please. But the food tasted great.

Her timing, however, could have been better. The coffee had gone lukewarm while she set the table just so. The eggs had lost their shine while she ducked to the pantry for jelly only to decide honey fit better. She caught the coffee too late and frowned at herself, the tiny kind of frown that says a person wants to deliver something perfect even when perfect is a bully.

"Sorry," she said, sliding plates. "I got bossed by the biscuits."

"They boss everybody," Jake said. He tried for a joke and almost made it. "Coffee's still coffee."

Annie knew where the conversation was going next and the kitchen felt small. It seemed like weeks had passed since they were drinking coffee together that morning with Blue between them, the quiet soft as flannel. Now the quiet had corners.

Blue clicked across the floor, nails like small typewriter keys, and parked under the table with a hopeful face. Tommy had peeled off to the barn to coil hoses. Maria had stepped out to call a neighbor about a casserole situation that sounded intense. The house had left them to it.

Annie set down a plate and sat. "Jake," she said, and the word carried more weight than four letters should.

He watched the steam that wasn't there rise from the coffee that had already cooled. He kept his eyes on the mug because mugs are safe. He was not.

She didn't circle. She told him the truth. If she skipped the Milan board vote on Thursday, it was more than just losing a vote. It put her personal trust in danger. Her father had already said there would be consequences, and he meant it. Those consequences probably meant she would lose her trust fund. She would have only the money she took with her to Montana, and that wasn't much.

She said it clean, the way a person gives a doctor the symptoms and waits for the part where the room decides what happens next. The words sat between them.

Jake stared past her shoulder, jaw tight. There was a scuff on the cabinet door he had been meaning to sand for four months. He stared at it like it might give him an answer.

"Maybe you should go," he said.

The scrape of a chair, then nothing. Silence filled all the corners. The fridge hummed softly. Outside, a light wind found the chimes and changed its mind. Blue lifted his head, then put it down again, confused by rules that were not about fetch.

Annie was heartbroken. It wasn't a dramatic thing. It didn't throw a glass. It was a small, precise ache. She had told the truth, and the truth had emptied the room of its warmth for a second.

She touched the fork, then let it go. "Okay," she said, and the word did not mean okay. It meant I heard you, and also, please do not move farther away.

Jake put his hands flat on the table. "I mean," he tried again, slower, "maybe you should go if the cost of not going is the kind of trouble that doesn't end. Your father doesn't make idle threats. If he pulls that money, he pulls leverage. If he pulls leverage, he might pull blood next time."

"I know," she said. "I grew up knowing."

"Then go," he said, and he hated how fast it came out.

She swallowed. The coffee ring on the table had a little tail where a drip had gone exploring. She fixed it with a thumb and a napkin and felt foolish for needing something to fix in a moment that did not want fixing.

"I don't want to leave," she said.

"I don't want you to leave," he said. "But I don't want to be the reason you light a fuse you can't stamp out."

She nodded, a small movement that made the knot in her hair threaten to quit. She pushed it back again and laughed once, the short sound a person makes to keep the air moving. "Eggs are cold," she said.

"They're good," he said, and he meant it. Cold eggs can still feed you.

Blue belly-crawled until his head rested on her boot. Annie dropped a hand, found the soft spot behind his ear, and rubbed until his eyes went to slits. Comfort moved in tiny circles.

"You told me to write the plan with you at the center," she said. "This is me trying."

"I hear that," he said. "This, what we are doing right now, feels like the part where we put the center on the table and measure it."

She breathed out through her nose, slow. "He will punish me if I do not show. He could make me punish you by extension. He has done worse to men he says he respects. He thinks consequences teach."

Jake gave a short, humorless breath. "Consequences teach plenty. I just never liked the class."

Annie looked at the window. She saw the yard, how the light danced across it. "If I go, I go for a day. I vote, I don't let him use my empty chair as a story. I come right back. That is the promise I made you."

He nodded. "I heard you."

"But when you said maybe you should go," she said, voice soft, "it felt like you were opening the door wider than a day."

He looked at her fully and the room changed shape. "I might have been trying to keep you safe the only way I know. People leave when they chase safety. I learned that a long time ago. It's not your fault I know it that way."

She put her hand flat on the table, fingers splayed like a starfish holding on. "I'm here. I'm not promising what I can't keep. I'm telling you where my feet are."

He stared at her hand as if he could read the map there. He wanted to take it. He did not. Touch felt like a contract and he did not trust himself to sign anything with his mouth still full of fear.

"Eat," she said.

He ate a bite. He chewed like a man thinking about numbers he cannot see. He swallowed and tried again. "I trust you," he said, quietly, like it could break if he spoke too loud.

"I know," she said, and the words warmed the room a degree.

They worked on the cold eggs like they were hot. Maria's

honey made the biscuits better. The potatoes were perfect at any temperature, crispy all the way through.

"So," Annie said, practical as she turned the wheel, "if I go, I take the first flight out Wednesday night or brutally early Thursday. I sit, I vote, I do not linger. I tell Dante thank you for the roof he built and no to the walls he keeps trying to add. I fly back Friday morning in time to prep the pop-up. We start our project. If flights fail, I drive or I hire a plane. I am not kidding."

"I don't think you can drive from Milan to Montana," he said, a smile almost finding him.

"Alright," she said. "then I'll walk."

He shook his head. The edge of a grin made a brave attempt. "You're impossible."

"Frequently," she said. "It keeps me interesting."

Silence came back, not the sharp one from before, the worn kind that knows where the chairs go. The kitchen sighed. The clock remembered it had a job and went back to it.

"I hate that he can hurt you with money," Jake said. "I hate that I am not the kind of man who can make that part not matter in a day."

"You are the kind of man who can make it matter less," she said. "You do that by being exactly who you are and not an inch less."

He looked away and then back, like he had checked the horizon and decided to stay. "Alright."

She stacked plates. He took them from her and set them by the sink. They did the dance of two people who want to be close without crowding. Blue supervised like a foreman.

"Say it again," Jake said, not looking at her. "The exact part about the trust."

"If I miss the vote, I lose control of my proxy. He can reassign protections. He will call it administrative, then he will lock me out for a cycle that could stretch. He could cut me to whatever cash I brought with me. In this case, that is a little card and a little envelope, both of which would run out if I blinked wrong."

"Do you care about the money, or do you care about what he thinks the money buys him?" he asked.

She rinsed a plate, set it to dry. "I care about not giving him a reason to write my story in my absence. I care about standing in the room when my name gets used. I care about not letting him use generosity as a leash."

"That one," he said. "That last one."

She met his eyes. "He is used to women being grateful in a language that lets him keep the pen. Women who bow at his feet."

Jake huffed what might have been a laugh if the day had started softer. "I believe you."

"You should," she said. "You've seen me work a fence line and a banker in the same hour."

"I have," he said. "You were mean to that mud puddle."

"It had it coming," she said.

They smiled.

"Will you be mad at me if I tell you I don't like you going, even if I think you should?" he asked.

"Not mad," she said. "Seen."

He nodded. "Seen is good."

She dried her hands and crossed to him. She stood close enough to feel the warmth without asking for rescue. "I want to stay," she said again, because sometimes the echo is the point.

"I want you to stay," he said again, same reason.

The wind pushed a little at the kitchen window and then left it alone. The day had work lined up. So did they.

Annie reached for the coffee and took a drink even though it was lukewarm. "This is terrible," she said.

"It is," he said. "We should reheat it."

They did, and the small act changed nothing and something at once. Heat rose in soft curls, almost forgiving. She held the mug with both hands and let it warm her fingers. He leaned on the counter with his hip and pretended not to watch her breathe. They stood there, two stubborn people holding one delicate morning together with coffee and choices.

"Maybe you should go," he said again, but softer, the kind of maybe that means I will wait right here and work the ranch while you handle the dragon that carries your name.

"Maybe I should," she said, and this time it didn't feel like a door swinging wide. It felt like a line drawn clear, not to divide them, to mark where they would meet again.

She took a bite of biscuit and closed her eyes for the small joy of it. He reached for the honey and handed it over without looking, like he had known she would ask. Blue sighed the deep sigh of a dog who has decided his people might be alright.

The kitchen breathed. The house settled. Outside, the yard shook off the last of the morning chill. Inside, they stood close and chose each other in the only way that counted today.

Not with promises. With plans.

It seemed the decision was made. She would go. Back in her cabin, she pulled a bag from the closet and began to fold. Jeans, worn boots, the laptop, cables coiled like a question. In the top drawer she found the carved bridle piece with the single letter A, smooth under her thumb. She pressed it to her chest and closed her eyes. A tear slipped, quick and hot, then she wiped it away.

She packed like a person who doesn't trust time. Neat stacks. Quiet choices. Two shirts rolled tight. The wool sweater that smelled like smoke and porch wood. Toiletries in a zip pouch. Chargers in a cloth bag. Habit ruled the small things when the big things felt wild.

Her phone buzzed with a reminder. Call Mr. Davidson. Confirm Thursday. She'd call. First, she needed a bag that said I'm leaving and I'm coming back in the same breath.

The closet held two kinds of shoes. The boots she already wore, clean but honest, and a pair of stilettos wrapped in tissue from a life with marble floors. Ricardo's message from last night rose up again. Bring heels. She didn't give him the grin he wanted. She slid the heels in anyway, not because he asked, because they were hers before he learned to name them. Boots and stilettos could sit side by side without a fight. Both were tools.

She tucked the bridle piece into the small inside pocket, the one that used to hold a compact. The leather warmed in her palm, like the letter liked heat. A for Annie. A for Antoinette. A for the line in the dirt she kept drawing until it stayed put.

A soft knock.

"Come in," she said.

Jake stepped inside and looked at the bag first because it was the loudest thing in the room.

"You talked to flights?" Jake asked.

"Not yet," she said. "I will in ten minutes. I wanted the room ready before I said it out loud."

He nodded.

Silence moved between them, careful, not empty.

"I was going to leave you a note," she said, "but here you are."

"I'm here," he said.

"I'm going to go, vote, say no to anything with a string, and come back," she said. "I'm taking the quiet with me through security like it's allowed."

"I'll meet you at the gate," he said, half a smile. "Not the airport one. The north pasture. Coffee hot this time."

"Deal," she said.

He picked up the cables, set them down, like he needed to touch something that could be untangled. "I don't like this," he said. "I also don't like men who think money buys a map to your bones."

"It doesn't," she said. "It never has. It bought me a roof. I'm grateful. But gratitude's not a leash."

He looked at the stilettos in the bag and lifted one eyebrow. "Packing weapons?"

"Only legal ones," she said. "They're for walking past marble without flinching."

"Boots look better on you," he said.

"They do," she said. "But sometimes the room hears you better if your shoes click."

He laughed once, the good kind that rescues a minute. "Click in and out."

She touched the bridle piece through the fabric and felt the letter. "I will."

"You want help?" he asked.

"Just one thing," she said. "Tell me to come back."

"Come back," he said, right away.

"Thank you," she said, and felt a latch catch.

Annie zipped the bag and set it by the door. Bags speak loud even when they're small. She opened the airline app. Routes lined up like dominos. She chose one that would drop her in, let her sit, vote, refuse lunch, and leave. She booked and sent two short texts to Maria and Tommy. Leaving for a day. Back in time to bake.

Next, she messaged Mr. Davidson. Confirming attendance. I'll send projected bookings on return. Review holds at current date, yes?

Jake watched her thumbs move. "I just cannot get over how good you are at this," he said.

"I've had practice," she said. "I'd rather practice here than there."

He glanced at the bridle on the hook by the door, the one missing the little piece in her pocket. "I forgot you kept that."

"I didn't," she said. "Helps to hold something that's seen the work."

He lifted the bag and set it down with care. "Light enough to move fast."

"I want to move fast," she said. "I don't want anyone spinning a story I have to unspin."

Blue shook and sneezed. He pressed his head to her knee. She scratched. "You're on gate duty," she told him.

He wagged like he understood.

Jake checked his watch and ignored it. "We've got an hour before the next round of chores starts. You want to sit and not think, or run your list out loud?"

"List," she said.

They sat on the bed with Blue between them like a warm log. Annie went down the list. Flight timing. Connection risk. Agenda. The tactic for when her father tried to praise her into a corner. The correct answer to be reasonable when it means be compliant. She had that one ready. No.

"Eat before you go in," Jake said. "Hold the pen if he hands you a document. Sit where you can see the door."

"You'd run security in Milan in an hour," she said.

"I've watched people make simple days hard," he said.

She stood. "I should tell him."

"You want to call him from here?"

"No," she said. "From the yard. I like the wind for company."

"I'll walk you," he said.

They stepped into bright, thin late morning. She dialed. She confirmed. She didn't promise dinner. The call ended clean.

She watched a small cloud climb the ridge. Her shoulders set, not tense.

"Thanks for walking with me," she said.

"Always," he said.

Back inside, she slid the bag under the chair where it couldn't glare. She wrote a note and tucked it under the salt shaker so he'd find it at breakfast if morning went sideways. Back soon. Hold my coffee.

"Need anything else?" Jake asked.

"Yes," she said. "One more look so I can take it with me."

So he stood and let her look. She memorized the light on his jaw, the steady in his eyes. She tucked that picture into the same pocket as the bridle piece.

"Alright," she said. "That's enough."

"For now," he said.

"For now," she agreed.

He reached for the bag and left it alone. "I'll be outside if you need a hand."

"I know," she said.

He stepped out. Blue followed, then circled back to lie across the threshold like a guard.

"Back soon," she told him.

He sighed like he'd already accepted the plan.

She stood, checked the locks she never locked, and laughed at herself. She turned off the lamp, then on, then off. The room held her shape for a breath and then settled back to itself, quiet, ready to wait.

The decision was made. She would go. The promise was made too. She would come back.

Night took the yard and left the stars bright and cold. Annie stood at her cabin door. Sleep, pack, fly, vote, return. No, she thought. Not like this. I can't leave this place without one more look at the ridge.

She crossed the yard, breath white as flour. The ranch gave up its small sounds. A board eased in the porch, a latch clicked. Blue lifted his head from his bed on the stoop, thumped his tail once, and let her pass.

In the barn, Spike lifted his head. "Just us," she whispered. She saddled Rusty by feel, slow and neat. Leather creaked. Cinch snug. He stood for her the way friends do. They stepped into the dark together.

The ranch lights pricked the valley, stubborn and imperfect, a map of what mattered. Frost crisped under hoof. Annie pressed her knees and Rusty took the grade honest, shoulders sure. The ridge waited.

"I'm not done here," she whispered. They climbed in a rhythm that felt like prayer, hoof after hoof, breath after breath. She let him choose the line. He always found the dry ground when she couldn't see it.

At the top she stood in the stirrups and looked. Below, the house sat square and stubborn. The barn breathed. The yard lights made a constellation, a rough draft of home. She thought of the vote. The proxy. The trust. Her father's voice shaped like a verdict. Her throat tightened, then eased.

She turned Rusty toward home and gave him his head. He stretched, sure, and the night peeled tears from her eyes. She laughed. It felt like flying and being ten and stealing a wind. Her jaw set like Jake's when he meets a problem he plans to outlast. Her heart set like her own.

I'm not going, she thought. The words didn't arrive like a drum. They arrived like dawn, plain and absolute. I'm not going. She said it into the dark, and the dark didn't argue.

The slope eased. The barn opened its shadowed mouth to meet them. She stood again and let the choice fill her lungs. "I'm not going!" she shouted. It bounced from the boards and came back thinner and braver. A light flickered in the kitchen and went out. Blue barked once, a seal on the decree.

She swung down and put her forehead to Rusty's. "Thank you," she told him. She slipped the bridle, loosened the cinch, and lifted the saddle, careful with the blanket. She brushed him until his coat rose soft under her hand, until her breath matched his. "We're alright," she said, and believed it.

Back in the cabin she set the phone on the table and opened the airline app. Her thumb hovered. Fear tried a last disguise, one that calls itself wisdom. She smiled. She canceled the trips. One by one the boxes asked if she was sure. Yes. Yes. Yes. She texted Maria and Tommy again. Change of plan. I'm staying. I'll explain in the morning. She screenshotted the confirmations, emailed herself the proof, and deleted the holds. The hiss in her head went quiet.

She opened messages and typed to her father. I changed my mind. I'm not going. She didn't add anything. She pressed send. The text slid away like a boat cut loose from a post. She felt lighter and a little scared, which is often how freedom starts.

She unzipped the bag and put the almost trip back where it belonged. Shirts sighed into the drawer. The wool sweater returned to its hook. The stilettos went back into tissue, then onto the shelf where she could see them. Tools, both pairs. She coiled the cables the right way, not like questions, like answers. The zipper closed on nothing.

In the top drawer the carved bridle piece waited, the single letter smooth under her thumb. A. Annie. Antoinette. A choice. She pressed it to her chest and closed her eyes. A tear slipped, quick. She wiped it and didn't apologize. Water grows things. She rubbed the leather with a soft cloth until it showed a quiet glow. Tender work. It didn't need much. It mattered anyway.

On the counter she wrote a note to the morning so it would know how to behave. Coffee at first light. Call Mr. Davidson. Tell Jake. Bake if there's time. Laugh on purpose. She stuck it under the salt shaker so she couldn't miss it. The clock said too late to knock. The sky agreed. She would tell him over coffee, hot this time, with the sun on the table and Blue underfoot.

She washed her face and watched herself in the mirror the way you watch a stranger you're ready to trust. She looked like a person who had refused one story and chosen another. She touched the glass with two fingers. "I'm staying," she said, and the room warmed a degree.

Outside, the ranch listened, because places listen when people make vows. The wind slid along the eaves and went quiet. In the barn Rusty stamped once and settled. Somewhere a board relaxed and told the nail it had it from here.

Annie turned off the lamp and climbed into bed. The sheet

felt cool and honest. She slipped the bridle piece under her pillow the way a child hides a treasure. Her phone lit once. She turned it face down and let the screen go dark. She didn't owe anyone an explanation, not tonight. Morning could have its turn later.

Sleep found her the way a horse finds the line home, without fuss. When she drifted she saw the ridge and the glory of stars and the yard lights making their rough map of hope. She saw Jake at the table, hat pushed back, coffee steaming. She saw Blue doing that full body wag that makes a person believe in simple joy. She saw the word she had chosen float and settle where it belonged.

Stay.

She kept it.

CHAPTER TWENTY-ONE

ULTIMATUMS AND UNRAVELING

The air seemed cleaner. The sky brighter. Everything was clearer. Annie woke with bright eyes and an excitement she hadn't felt since childhood, the kind that starts in the ribs and makes a person want to run. Not a soul in the world would've known she'd just thrown away millions in her trust fund by not showing up to the board meeting. She'd slept anyway, sound, and somehow woke lighter.

Strange as it was, she woke up before Jake. She remembered that first morning she was here. "Five AM sharp," Jake had said. She smiled, remembering how just a few months ago she didn't even know 5AM existed. She crossed the yard, boots quick on cold boards, breath fogging. Blue pricked his ears from the porch, wagged once, and trotted ahead to announce her.

She knocked on the main house door before Jake was really moving. "Surprise… I'm not going!"

Jake blinked, then blinked again, sleep hanging on. "What… what do you mean?"

"I'm not going," she said again, steady this time. "I don't care what he does or what happens. This place matters more. You matter more."

He stared at her a beat, and whatever argument had been loading in his head powered down. He stepped back. "Come in. Coffee."

They sat at the kitchen table, the same table that had held too many hard words the day before. Steam rose off fresh mugs. The house made friendly morning sounds; a heater ticked, the fridge hummed, Blue settled at their feet like a living rug.

"Okay," Jake said, palms around his cup. "If that's the case, we work your project. We find out fast if it can carry weight. We need to know if it'll work or not." He drew a breath. "Alright. Let's do it, together. I'll ride Spike for your photo. Keep it short."

"Short and pretty," Annie said.

He nodded. "I'll pretend to fix that fence on the north pasture again, you know, for pictures."

"Great idea," she said, grinning. The fear that had been living under her ribs took a step back. "Next, we need more string lights. Rich people love starry lights. Then we clean up everything and get this ready to happen."

"Thanks," he said, and the thanks meant more than the word usually does.

They built a list of names and numbers, quick and focused. Maria texted eight names in five minutes, each with notes, two flagged as sure things. Tommy added four more and included who they trusted at church to spread a whisper that would grow legs. Annie wrote copy for a simple social media post, no fluff, just what, when, how much, and why. Sunset ride available, not guaranteed. Founders' Night, twelve spots only. Quiet hours. Real food. Deposits required.

Annie was busy with pictures as Tommy showed up. "Make sure you spell out we got bathrooms and show pictures too," Tommy said when she read it aloud. "City folks like to see we got 'em."

"They'll sparkle," Annie said. "We'll take the mirror off the wall if we have to and shine it on the porch."

She and Tommy walked the yard and framed shots. The barn door slightly ajar, warm light spilling. A quilt over the rail, hand stitched, clean. Two mugs steaming on a whiskey barrel. The ridge with the promise of stars even though the sun hadn't given up yet. Blue nosed into frames and out again like an unpaid extra with excellent instincts.

"Show me that path of lanterns from the house to the yard," Annie said. "I want the line to read like welcome."

"On it," Tommy said. "And I can lift the string lights one notch higher if you want that soft roof look."

"Do it," she said. "Magic only matters if people can see it."

They split jobs without talking about it. Jake saddled Spike and rode to the north fence for the I'm-fixing-something shot, then set a real staple because he couldn't stand pretend work sitting there all day. Maria scrubbed the bathrooms until the fixtures winked. Blue inspected everything twice. Annie kept the phone in her back pocket, camera at the ready, eyes tuned to what would feel true on the screen. She shot tight and honest. No filters. No lies.

By midmorning, the post went up with six photos and twenty clean words. The notifications chirped, then slowed, then started a steady hum that grew teeth.

By early afternoon, pings started landing like hail on a metal roof. Deposits hit faster than anyone expected. One couple booked from Denver. One from two towns over. A teacher asked if there were quiet corners to read. A lineman's wife said they needed a night where nobody needed them.

Annie watched the cart total blink and then hold. She let herself breathe for the first time in what felt like a week. "We've got twelve," she said. "Wait. Thirteen on the pop-up next weekend if we open it."

Jake scrolled with a frown that wasn't worry, it was awe trying not to make a scene. "That's rent on one more month of hope," he said, extremely impressed.

"It's proof," she said. "The idea isn't just cute. It works."

They kept moving. Tommy strung more lights from tree to eave and back again, the bulbs throwing a warm promise over the yard even in daylight. Annie chalked a small board with the evening timeline, not for guests, for them. Prep, greet, ride if safe, eat, stargaze, thank you, goodnight. No speeches. No sales pitch. Just the truth and a clean place to stand under it.

"Show the bathrooms," Tommy reminded, tapping the list.

"On the list," Annie said, and added a small star. "Priority sparkle."

Maria dragged a broom across the porch with a fierce rhythm. "If they see my floors, they'll cry. In a good way."

"They'll cry from joy," Annie said. "And because the biscuits are illegal."

"I'll allow it," Maria said, pleased.

Jake came back from the north fence, hat tipped back, Spike blowing easy. Annie caught a candid of him swinging down, one palm on the saddle horn, the kind of picture that sells not because it's pretty, because it's honest. She lowered the camera and caught the real thing with her own eyes, the better lens.

"Short and pretty," he said, handing her the reins.

"Perfect," she said.

He looped the reins and brushed Spike's shoulder with the flat of his hand. "We'll need firewood at both pits," he said. "And I'll check the gate latch by the cottonwoods. It stuck last week."

"I'll put it on the list," Annie said, scribbling. "Firewood, gate, bathrooms, biscuits, stars."

"Add coffee," Jake said. "Hot this time."

She laughed. "Deal."

The pings kept coming. She let the numbers stack to a line that made sense, then grabbed her folder of proof. Receipts. Names. Time stamps. The quiet math of momentum.

"Time to feed the banker," she said, and took a breath to steady her voice. She composed the email to Mr. Davidson, attached screenshots and a short note, then sent a single clean sentence to sit under it: Booked to twelve for Founders' Night, deposits cleared, next two weekends in motion. She hit send and felt the old dread try to climb back into the room. It didn't get far.

Jake watched her face, not the screen. "You good?"

"I am," she said. "He'll either play fair or he won't. Either way, we're moving."

"Good," he said. "Movement is a good thing."

They ate late at the table, bowls in hand, blue dusk already leaning against the windows. The day had the tired that means satisfied, not wrecked. Blue fell asleep sitting up and tipped over like a log. Tommy caught him with a laugh and made a pillow from a folded towel. Maria slid a biscuit toward Annie without looking and said, "Eat," which is how love talks in kitchens.

"Tomorrow we shoot the Sky Cabin pop-up, right?" Tommy asked.

"Right," Annie said. "Bunkhouse scrubbed, quilts washed, star map on the table, kettle whistling. No gilt, no fake."

Jake raised his cup. "To no fake."

"To no fake," they echoed.

Annie looked around the room and took a small mental photograph. Jake's hat on the chair back, Maria's pencil behind her ear, Tommy's grin half-cocked, Blue's paws twitching. The house held it all like a cupped hand.

She stood to rinse bowls and caught her reflection in the dark window. She didn't look like a woman who had just lost a fortune. She looked like a woman who had found a place to spend herself on purpose. The sky outside was getting ready to bring stars, and the string lights were already making their little promises.

"Let's make this happen," Jake said, voice low, like he didn't want to spook the luck. "Magic only matters if people can see it."

Annie nodded. "Then we'll turn the lights on."

She pressed send on a final packet to the bank, the neat bundle of proof a ranch sometimes needs to keep breathing: deposits, schedule, list of names, photos that felt like truth. She clicked her laptop closed and rested her palm on the lid.

Outside, so much work to do. Inside too, so they got back to work, which is another word for hope when you do it together.

Annie never did show up for the board vote.

Her father was beyond furious. A rich, mad Italian on a mission. Calls went out. Papers were read. Promises were made to men who only spoke in invoices. By noon in Milan he'd decided talk was pointless. He wanted ground. He wanted a door to knock on and a face to scold. He wanted to look his daughter in the eye and win.

Dante Contadelucci and his lawyer boarded his jet with clipped steps and silent luggage. The flight attendant felt the weather in the cabin, cool and expensive. Because of the time difference and the speed of his jet, Dante could leave at 1 p.m. and, on Montana clocks, be on the ground at 2 p.m. It pleased him to bend time on the page, to make the world fold just so when he pressed his name against it.

The jet cut across clean blue and dropped toward a strip that was more dust than runway. Heat shimmered even though the air wasn't truly hot. The place stretched out in long browns and long silvers. Then a square patch of green. Dante felt the land's size press against the windows. Milan is a chessboard. This was a table with no edges.

He stood at the top of the steps and tasted it. Sun. Hay. Oil. A drift of cattle on the wind. The smell got past city suits and money fast. Dust lifted and clung to the cuffs of his trousers, and the cuffs alone said plenty. Montana didn't care who he was. It didn't even know.

Ricardo was waiting at the bottom of the stairs, already smiling the smile you can't trust. The kind that says I'm on your side while counting the chairs. He wore desert boots he'd bought yesterday and scuffed on purpose in the hotel lot so they'd look like they'd lived. He'd chosen a jacket that could survive a snapshot, and he held two pairs of sunglasses like props.

"Dottore," he said, syrup over steel. "Welcome. You made good time."

"Of course," Dante said. He didn't take a hand Ricardo offered. He nodded instead, a royal allowance. Behind him, his lawyer came down careful, briefcase gleaming. Ricardo's lawyer followed with the same briefcase in a darker shade.

They crossed the tarmac in heat that had opinions. The SUV waited with its own kind of grin. Dante sat back, already calculating the way the light would fall across the ranch house door when he arrived. He liked settings that helped him win before he spoke.

"How long?" he asked, staring straight ahead.

"Forty minutes if we behave," Ricardo said. "Thirty if the road behaves."

"Behave," Dante said. "I want control, not dust."

Ricardo smiled at the windshield. "You'll get both today."

Dante's lawyer, a quiet man who liked precise verbs, clicked open the briefcase. "We have options prepared. If she's present, we deliver choice A. If she's absent, we deliver choice B. If she's resistant, we file the protective amendments. We can freeze distributions within the hour."

"Freeze them," Dante said. "All of them."

"You'll look harsh," Ricardo said lightly. "Which is fine, but optics matter for the brand."

"My name is not a brand," Dante said. "It is a promise."

"Exactly," Ricardo said, delighted. "And promises need theater. Lucky for us, we have a ranch. We can use this setting to tell a story about duty, about returning to roots. Photos by the fence. A clean statement to the press if needed. Antonietta can still be part of the story if she wants to be wise."

"She chose foolish," Dante said. The word sat hard between them. "She chose to humiliate me."

Ricardo adjusted a cuff. "Or she chose wonder. She's been very busy selling stars to people who like to buy them." He held up a printed copy of Annie's post from the morning. Founders' Night. Twelve spots. Deposits taken. A blurry Jake in one photo, Spike's ears forward like a crown. "She moved product," he said. "Honestly, I'm impressed. But it's still a phase."

Dante didn't look at the page. "Do not call my daughter a phase."

"Never," Ricardo said, unbothered. "I'm calling the ranch a phase. The city is permanent. The board is permanent."

Dante watched fence after fence tick past. Lines in the dirt that meant something to men who put them there with their hands. He felt annoyance and, underneath it, something else he didn't name. He pressed his palm flat against his knee until the feeling filed itself away.

They left the paved road for gravel. The SUV softened the rattle but didn't kill it. Cottonwoods made a narrow river of light and shadow. A hawk wrote its name on the sky. Ricardo took the turn a touch too fast.

"Slow," Dante said.

"Of course," Ricardo said, slowing.

Dante's phone buzzed. A message he didn't read yet. He knew what it would say. Lawyers moved faster than apologies. Money moved faster than love. He'd taught both lessons for years. He wasn't a cruel man, he told himself. He was an efficient one. Efficiency looks like cruelty to people who prefer mess.

"Sir," the lawyer said quietly, "I also have a letter drafted if you want to leave it on her table as a formal notice."

Dante nodded once. "We leave nothing that can be ignored. We speak. She answers. We leave with clarity."

Ricardo turned off the gravel onto two ruts that counted as a lane. The land opened. There, in the middle of all that honest space, the ranch sat stubborn and imperfect, lights pricking the bright of afternoon. It didn't bow to him. It didn't pose. It simply was.

"Charming," Ricardo said, that word he uses when he means useful.

Dante didn't answer. He saw a yard swept clean. String lights strung like a low sky. Two mugs on a barrel. A path of lantern hooks marching from the house to the gate. A bathroom window that flashed once like a wink. He filed every detail because that's what men like him do. Even his anger took notes.

They rolled to a stop. Dust went past them and went on with its life. Dante stepped out first. The heat hit again. So did the smell of cattle and hay. A horse stamped, close but not visible. A dog barked once, the kind that states a fact and waits for the next one.

Maria came out onto the porch with a dish towel in her hand and the kind of look that could measure a person without touching them. She didn't flinch when she saw the suits. She didn't hurry either. "Afternoon," she said. "Can I help you gentlemen find the right door?"

"I'm here for my daughter," Dante said, each word laid down like a tile. "Antonietta."

Maria wiped her hands, slow. "She's not here right this second. She's at the bunkhouse, making it shine. You can wait, or you can walk."

Ricardo stepped forward with a gleam he couldn't hide. "We'll walk," he said.

"Suit yourselves," Maria said. She looked at Dante's cuffs, dust hugging the hem. "You might want to lift your pants. The path's clean, the ground isn't."

Dante didn't lift his pants. He'd already lost enough ground for one day. He followed Maria's chin toward the side yard, lawyers at his back like punctuation. Ricardo kept up a running commentary, soft enough to pretend polite. "We'll take photos by the string lights later," he whispered. "You'll look paternal. She'll look redeemed. The story will sell."

Dante didn't answer. He was busy holding his temper like a glass of water filled to the lip.

They rounded the barn. The bunkhouse stood ahead, windows open to let the soap out. Annie's quilt hung over the rail like a flag. On the table by the door, a star map waited under a smooth stone.

Blue trotted up first. He gave them the once-over, polite but not impressed, then peeled away to find someone he trusted. A moment later Annie appeared in the doorway with a bucket and a rag, hair pulled back, sleeves rolled, eyes bright, all work and light.

She stopped when she saw them, not from fear, from the need to put words in the right order before the air stole them.

"Antonietta," Dante said.

"Papa," she said, steady.

Ricardo's smile widened. The lawyers shifted their cases from left to right, a small, hungry ballet. The Montana sun stood there like an honest witness. Dust clung to cuffs that never learned to kneel. Milan had flown a long way to tell the prairie how to behave.

Montana didn't care. And this world was not where a Contadelucci belonged, not by Dante's rules. But she had made her choice.

She didn't look away.

They cleared the long table in the bunkhouse and called it a boardroom. Phones were propped on salt-shakers.

She started tapping her foot, sharp and quick. She was impatient and close to certain this circus was useless. She had canceled flights. She had told the only person who mattered. Yet here they were, acting out a power she'd already stepped out from under.

Dante set a leather folder on the wood, flipped to a blue tab, and pushed papers toward her. "You'll sign away your voting rights," he said. "We're making this legal. Quick and clean."

"It protects you," she said.

Annie kept her voice level. "No." She let the word sit. "You do what you gotta do. But I'm not signing nuttin'." She rounded the vowels on purpose, her best try at a Montana drawl, and let herself grin.

Ricardo let his smile sharpen. "You'll be out of those boots soon and back in heels," he said. "I'll have the car for the airport ready and waiting for you."

"Don't wait," she said.

Dante's lawyer slid a pen across the table. "If you refuse, you understand the consequences. Freezing distributions. Amending controls."

"Big words for taking things," Annie said.

"We will secure the trust against irresponsible risk," the lawyer said.

"By which you mean my money," she said.

"Yes," he said. "You will have zero control and you will have no way of regaining control. Even upon the death of..."

"This is useless," Annie interrupted. "People buy the sky," Annie said. "They also buy honesty. That's what I'm focusing on now. Not any trust fund, Not any board vote."

Dante's jaw flexed, then went calm. "Antonietta," he said. "I will forgive your tone. I will forgive this playacting. I will not forgive public disobedience. Sign, and we'll keep this in the family."

She laid her palms flat. "We are family whether I sign or not. That was your choice the day I was born. This is mine. I'm not signing."

Silence had weight. A pipe ticked. Outside, a fly banged a screen.

Ricardo angled his phone, framing her like a headline. "Stubborn can be charming," he murmured. "For a week."

"It's been longer than a week," Annie said. "And I'm more than charming."

Dante looked at her like a man eyeing the last card in a hand he'd already lost. "You will regret this," he said. "When you are out of money. When this little ranch project fails. When the headline ends. When the man leaves…"

"The man is outside fixing a gate again because he likes things that work," she said. "And the headline is a star map and a plate of biscuits. I can live with that."

He pushed back his chair and stood. "Final time," he said. "Sign."

"Final time," she said. "No."

The lawyer cleared his throat. "Then we enact the freeze notice of reassignment. I'll file within the hour."

"Do your job," Annie said.

"You do like to make work for people," Ricardo said.

"Funny," she said. "I'm working right now."

Dante gathered the papers. "We are leaving," he said. "I'll have your voting rights removed by nightfall. Your trust will be revoked even sooner."

"You do you," she said. "I'll do me."

He blinked at that. Only a beat, but she saw it land.

"We're done," she said.

"We're not," he said. "We will never be done."

"Then we'll be not done from here," she said.

He looked at the boots peeking from under the table. "Those are not your shoes."

"They are now," she said.

The door stood half open to let the soap smell out. Jake had come up the steps when Tommy flagged him by the barn. He meant to stride in and plant himself at her side. He stopped when he heard her voice. Firm enough to build on.

He set a palm to the jamb and listened. Papers. Pen. Low lawyer murmur. Her no, calm as bedrock. He wanted to believe she was doing it for him, for the ranch. Doubt still kept one hand on his shoulder. He let it sit and didn't let it steer.

Inside, Annie tapped once more and made her foot be still. She stood to end the theater. "I've got guests to prep," she said. "Founders' Night is tonight. You're welcome to buy a ticket."

Ricardo laughed. "I don't buy tickets. I am tickets."

"Then you're not on the list," she said.

Dante's lawyer gathered notes. "We'll serve the notices."

"Of course you will," she said.

Dante paused at the threshold where daylight made a clean line. "You will ask me later to undo this," he said.

"No," she said. "I'll ask you later to come for dinner and be my father."

He left. Ricardo followed, smile back in place, phone low and ready. The lawyers went after them.

Jake stepped in, hat in hand. He stood where she could see him. "You alright?"

"I am," she said, her voice steady. "I am."

"I was coming to save you," he said.

"I noticed," she said. "I saved me instead."

He nodded. "That's better."

Blue pushed past his leg and stuck his nose in her palm. She scratched his head and laughed.

"Founders' Night still on?" Jake asked.

"Still on," she said. "We've got a sky to sell and a fence to fix. Which one do you want?"

"I'll take the fence," he said.

"Figures," she said.

He looked at the clean spot where the papers had been. "You held the line."

"I did," she said. She lifted her foot and set it down, a little stomp that said the dirt belongs to whoever stands on it. "And I'm not tired."

"Good," he said. "We've got work."

She grabbed the rag and the bucket. Soon the bunkhouse would be smelling great. Like something new. They walked out into a day that had decided to be honest. Outside, the wind shifted, and the sky looked ready to keep their secrets tonight.

Founders' Night was going great. The lantern path glowed like a quiet runway. String lights threw a soft roof over the yard. Two mugs steamed on the barrel exactly like the photo. Maria's biscuits vanished in waves. Someone whispered, "The bathrooms sparkle." Three people nodded like they'd just seen a miracle. You could read five-star Google ratings on their faces.

Annie moved through it, light on her feet, taking payments, refilling cider, pointing at constellations with the star map folded to the right page. Jake stayed near the barn door, easy and calm, hat tipped back. Blue made his rounds and collected love. Tommy floated wherever a hand was needed. People kept saying the same sentence. It feels honest here.

Night carried the warning before anyone saw it. A thread of scent that didn't belong. Sweet, then bitter. Annie paused and lifted her head. The music from somebody's truck went soft. A guest turned and squinted at the barn. The glow came next. Orange at a seam where no light should be. Then a thump, a pop, and a thin line of smoke unfurling like a bad idea that had been waiting all day.

The barn was on fire from the inside out. Too fast. Too sudden to be chance.

They ran without thinking. Tommy grabbed the nearest hose and dragged it hard. Maria shouted for folks to clear the yard and go to the east fence if they wanted to stay and watch from safety. Annie hit the latch on the side door and heat hit her like a wall. Smoke rolled thick and low. She dropped to a knee, coughed, and pushed forward.

Stalls thrown open. Tack hauled into the yard. Panic in every sound. Wood complaining. Nails letting go. Spike was not in his stall. His halter hung, the lead rope gone. Blue darted to the next corridor, stopped, barked once, and looked back hard. Annie followed the sound, hand on the wall, eyes stinging.

She found him in the far corner, tangled where a lead had wrapped itself through an eye bolt and turned mean. Spike's eyes were wide and white. He fought air he couldn't breathe. Heat pressed her back. She fumbled for the pocketknife she kept in her back pocket because Tommy had made her carry one, and now she was grateful he had. She sawed at the rope. Smoke clawed her throat. She coughed so hard a spark of black danced at the edge of her vision.

"Easy, boy," she said, voice ragged. "It's me. I've got you." She cut and cut. The rope gave an inch and then another. She pushed at his shoulder. He shoved back, blind with fear. She pleaded out loud because sometimes words hold a body together. "Come on, Spike. Come on, please."

Jake barreled through the haze, towel over his mouth, shoulders squared against heat. He reached her as a beam cracked above them like a gunshot. He felt the shift in the air that means hurry now or don't get another chance. He grabbed her with one hand and the halter with the other. "Move," he said, voice calm, and that saved them more than the hose did.

The rope let go with a mean little snap. Spike lurched. Jake hauled. Annie shoved his flank and then shoved herself. They ran crooked, lower than they knew, while smoke tried to make a new wall in front of them. The doorway showed as a dark rectangle of mercy. They hit it just as the roof found a weak point and folded in on itself. Sparks blew across the yard.

They tumbled into hard night and cold air, coughing water and smoke. Blue leaped and then backed off, dancing in place, eyes wild, as if to say, You did it, now keep doing it. Maria was there with a wet bandanna and a bottle. Tommy took Spike's halter, hands fast, voice low. "Easy, big man. Easy. It's just noise."

The guests moved like a flock. Some filmed, most didn't. A teacher cried and handed Maria her sweater. A lineman shook out hose and found the hydrant spigot by instinct. Someone called the volunteers and then called two neighbors who had water tanks and opinions about fire. The yard turned into a quiet, busy machine.

Annie's lungs burned, then found air and held it. Jake put a hand at the back of her neck and felt her pulse. He didn't ask if she was alright. He looked. She met his eyes and gave a small nod. He nodded back and scooped an armful of bridles from a peg near the door they had just left. He tossed them clear. Metal clanged. Leather skidded. They saved what could be saved.

Flames took the rafters like rumor takes a town. The center gave with a sound that felt personal. Sparks went high, then drifted toward the cottonwoods and died in the damp grass because Tommy had soaked that strip after the storm and sometimes past work comes back as grace. The volunteers arrived with lights. Neighbors rolled in with tanks and flatbeds. Water hit the fire and turned anger to steam.

Sabotage felt certain. The way it caught. The way it jumped seams that shouldn't have met. It was neat. It was cruel. It was exactly the kind of work Ricardo admired. Annie filed that thought where she could take it out later and look at it without shaking.

Spike shook from poll to tail and stayed on his feet. His lashes were singed at the tips. His breath rasped then smoothed. Annie put her forehead to his and let him smell her. "You're alright," she said. "You're alright." She found the bridle piece in her pocket and squeezed it once like a prayer stone.

Maria counted heads twice and then once more. Every guest accounted for. One skinned knee. One scorched sleeve. No one missing. Blue finally lay down, chest heaving, eyes on the door like a soldier.

The barn finally settled into ruin. The volunteers did their steady work, talking in simple sentences, asking for nothing they didn't need. Jake stood with them, jaw set, shirt stuck to his back, offering his muscles to anything that would use them. Tommy kept the hose where it needed to be and quietly pulled the sound system wire before the fire could find an outlet and try a new trick.

The guests stood along the east fence and watched the team do something hard with grace. The teacher who had asked about quiet corners for reading came up to Annie with tears on her face and said, "I've never felt safer in a disaster." The lineman's wife pressed cash into Maria's hands and said, "For lumber. Or biscuits." A couple from Denver booked the pop-up on the spot with shaking hands and said it was because the stars looked braver now.

Despite all of this, Founders' Night was a huge success. Not because the fire made good theater. Because the night told the truth and the people in it answered. Deposits cleared. Tips landed. Three different guests asked how to help rebuild. One posted a photo of the lantern path and wrote, Honest people. Honest place. Ten out of ten. Would trust with my life.

Annie sent a short update to the banker with the facts and none of the smoke. Guests safe. Twelve completed. Two commitments for next weekend. Incident contained. Community present. She hit send and put the phone away. Tonight was not about emails. Tonight was about breathing.

Jake came to her then, hair damp, eyes tired, alive. "You went in," he said.

"I did," she said. "You came for me."

"Every time," he said, as if that had already been settled.

She let herself lean on his shoulder for the length of a breath and then stood up straight. "We've got people to thank."

"We do," he said.

They walked the fence line together, shaking hands, taking names, promising coffee in the morning for anyone who came back with a hammer. Blue trotted at their heels with a new dignity, like he had been promoted. Spike watched from the safe side of the yard, ears forward, a king without a barn and not less for it.

The last flames hissed out. Steam floated. The string lights still shone, stubborn and kind, as if to say the sky would keep its part. Annie lifted her chin to the stars and felt her ribs unclench. She had chosen. The night had tested the choice and not found it wanting.

She looked at Jake. He looked at her. They didn't say much. They didn't need to. The work had more to say, and it would keep saying it in the morning. For now, they stood in the glow of a hard won yes and let it count.

By morning the sheriff had tire tracks to follow and questions with teeth. The air still smelled like wet char. Steam slipped out of the ruin in thin white threads.

Deputies marked the ground with bright flags. One knelt where the heat had run hottest, palm over scorched earth. The sheriff, a square man with a soft voice, walked the edge of the wreck in a slow square. He checked tracks, hinges, a latch twisted wrong, a padlock with a new scar. He sniffed and frowned at something sweet that shouldn't be there.

"Patterns," he said. "They always leave patterns."

Annie stood, hands tucked in her jacket sleeves, watching morning write itself on soot and frost. This was her yard. This was her mess and her miracle.

Jake stayed close enough to read her pulse without touching. He answered early questions in short, clean sentences. Yes, he'd been at the door when the glow showed. Yes, he'd heard a pop. No heater running. Soaked the cottonwood line last week. No wiring trouble in years.

Neighbors arrived with hoses, plywood, and casseroles. Trucks rolled in like a small army. Folks who had tutted at Annie's city ideas last month climbed out with crowbars and coolers and stood beside her. Someone set ladders against nothing because ladders make people feel ready. Someone else started coffee big enough to baptize doubts in.

Maria spoke in a voice that carried. "Listen up," she said from the porch. "Strong backs with Jake and Tommy on salvage. Sorters with me at the tack table. Lumber by the cottonwoods. Food to the kitchen. Nobody blocks the sheriff."

A murmur moved across the yard. People fell into lines without fuss. Spike stood in a temporary pen, ears forward, watching which way the day would lean.

The sheriff took notes while work started around him. He asked questions, polite and precise. "Anyone come by who didn't belong? New locks? Old grudges?" He pointed where a tire had cut across the ditch like a person in a hurry. "That's not a neighbor," he said. "Neighbors know the turn."

Annie gave names when asked, not many, just the ones who had earned a spot on a list that starts with check. She said Ricardo last and washed the taste away with coffee.

By 10AM, the yard became a barn raising in reverse. Salvage first. Sift next. Volunteers found halters they could save, metal bins that only looked dead, and boards that would work once you cut the black off. Jake's hands were black to the wrists. Tommy's shirt looked like it had been through a war. Annie's braid slipped and she didn't care.

Maria stood at a folding table with a Sharpie and tape, writing labels: BRIDLES, CLEAN. HARDWARE, GOOD. SCRAP, BURN. She called Annie family, simple as that, in front of three women who'd called her that city girl with nice boots. "Family eats first," Maria said, pointing at a pan of something golden. That settled the whispers. The women took plates and set to work.

The sheriff eased up the steps and took off his hat. "Ms. Contadelucci," he said. "We'll have more for you this afternoon. I've got casts to make and calls to place."

"Thank you," she said.

"You got people," he said, surprised by how many. "That helps." He put his hat back on and went to check the ditch again.

By noon the sun had a little heat. Steam faded to memory. Two neighbors framed a temporary wall for the feed room. A lineman fixed the gate latch because he couldn't stand to see it hang wrong. The teacher from last night handed out plates with the focus of a field general. The ranch absorbed all that intention and stood a little taller on it.

The same faces that once doubted Annie now stood shoulder to shoulder beside her. It wasn't a parade anymore. It was a promise with boots on.

When the yard finally quieted, helpers gone to naps and chores, volunteers back to their lives, the sheriff off to match tread to tread, the ranch exhaled. The quiet wasn't empty. It held what people had left behind: sawdust, footprints, and a casserole cooling on the counter, the sensible kind with corn-flakes on top.

Jake and Annie sat on the porch steps, hands close on the same stair. The wood was warm from sun, gritty with ash. Crickets started early. One black beam still breathed a thin ribbon of white.

They didn't talk for a while. There was too much and not enough to say. Their shoulders leaned almost toward each other and then held their own weight. A kind wind pushed through the cottonwoods. Somewhere, Blue dreamed and twitched.

Annie looked at her palms, the lines packed with soot she hadn't washed out. "I thought I'd be wrecked," she said at last. "I'm not. I'm tired and mad and grateful all at once, but I'm not wrecked."

"You're standing," Jake said.

"We are," she said. "We're standing."

Their fingers shifted, almost touching, then stopped. Close was all they could manage. For now. It felt right.

He nodded at the ruin. "We'll build again."

"We will," she said. "We'll call it the Phoenix and then never call it that again."

He laughed, soft. "Deal."

A hawk traced a slow arc above the ridge. Annie let her shoulder tip an inch. Jake didn't move away.

"Tomorrow," he said.

"Tomorrow," she agreed.

They watched the first porch light come on without asking, a timer Maria had set years ago, faithful to its one job. The bulb rolled a small honey circle across their boots. The night took their breath and gave it back, easier now. The crickets kept time. And the ranch, stubborn as ever, settled into the long work of being alive.

CHAPTER TWENTY-TWO

TERMS

At first light, Annie and Jake sat where they always seemed to end up, elbows near, mugs warm, Blue between their boots. The house was quiet in that respectful way a place gets after a hard night. Coffee steamed. The sky edged from darkness to light.

Annie's eyes brightened like someone had flipped a switch behind them. "Act of God," she said, half to the mug, half to him.

"What?" Jake asked. "We praying or planning?"

"Both," she said, already on her feet. "Do you have a force majeure clause in your contract with the Millers?"

"A what?" He frowned. "In English."

"An Act of God clause," she said, moving to the office corner. "Show me the contract."

Jake ruffled through the drawer under the ledger, the one that held everything important and half the things that weren't. He pulled a fat manila folder, flipped past receipts and scratch paper, and found the stamped pages. "Here," he said, handing it over.

She took it and read like she'd been born doing it. Thumb sliding. Eyes catching on numbers, dates, verbs. She didn't skim; she hunted. She stopped, tapped the margin, and grinned. "Yes."

"What yes," he said, trying not to hope ahead of the facts.

"The barn fire," she said. "It's in scope. Force majeure covers 'fire, acts of God, or events beyond reasonable control' that prevent performance. We can ask for a mutual release. No penalties. Clean break."

He ran a hand over his jaw. "And they just say sure?"

"They'll say sure if I give them nowhere good to stand," Annie said, already pulling the laptop closer. "We've got the sheriff's case number. The claim number. Photos. We're not dodging. We're documenting." She looked up. "Okay if I write on your behalf?"

"Please," he said. "Make it sound like those emails that make men sit up straight."

She smiled, soft and quick. "That I can do."

She typed with a calm speed that made Jake's chest ease a notch. The subject line was simple: **Force Majeure - Mutual Release Request**. The body was cleaner still.

Given the fire and the claim in process, I'm invoking force majeure and asking for a mutual release. No penalties either way.

Sheriff case F89632.3. Claim #AC-219. Photos attached.

- Jake Spyker, Spyker Ranch (sent by Annie Contadelucci, on his behalf)

"On your behalf," she said without looking up. "Not in your voice. Yours matters later."

"Fine by me," he said. "Send it."

She clicked. The email left.

They didn't pace. They didn't pretend they didn't care. They stood by the window and drank coffee like it might be a shield. Maria moved in the kitchen behind them, quiet as a cat who knows how to make biscuits without loudness. Tommy bumped the screen door with a shoulder and said he'd check hoses, then read the room and vanished.

Minutes later the reply landed with the neat little chime that never sounded so good.

"Open it," Jake said.

Annie did. She read once, then again for the pleasure of it. "Agreed," she said, breath leaving on the word. "Effective today. No further obligations."

Jake leaned both hands on the table and let his head hang for a second, not like a man broken, like a man who just took off a pack he'd been carrying too long. "Just like that," he said.

"Just like that," she echoed. "Because it was fair. And because we asked right." She forwarded the thread to his email, printed the PDF, and wrote RELEASE on the top in her neat, bossy hand. She slid it into the folder, then into the drawer under the ledger where he kept the things he couldn't lose.

Blue thumped his tail against the floorboards, picking up what words can't carry. Maria slid a plate across the table with two biscuits and honey. "Eat," she said. "Then go win the next fight."

"This was big," Jake said, still looking at the table like maybe it might float if he stared hard enough.

"It was," Annie said. "And it's done." She reached for his mug and topped it off. "Next."

He watched her for a beat he didn't hide. "You're good at reading storms," he said. "On paper and in the sky."

"I had good teachers," she said. "Half of them mean, half of them helpful." She tipped her chin toward the window where the light was growing. "I like the helpful better."

Tommy reappeared with a coil of lights and a grin. "Heard the chime from the porch," he said. "Was that the kind that pays off or the kind that asks for money?"

"Pays off," Annie said.

"Praise be," Tommy said, letting his eyes tip upward.

They ate in the kind of silence that comes from relief, not awkwardness. Outside, the yard stretched and yawned. The burn still held its own weather, a faint sweet-sour in the air, but the morning was busy with normal sounds again: a hinge, a far-off truck, a bird that insisted on starting songs it never finished.

"Alright," Annie said, sliding her plate away. "I'm going to pull together a packet for Mr. Davidson. Founders' Night receipts, deposits, claim number, and a short plan for the next two weekends. I'll ask to keep the review steady."

Jake nodded and stood, the old habit of motion returning. "I'll go check that east gate and the temporary feed room. If the sheriff calls, I'll wave you down."

"Good," Annie said. "We keep each other in the loop, yes?"

"Yes," he said, and meant it.

He reached for her mug, then thought better of it and reached for the biscuit basket instead. She watched the almost-touch and didn't rush it. Close counted.

Feeling like she was on a roll, Annie pulled together everything for Mr. Davidson: Founders' Night receipts; fresh deposits; the claim acknowledgment; photos of safe operations; a simple plan for the next two weekends; and a clean ask to keep the review steady with a 60-day extension to bridge the rebuild. She hit send, then set up escrow for deposits, promises are prettier when they come with a ledger that balances.

The call came quicker than she expected. Davidson's voice was calm and careful, the tone of a man walking policy around a corner. "I'll do my best," he said, "but policy doesn't like fire, or feelings. Committee makes the final decision. I'll communicate next steps to Jake directly via email."

"Understood," Annie said. "Thanks for taking the time."

She hung up and went back to work counting hope. She wrote a short update for guests. She was open, safe. She talked about the bathrooms sparkling and posted two daylight photos that felt like the truth: string lights unshowy, Blue sitting noble beside stacked salvage.

Jake was fidgety. He was outside, then inside. Making up stuff to do. Now, he had worked his way back inside, back at the desk and he was tightening a stubborn hinge when the laptop chimed. He wiped his hands, clicked, and read the response once, then twice. The bank would hold the review at sixty days and accept escrowed deposits toward the principal. However, they were still denying any new funds and demanded a good-faith curtailment soon. Mr. Davidson would deliver the figures personally.

Jake stared at the paragraph that did the real cutting, 'good-faith curtailment'. He knew, however much it ended up being, it was more than he had or could gather on the fly. He clicked print on the email. Then he folded the paper and slid the warm page into the drawer under the ledger. He told no one.

He ran numbers, circled dates, picked out the cows he could sell without breaking the herd's back. Pride did the talking. Survival did the math.

Outside, the yard kept humming. Tommy strung a fresh line of bulbs from tree to eave. Maria labeled bins - HARDWARE; BRIDLES; TOOLS - and set bread to rise. Annie took three photos for Davidson's committee and typed captions: **Deposits cleared. Volunteers scheduled. Operations safe and contained.**

"Anything from the bank?" she asked, breezing past the office door with a coil of twine on her shoulder.

"Not yet," he said, and immediately hated the lie. He wasn't hiding to punish her. He was buying time to turn no into something he could lift.

Annie printed one more copy of the release and tacked it to the cork board by the door with a thumbtack that bit clean. She stood there a second and let her eyes rest on the word NO FURTHER OBLIGATIONS. Not a prayer, not a victory lap. Just a small thank you to the right clause at the right time.

She nodded, trusting the pace of the day. "I'll be over at the bunkhouse prepping it for the Sky Cabin pop-up. Yell if Davidson emails."

"Will do."

He watched her go and pressed his thumb against the drawer

edge until the wood remembered it was harder than skin. Blue laid his head on Jake's boot and sighed, a sound that usually made the world feel simpler. Today it only made it honest.

Outside, Jake walked the line from the porch to the cottonwoods, reading the ground the way other men read books. He paused at the edge of the ruin, not to worship it, not to fear it, just to admit it was there. "We need one less weight on the rope," he said, mostly to Blue, who wagged like he understood metaphors.

Annie closed the bunkhouse door and started setting up the next part of her plan. Investors would bring in real money. She put her business training to work.

Jake poked his head in the bunkhouse, "Annie."

She looked up. "Yes?"

"Thank you," he said. "For seeing the line in the paper I didn't know to look for."

"You're welcome," she said. "You see the lines in the ground I'd trip over. We even out."

He lifted a shoulder, not quite a shrug, more of a yes that didn't want to be loud. "We do."

By early afternoon the wind came up and then reconsidered. The burn's sweet-sour faded under the smell of yeast and coffee. Annie chalked the evening timeline on a small board - prep, greet, ride if safe, eat, stargaze, thank you, goodnight - and added Tommy's favorite line at the bottom: **Bathrooms sparkle.**

She stepped into the office corner to grab new chalk and caught Jake staring a hole through the ledger. "You good?" she asked.

"I'm fine," he said, too quick, then softened it. "I'm fine. Gate's fixed. We'll need firewood at both pits."

"I'll add it to the list," she said, and did.

She tacked one more page to the cork board under the release. **TODAY'S TERMS**

Tell the truth.

Take the help.

Keep the doors open.

Count the cash.

Count the stars.

She read it once, felt foolish, left it anyway. Sometimes people need to read the obvious before they do it.

Time continued across the yard and made everything look a little more possible. The Miller problem was gone, clean as a cut rope. Annie didn't know it yet, but the bank problem sat in a drawer with sharp edges. Work filled the space between.

"Ready?" Annie asked from the doorway.

"Ready," Jake said. He meant it in the only way that mattered: ready to keep going.

They stepped off the porch and back into the day they were building, one clause, one receipt, one fence, one star at a time.

CHAPTER TWENTY-THREE

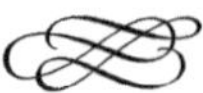

BONE AND GRIT

*A*nnie moved from the bunkhouse to the office, camera in one hand and laptop in the other. She closed the door until the latch kissed, and the busy sounds of the yard softened to a hum. The room smelled like cedar boxes and coffee gone cool. She set the laptop on the scarred table, stacked three ledger books to lift the webcam, and angled the chair so the window threw clean light across her face. Camera on. Slides clean. Hope steady.

"Good morning," said the woman who'd emailed from an investment firm address. Tortoiseshell glasses. A neat bun that didn't move when she smiled. A second square popped in, a man in a fleece vest with a trail map pinned behind him. Boutique money, the kind that likes story but wants the math to sing.

"Thanks for making the time," Annie said. Her voice sounded like she was already standing up straight. She tapped the first slide. "Spyker Ranch. Grit with a little silk. Founders' Night sold out in under eight hours. Deposits cleared for two more weekends. Insurance claim filed. Operations safe and contained." She gave him the details, clean and quick, then waited. Just the way this type of investor wanted to hear it.

She didn't gild anything. She didn't apologize for the burn. She put the truth in order and let it breathe.

Slide two covered margins. She walked them through the basic tier, the add-ons, and the pop-up Sky Cabin nights using the bunkhouse. "No gilt. No fake," she said. "Quilts washed. Star map and kettle. A promise of quiet."

Slide three handled cost control. Volunteers on rebuild. Vendor release in hand. Escrow for deposits. "We're not spending hope," she said. "We're spending cash we've already earned."

Slide four told the story. Three photos. Two mugs steaming on a whiskey barrel with Blue in perfect focus between them like he'd planned it. The ridge under a sky that looked ready to keep secrets. Jake swinging down from Spike with one hand on the horn, candid and honest.

"Your revenue sources," the woman asked. "Besides the weekends."

"Cabin vouchers we presell," Annie said. "Starlight Supper add-ons. Ranch Hand for a Day with strict caps. We've got corporate off-site interest, but we'll table that until the bones are rebuilt."

"Customer acquisition cost," the man asked, already half convinced.

"Near zero right now," she said. "Whisper network, repeat bookings, one local paper story we didn't pay for. We won't buy ads until we can seat them."

"And risk," the woman asked. "Beyond the obvious."

"Bank timing," Annie said, refusing to flinch. "They're holding the review at sixty days and counting escrowed deposits toward covenant. They denied new funds and that is why we are looking at investors. We're bridging with booked revenue, insurance, and you."

They nodded like people do when they've heard the right answer even if they don't love the shape of it.

"Use of proceeds," the man said.

"Temporary structures and safety first," Annie said. "Guest comfort right behind it. A generator we won't regret. A small cushion so one bad weather weekend doesn't eat our souls."

The woman's smile turned warmer. "Send your weekly cash snapshots and we'll send a conditional. Thirty days to show profit. We'll fund in tranches against proof. No personal guarantees. Our lien stays behind the bank. If you hit your numbers, we stay. If you don't, we part decent."

Real money, with a clock.

"Understood," Annie said. She didn't pump a fist. She didn't let relief get loud. "We'll make the target."

"We like grit paired with elegance," the woman said. "You've got both."

The call ended. Annie stayed still long enough to feel her heartbeat land where it belonged. She looked at the empty screen, then at the cork board, then at the little carved bridle piece she'd tucked under a clip. She pressed her thumb to the A and breathed out.

Would it be enough. It had to be. Thirty days felt like a number you can hold in your hand and still respect.

She printed the conditional and filed it behind the bank folder, not in front. Hope first, sure, but not blind. She drafted a short email with attachments, receipts, deposits, and a one pager with their thirty-day plan, then saved it to send after she'd checked it again with a calmer head. She didn't text Jake. Not yet. Hope felt fragile. She wanted it solid before she handed it to him.

Outside, the ranch kept moving like a well-tuned muscle. She could hear Tommy laughing at something heavy, Maria singing, and the low murmur of neighbors who'd stayed to help. Annie opened the door and the sounds swallowed the quiet whole.

"How'd your camera talk go?" Maria asked, eyes on the dough.

"Clean," Annie said. "We've got a path if we walk it straight."

"Then walk it," Maria said. "I'll feed you while you do."

Annie grabbed her notebook and slipped into the yard. She wrote notes as she walked. Weekly snapshots. To-Do's. Plans. Ideas. Finally she added the last and circled it. Tell him when it's real.

Jake crossed the drive with a set of braces on his shoulder and a hammer hanging from two fingers. He didn't look like a man who'd decided anything except the next right nail. For a small, stupid second she almost stopped and told him everything. Thirty days. A way across. She didn't. Not yet. He set the braces down under the cottonwoods and met her eyes.

"You need anything," he asked.

"Just you," she almost said. "Just the gate latch when you get a minute," she said instead.

"On it," he said, and meant it.

Blue found her and shoved a toy into her knee, and she threw it, grateful for instructions she couldn't mess up.

The wind had moved the smoke smell down the road. Somebody started a radio low. Someone else laid out salvaged boards that could live again after a date with a saw. Annie walked the line of volunteers prepping for the barn raising. She thanked them by name, because names matter. She caught Tommy's eye, and he tilted his chin at the mailbox like it was plotting something.

"You want me to sweet talk it," he asked.

"Please do," she said.

He shook the post and declared it appeased. It made her smile even when she didn't think she had smiles left.

Back in the office she opened the draft email to the investors, scanned it, fixed a stray comma, and hit send. Then she opened a new doc and wrote the thirty-day plan in ten clean bullets. No manifestos. No fluff. She titled it **Bone and Grit: 30 Days** and printed two copies, one for the cork board and one for her pocket.

It read like a dare she planned to win:

1. Keep the bank review steady.
2. Hit weekend occupancy targets.
3. Presell vouchers and cap at honest.
4. Weekly cash snapshots every Friday by noon.
5. Safety first, then comfort.
6. No spin.
7. No shortcuts that steal later.
8. Talk plain.
9. Take help.
10. Count the stars.

She pinned it under the 'Act of God' release and stepped back.

The doorframe clicked and Jake leaned in, hat pushed back, a smear of soot on his forearm. "You got a minute," he asked.

"For you," she said. "Always."

He set a small metal box on the table and popped the lid. Inside were screws sorted by size and temperament. "Found these buried in the shop behind a tired tarp," he said. "Thought you'd be proud of me for not tossing chaos back on chaos."

She laughed, soft. "I'm proud."

He watched her face as if he could read what she wasn't saying. She held his gaze and let him see steadiness. Not yet. His eyes dipped to the cork board and paused on **Bone and Grit: 30 Days**.

"Good title," he said.

"Stole it from the day," she said.

He nodded once. "I should get that latch before it forgets who's boss."

"Go be the boss," she said.

He left. She stood very still and listened to the ranch breathe. Hope tapped in her ribs. She let it stay.

Tommy tested the generator, and Maria painted a sign that said **WELCOME** in a hand that made the word look truer, Annie took the bridle piece from the cork board and held it. She tucked it into her pocket and walked the perimeter. Shoes bit gravel. She kept her eyes on the fence line the way Jake would have looked at it. She didn't pray with words. She prayed with the list in her pocket and the work in her hands.

A couple from Denver messaged to say they were bringing raincoats just in case and did the Sky Cabins have kettles. Yes, she wrote. Yes, they do.

She stood on the porch and let the yard tell her the truth. It told her they weren't safe yet. It told her they weren't lost either. It told her bone and grit beat pretty speeches every time.

She thumbed open her phone and typed a text to Jake. Need to tell you something. It's good. She stared at it, then deleted the message. Not because the good wasn't true, because she wanted it truer. She slid the phone back in her pocket and went to help Tommy.

While working she kept thinking, 'Thirty days. She could do thirty days.'

Out by the fence, Jake looked over and caught her in the yellow wash. He tipped his hat. She tipped her chin. 'Is he flirting with me?' She thought.

Blue ran a tired circle, then flopped with a sigh. The ranch breathed with him. And the plan, bone and grit, held. But hard decisions were only minutes away.

Jake knew cattle well, they're herd animals with social rules older than dirt. Take a few out at the wrong time and the rest feel it in their bones. Pairs look for each other. Young ones key off old ones. Boss cows argue, then settle it with a look and a step. If you respect that, a move can go quiet. If you do not, the day chews you up.

Jake knew that the hard decision had to be made. They would

be selling off a bunch from the herd soon. So, to make it easier on those that remained, they were moving them to a pasture with better grazing. The storm had left mud that did not dry right. Hoof prints had filled with water and stayed that way. It was gonna be a long day.

Maria drove the feed truck slow, salt and mineral in the back, radio low. Tommy rode out with Blue tucked close to his boot, the dog ready to work with that flat, serious look he wore when cows were in the picture. Annie swung up on Rusty, the gentle gelding with a kind mouth. Jake took Spike because Spike knew his job.

They eased the gate and let the front-line flow. No yelling. No hurry. A cow sniffed the new air and made up her mind to go. The rest read the signal and followed. The sun had not burned the wet yet, so the dirt held teeth. They kept to the edges where the grass knitted better.

"Keep them nice and round," Jake said. "No sharp corners. Pairs together if you can help it."

"I can help it," Annie said. Her voice sounded like she believed herself. Rusty flicked an ear and took the hint.

For a while it worked. Calves bawled the way calves do when they do not love change. Cows answered and checked noses. They climbed out of a shallow draw that had gone slick after the storm. Jake rode high and watched angles. Tommy cut off the thought of a break before the thought got brave. Blue slid low, slow, and useful.

The footing turned dirty on the north side of a seep. A calf with a bright white face put a hoof where a hoof had no business and popped sideways. He got spooked by his own mistake and shot forward, then hard right. The line shivered. Two more thought about going with him.

Jake did not think. He lit Spike and went hard. His rope snapped tight on the horn and then snapped again, his shoulder doing something it did not want to do. Pain slapped him so clean he felt it in his toes. He cursed once, a word that did not help anything, and he went pale white.

"Hold," he barked, but the bark sounded like it came from someone else.

Annie did not ask. She pushed Rusty into the hole he had just left and made her voice cut through the rising noise. "Tommy, hold your line. Rita, ride up and bump the left. Mrs. Pacheco, let your old girl step, then stop her there and be big."

Blue shot to the gap and laid a neat pressure on the wrong-minded calf. Annie pointed a finger without looking. "Not that way, little man. Come on. Back to your mama."

She kept her seat loose and her hands steady. Rusty took her weight and turned like a good teacher who wants you to get an A. Annie put the line back where it belonged. She did not rush. She did not chase. She took air out of the panic and gave it back to calm. The calf spun once, saw the wall she had made out of quiet horses, and thought better of his great idea. He ducked left, then left again, and found the path he had fallen off. His mother bawled and he bawled and they made a straight beeline for each other like magnets.

"Good," Annie said, low. "Go on."

Neighbors who had come to help stared and then nodded. One of the neighbor boys said it out loud with a kind of surprise that made it sweeter. "She's the real thing."

Jake held Spike and his arm and his temper. The throb felt like it had its own clock. He swallowed the sour and watched Annie set riders like chess pieces that wanted to cooperate. She sent Tommy ahead to open the next gate, not the one closest, the one that offered better ground. She stalled the front with a slow figure eight so the back could catch up, then let the whole line breathe. No one ran. No one froze. They just moved.

"Check your right," she called. "There's a hole where the creek cut. Give it a wide berth. If a cow looks like she wants to argue, let her talk to me."

They cleared the seep and found firmer sod. The herd settled into the kind of walk that eats ground without drama. Annie rode the drag a minute to count calves, then traded with Rita at the swing so the old mare could breathe. She praised Blue when he slid back to heel and gave him water from her glove.

Jake tried to roll his shoulder and got a nasty flash that shut that idea down. He sat still until the ache fell from white to steady. Annie angled over, gave him one look, and did not make it small.

"Out of the saddle," she said.

"I'm fine," he said.

"You are important," she said. "Get off."

He slid down and the ground tilted. Spike breathed warm on his neck like a friend. Annie was already off and had his rope in one hand and the other on his bad side.

"Cold," she said. "Now." She took his hand and put it on the cool shadow under Spike's mane. It was a silly thing that worked. The shock of it gave him a breath that had room in it.

"Let me see," she said.

"I can ride," he said.

"You can ride in five minutes," she said. "You can be stubborn forever. Pick one."

He picked five minutes because he trusted her more than he trusted his pride in that second. She looped a scarf high and snug, not a sling, just a reminder to act like he had only one good wing for a bit. He did not thank her out loud. She did not need that, and he did not have it in him yet.

They moved again with Jake on the ground for a stretch while Tommy held the point and Annie floated the middle. The bad patch gave way to a gentle climb. The new pasture rolled open. Grass pushed up soft and thick. The air lost its mud taste.

They brought the herd through the gate and let the front spread and drop their heads. Cows tested the grass and decided it pleased them. Calves kicked like kids at recess. Annie held them a minute more, then turned her horse and cut a clean line back to the latch. She ran the chain, checked the post, and looked like she owned the day.

"That was clean," Rita said, easing her mare next to Annie. "Textbook, if textbooks bothered to tell the truth."

"Thank you," Annie said. "I had a good book to steal from. Jake, your pages."

"His pages are greasy and live in the glove box," Tommy said, grinning. "But alright."

Laughter loosened what the mud had tightened. Maria pulled the truck along the way and passed canteens and sandwiches through the window.

Jake swung back up because that is what he knew. His shoulder sent a hot telegram and then calmed to a growl. He watched Annie collect Blue with a whistle he had taught her last week. She did not blow it hard. She did not need to. The dog read her and did the thing.

They rode the fence on the far side to be sure there were no insults hiding where the eye cannot see from the gate. Annie spotted a loose wire and fixed it with the little tool she had clipped to her belt, the one she had adopted like a pocketknife becomes a habit. She did not call for Jake. She did not make a show of doing it herself. She just fixed it and moved on.

By late afternoon, the sharp edges had rounded. The herd lay down in twos and threes. Birds said what birds say when the worst is over. The sky started thinking about gold.

On the ride back, the neighbors fell into a lazy line and let their horses talk to each other with flicked ears and swung tails. Someone told the story of a calf that once swam a creek because he thought it was a game. Someone else swore she had seen a coyote climb a tree like a cat. The day let go of its jaw.

They reached the yard and slid off, slow and creaky, the way people do who have earned supper. Maria pointed at the porch with a look that said wash your hands and then eat. Tommy took the bridles. Blue found a puddle and took it as a personal invitation.

Annie led Rusty to the rail and loosened the cinch, then rested her forehead against the gelding's neck. She said thank you in a whisper and patted twice. She turned and caught Jake watching her with a kind of focus that can break a person if they are not ready for it.

"You alright?" she asked.

"I will be," he said.

He meant his shoulder. He meant more. He would not name it yet. Naming makes things real, and the sun was not quite down.

Neighbors drifted off with waves and see you tomorrows. Tommy stacked saddles. Maria clucked her tongue and herded them toward food.

Jake stood on the porch step and looked out towards the new pasture. The herd lay like stones in a creek, right where they should be. The gate held. The day had not eaten them. His shoulder complained and then remembered it had met worse.

He looked back at Annie. She was talking to Blue, who listened like he planned to run for office. She laughed and it lifted the yard a notch. He felt something shift inside him, quiet and not small. It did not have a word yet. It would. For now, it sat where a man keeps the things he does not risk dropping.

He did not say thank you. He did not say stay. He said the only thing that fit without breaking anything important.

"Good work," he said.

"You too," she said.

He watched her through the throb in his arm and felt the shift again, the one he could not name. He let it be, and the evening let him.

That night they sat by a low fire, the sky full of stars. The generator hummed a steady note from the yard, softer now that the work was done. Smoke curled in a thin ribbon. Blue laid with his chin on his paws, ears pricking every time the coals shifted.

The string lights cut a shy path to the gate, not competing with the sky.

Jake's shoulder ached in a way that felt honest. He rolled the thought of the email in his head, the white page, sentences that said no in polite words. He tried to think of a better start than I failed and could not find one that was true.

He finally spoke about the money. About the bank email. About the plan to sell down the herd in pieces that would not break the herd. He told her which cows he had circled and why. He said what he thought the curtailment figure would be and did not look at her. He did not talk about feelings, not yet. He talked about failure and fear, in plain ranch numbers and the silence that follows them.

Annie listened with both hands wrapped around a tin cup. Steam left in small ghosts. She did not interrupt. She did not feed him pretty. She let the facts sit in the air between them and settle. She watched the fire find a new pocket and flare, then calm. She thought about her thirty-day clock and her promise to tell him when the good had bones.

When he finished, the night felt like it had leaned closer to hear.

"You're worth fighting for," she said, very quietly. "So is this place."

The words did not arrive like trumpets. They arrived like a hand on a close friend's shoulder, steady and warm. He looked at her then, and whatever he had been bracing for did not come. He saw a woman who had ridden a messy day clean and still had room for one more truth.

She leaned in and kissed him. He did not pull away. He tasted smoke and honey and a promise that did not need a speech. His bad shoulder forgot itself for a second. Her hand found his jaw and rested there like it had found home.

The fire cracked. A spark lifted and went dark before it could worry anyone. The generator gave a cough and settled again.

Somewhere a cow called to a calf and the calf answered. Stars held their ground. The night did too. Blue shifted closer, sighing.

It was not the end of their trouble. It was the start of something that could carry trouble better. They sat a long time without talking, feet toward heat, shoulders close, choosing the same fight in the same breath.

CHAPTER TWENTY-FOUR

THE EDGE OF GOODBYE

The notice came the way bad news likes to arrive, right on the front steps. Gravel crackled, then went quiet. The banker's sedan eased to a stop like it had been trained for this one chore. Davidson climbed out with a folder tucked tight under his arm and the kind of careful face a man wears when the script is short, and nobody will like it.

Jake met him at the top step. He didn't bother with his hat. He didn't bother with small talk. Davidson held the papers with two careful fingers, as if the ink might smear onto him if he got careless.

"Mr. Spyker," Davidson said. "I'm sorry."

The apology sounded like policy. It sounded like a line a person learns on the first week of the job. His tone was kind, but the words had already been decided somewhere far from porches and dirt.

Annie stood in the doorway with her palm on the jamb. She felt the house breathe around her. She watched Jake take the envelope without flinching. The paper looked heavier than paper has any right to look.

Davidson cleared his throat. "We delivered by email as well, but the committee asked me to hand these in person. Questions can go through me, of course."

Jake nodded once. "Alright."

He didn't ask what was inside. He already knew. The top sheet flashed black type in the sun. Foreclosure accelerated. Huge payments due now. A date circled by the universe and not by them.

Blue stood up from the shade and planted himself between the men. His tail moved once and then stopped. Tommy paused at the gate with a coil of wire on his shoulder and did not call out hello. Even the wind seemed to hold its breath. A fly bumped the screen and thought better of it.

"I'll give you space," Davidson said. He looked past Jake at the yard, the salvage piles, the clean path, the string lights that sagged a little in daylight. Something in his face softened, then reset. "I'll be on the road if you need me."

"Thank you for bringing it yourself," Annie said, because somebody had to say a human thing.

He tipped his head to her. "You've done good work here," he said, and for once it didn't sound like policy. Then he turned, got in the car, and drove away slowly, as if speed might break something worse.

The engine's sound drained into the field. The dust settled. Jake stood with the packet in his hand and stared at the porch boards until the grain went double. He took one breath, then another, the kind a man takes when he knows the next part is on him and nobody else.

Annie didn't move. She felt the hit land in his shoulders like a body blow. She wanted to step forward. She wanted to take the papers and throw them at the sun and watch them burn. She kept her feet. You don't grab a man on a ledge, not until he asks.

Maria's skirt lifted an inch, then fell. The kitchen clock clicked once and remembered its job. Somewhere out by the cottonwoods a bird tried the opening line of a song and quit.

Jake looked down at the first page. He didn't read. He didn't need to. Every line lived inside the envelope like a weight. The numbers were going to have commas in the wrong places. The terms were going to be set like concrete. The words were going to pretend this was math, not a life.

He swallowed. His throat worked around a taste that had nothing to do with coffee. He slid a thumb under the flap as if the paper might fight him and then stopped. Not yet. Not on the threshold.

Annie's mouth was dry. She could see the day he'd have to pick which cows would go and which would stay, the way he'd stand at the rail and pretend it didn't take a piece out of him. She hated that this paper could decide any part of the ranch that had nothing to do with ink.

"Jake," she said, almost a whisper.

He didn't look back. He nodded once, simple and small. He stepped off the top stair and walked to the porch rail like a man taking a thin bridge over a deep drop. He set the packet there and laid a palm flat on the wood, steadying the world before he opened anything.

The yard stayed quiet. Even the wind kept its place. Humiliation burned like a fresh sunburn.

He opened the envelope and stared at the numbers until they blurred. So many zeros, he thought. He flattened the top sheet on the porch rail and counted the zeros again, then again, and only when the type refused to stay put did he realize his eyes had filled. He dragged a sleeve across his face and set his palm flat to stop the paper from shaking.

The world seemed to hold still like it respected grief. A grasshopper clicked and changed its mind. Blue eased closer, pressed his shoulder to Jake's boot, then parked, nose forward, waiting.

Annie walked up quiet enough that the boards did not complain. She saw the numbers over his shoulder before she saw his face. The columns stacked like ladders leading nowhere. Interest, penalties, a date that pretended it was only ink. Heat rose to her mouth. She held it.

"Jake," she said.

He did not turn. He kept his eyes on the page as if looking away might let the debt grow teeth. He set one finger on a line, read it again, and made a sound that was not a word.

She reached for him. He pulled back. Not far. Just enough to say there was a ledge here and he preferred to stand on it alone. His jaw set. The muscles in his forearm jumped.

"It's too much," he said. The words came out low and hard. "Save yourself. Don't throw your future away for a sinking ship."

The sentence landed between them like a tool dropped from above. The porch seemed to tilt. Annie steadied on the rail and took a breath that did not reach bottom. She looked at the paper, then at the man who would carry it before he asked anyone else to try.

"I'm not a passenger," she said, soft.

He shook his head, a single inch, the kind of denial that came from the boy who once watched a bank take a gate and then a field. Pride spoke first. Old lessons piled in after it. Survival lined them all up and barked orders.

"You don't owe this place your life," he said. "Not your name. Not your good years. Take your boots and your camera and go while you still can. Run, don't walk back to Italy. To your family. To your father. To your life."

Blue lifted his head like he objected to the plan. Maria's shadow moved behind the screen and stilled. Tommy's truck rattled past the lane and faded. The ranch listened.

Annie folded her fingers into her palm until the urge to shake him passed. She wanted to say she had a way. She wanted to push back with numbers that might stand up in a wind this mean. The words lined up and then stopped, not from doubt, from care. He was bleeding and a pitch is not a bandage.

"I hear you," she said.

He let the paper curl and then forced it flat again. His eyes were clear now. The blur burned off, leaving anger he did not want and shame that did not belong to him.

"I won't drag you down," he said. "I won't let you write checks with your heart that your life has to cash."

The wind found the cottonwoods and told them to speak. Leaves answered, soft and dry. Annie set her hand on the rail beside his, not touching, close enough to count as a promise she had not spoken.

"It's not a sinking ship," she said, barely above the porch hum. "It's our ship." He didn't answer. The paper fluttered once, lay still. Somewhere a calf called and the ranch breathed again.

She told Jake she thought she had a plan. The words came out even, careful as a rider's hands on a green horse. The porch boards gave a small creak under her boot and then went still again. Smoke from last night's fire pit drifted, thin as thread. The envelope sat on the rail like a warning no one could misread.

Jake shook his head. "No way you have a plan for that many zeros." His voice stayed low, the kind of low that keeps a man from breaking the things he can't afford to replace. Pride did the talking. Fear did the rest. Blue shifted closer to his boot and looked up like he wanted permission to fix what a dog cannot fix.

Annie stepped back, not retreating, making room the way you do for a skittish colt. Her eyes were bright, not with tears, with heat.

"I've been working," she said. "Numbers, bookings, calls. I think we can make a bridge."

"That paper says we need a plane," he said. He let the letter curl and made it flat again with his palm. "You can't build a plane out of string lights and good intentions."

She took a breath and let it out slow. "I'm not talking about pretty. I'm talking about real. Founders' Night proved it. The next two weekends are sold. The escrow is clean. I have people ready to help if we can show profit inside thirty days."

He looked at her then, really looked, and the old lessons flared. Banks do not care about charm. Zeros do not blink. Men who promise help often have a bill in their pocket you do not see coming. He had learned all of that the ugly way and he could not unknow it in a morning.

"Every time I think I can breathe, something bigger steps on our neck," he said. "I won't ask you to stand under that boot."

"You didn't ask," she said. "I walked here myself."

He rubbed his shoulder, and the pain gave him something to hold. "I'll sell down. I'll take the hit and keep the herd standing. I'll be the man who can live with that choice. You don't owe me your future to make it easier."

The words were clean and hard. They were also wrong. She felt it like a stone under her heel that she could not ignore. She thought of the bridle piece in her pocket and the A worn smooth by her thumb. She thought of the night sky and the taste of smoke when she had said stay without saying it.

"Look at me," she said.

He did.

"Do you trust me?" she asked.

He did not answer right away. Trust is not a light switch. It is a gate, and it remembers every hand that ever slammed it. He looked past her shoulder at the yard they had been holding together with wire, work, and stubborn. He looked at the string lights, a little tired in daylight, still trying. He looked at Blue. He looked at Annie, who did not blink.

He let out a deep breath. For a heartbeat the porch felt like a dock and the paper like a tide trying to pull him off his feet. He set his jaw, not in defiance, in decision. All he could manage was an imperceptible nod.

Annie did not rush the victory. She did not turn it into a speech. She stepped in just enough that their shoulders shared the same patch of sun. The hurt in the air did not vanish. It shifted. It made room.

"Alright," he said, barely louder than the wind. "Tell me the shape. Not all of it. Just the shape."

"Thirty days," she said. "We hit the weekends hard and clean. We keep costs quiet. The bank has the snapshots every Friday before noon. I have conditional capital that funds against proof. No personal guarantees. Their lien sits behind the bank. We buy time that the paper will not give us on its own."

He frowned, searching her eyes for any sign of a weak spot. "Conditional," he said. "Meaning it walks if we stumble."

"Meaning it walks if we lie," she said. "We won't."

"You keep doing all that you do. Keep this ranch moving. Keep it on its feet. You stay healthy and we prove this can be done. The bank has no other decision but to let us keep doing what we do. Remember, they don't want to lose money. And if they foreclose, they lose."

The corner of his mouth moved. It was not a smile, not yet. It was recognition. He understood hard bargains. He understood clean ones better.

"Alright," he said again. He set the envelope flat on the rail and smoothed the top page as if that could tame it. "We try it your way."

"Our way," she said.

He nodded. "Our way."

The yard remembered how to breathe. Maria's skirt twitched and this time she came to the door with two cups and a face that did not ask questions. Tommy's truck clattered back into the lane, and he leaned out the window with a look that said he could feel from the road that something had moved.

"Coffee," Maria said, passing a cup to each of them. "Drink, then work."

They did. The coffee was hot and bitter and perfect. Jake set the cup on the rail next to the letter. Annie folded the printout of the booking list into his hand and kept her touch there a second longer than necessary. Blue wagged once and then trotted off, satisfied that the people had decided to act like a pack again.

Annie pulled her notebook from her back pocket and flipped to a clean page. "First tasks," she said. "You gotta do something with that bull before he hurts someone. I'll lock tonight's timeline and call the adjuster for a site check. Then I send the snapshots to Davidson with the updates."

"Add to your list the gate at the cottonwoods," he said. "It sticks."

"On the list," she said.

They stood shoulder to shoulder while she wrote. The wind lifted the top sheet of the notice and then let it fall. The numbers were still what they were. So were the people facing them. He watched her hand move, steady. She watched his profile, steady. The space between them was not miles anymore. It was a shared step.

"Do you trust me?" she had asked.

He had nodded once. Now he found the rest of the answer. "Yes," he said, quiet and sure. "I do."

CHAPTER TWENTY-FIVE

SIRENS AND VOWS

*J*ake went to the corral alone. A panel rattled with a sour note that raised the hair along his neck. What is wrong with that bull, he thought. The big red stood off the shade, head high, eyes white at the edges. Flies worried his flanks. Something had spooked him and left the fear with nowhere to go.

Jake stepped in slow, hands out, voice low. "Easy." He read the air the way he always did. He heard the small teeth of wire, the heavy breath, the scrape of a hoof thinking about a wrong move. He reached the loose panel and set his palm to the pipe. It shivered. In the far pen a gate chain tapped a post, light and maddening.

The bull surged. No warning, just a hard choice made by an animal that did not like the shape of the world. Jake moved to stop it like he always had, fast and stubborn, body against muscle and panic. He tried to turn the head with the panel, tried to be bigger than he was, tried to make a narrow place look like the right place. Hooves struck. The ground came up and took him.

The world narrowed to dust and noise. Iron, dirt, a flash of sky. He felt the hit all through the old breaks that had learned to predict weather. Something inside his shoulder screamed and then went dull. He tried to pull his knees under him and the corral spun. He tasted blood and metal and a bad memory of other days like this. Not good, he knew. Not this time. And then the world went dark.

Blue barked so loud it changed the day. He threw himself at the rail and slid through the gap a dog has no business using. He planted between the bull and the man and made himself ten feet tall with nothing but sound and faith. The bull checked, surprised by a small creature with a lion's voice. He swung, stomped, shook his head, then lost interest and crashed down the fence line looking for a place with fewer problems.

Annie saw the motion from the drive. Dust rose in a mean twist. A panel jumped. A hat went down. She ran. "Help," she shouted, voice tearing the quiet. "Yard, now." Her boots slipped and caught. She slid on the dirt, grabbed a post, and found him.

"Jake." She dropped to her knees and put both hands on his face to make the world hold still. His eyes were open and glassy. His breath came in a short pull and a longer one that made her want to cry. She didn't. She pressed the heel of her hand to the cut at his temple until the blood slowed. "Stay with me."

Neighbors vaulted the fence like they were late to Sunday. Tommy hit the gate and made it bang, then took the hotshot and planted himself between the bull and anything that bled. One of the neighbors grabbed a rope and made a clean loop without asking permission. More neighbors came over the rail with boards and calm and years of good sense. Maria ran with a towel and a phone and her voice already talking to the dispatcher.

"Adult male. Hit by a bull. Breathing. Bleeding at the head. Shoulder likely broken. No, he is not walking. Yes, unconscious." She listened, nodded, then repeated, "We've got him."

Annie checked what she could with the small training life gives you when you live far from town. Airway clear. Breath tight but coming. Spine still. She wanted to cradle him. She didn't. She held his hand instead, the one without blood on it.

"Look at me," she said. "Right here."

His eyes seemed to find her through the fog. But really didn't. She held it. "You're alright," she lied, soft. "You're mine to keep."

Tommy shouted something and the bull gave up on the people and threw his anger at a water trough that deserved nothing. It clanged, rolled, and lay bruised. Blue kept up his thunder until the animal turned into another pen and someone slammed a gate hard enough to make the hinges complain.

Sirens pulled the road into the yard. Not loud at first, just a thin thread that thickened. Annie felt her body shake only when she knew the sound belonged to them. Neighbors moved like a practiced crew. The gate swung and the volunteers were there, blue gloves, clipped voices, a backboard that looked too clean for this place.

"Name," one asked.

"Jake Spyker," Annie said.

"Age."

"Thirty-three."

"Events."

"Bull in a tight corral. Hoof strike. Fall. Head cut. Neck. Shoulder bad."

They nodded and made the world a set of small tasks. Collar on. Lines checked. Vitals. Count. Lift on three. Annie kept his hand until they had to take him. He laid on the board seemly lifeless. Annie bent close.

"I'm here," she said. "I'm not leaving."

He never moved. At this point all she wanted was for him to say her name. But his mouth failed to say it. The medic glanced at her and gave a short nod that meant ride with us if you can keep your head. She could. She would.

As they carried him, the corral looked like a place after a storm. Boards crooked. Dust hanging. A hat under a rail. Annie wanted to fix it all with her hands. She wanted to pick the whole day up and set it back on the shelf. She climbed into the rig and took his hand again.

"Sirens," Tommy said from the doorway, voice rough. "Bring him back here."

"We will," Annie said. The doors closed and the world turned into white walls and beeping and the fast breath of a machine that meant help. She leaned close to Jake's ear and said it again, in case the noise had swallowed her first try.

"I'm not leaving. Not now. Not ever."

Sirens took the night. The hospital lights were too white, the air too clean. Doors opened like they belonged to another world and swallowed them. Annie held Jake's hand and talked to him as if words could call him back. She told him where he was. She told him his name. She told him Blue would be waiting at the gate. She kept talking because silence felt wrong.

It was bad. Jake was seriously hurt. For a moment, it was touch and go. A nurse with calm eyes said the words nobody wants, and then said the next set that gives you something to hold. He's breathing. We're watching the numbers. Stay here.

Annie sat in a hard chair near the trauma bay and counted breaths until counting felt like superstition. Maria arrived with a sweatshirt and a paper cup that burned her hands in a good way. Tommy showed up with dirt on his knees and a look that said he'd fight a bull with a spoon if it would help. They didn't ask questions. They sat. They made a small circle that felt like home in a place that didn't.

Bad news travels fast. Annie's phone buzzed on the plastic seat, a nervous insect that wouldn't quit. She looked because work is how she breathes when fear gets loud. Six couples canceled cabins for the weekend. The messages stacked with the same few words. So sorry. The fire. The accident. Refund please. She wrote back with a steady hand and no resentment. Of course. We understand. We'll welcome you when the time is right. She processed each one and felt the numbers slip a little, then a little more.

An email landed from the investor with the trail map on his wall. Short and polite. Pulling out. Stating "danger" as a bad investment. We wish you the best. She stared at the screen until the words blurred and then cleared. She closed her eyes and saw the spreadsheet she had built at the kitchen table, all those thin lines that depended on weekends staying whole. With Jake hurt, every plan shifted. The ranch did not have a spare man like him. It did not have a spare heart either.

Flashes of the papers from the bank clicked in her mind. The denial. The curtailment. The date that did not care if a man bled. She pressed her thumb to the edge of the phone until the pressure steadied her. There was one path left now. It tasted like pride swallowed whole. It tasted like the old life she had walked away from, still standing behind her with its hand out.

She looked through the glass where the curtain moved. A medic turned and nodded once, not a promise, a simple marker that time was passing and they were still fighting. Annie rose. Maria touched her elbow. "You need air," Maria said. "Go breathe and come back."

Annie found the family corridor that smelled like bleach and tired hope. There was a pay phone on the wall that nobody used anymore and a vending machine that believed in sugar. She leaned against the cool tile and opened a new message. The cursor blinked in a small box that felt like a courthouse door.

She hated that she knew exactly how to write to him. She hated that he would read it with a smile and think the lesson had finally taken. She loved a man in a room she couldn't enter, and love can decide the words for you.

She did not type the body. She wrote the only line that mattered and let it carry everything she couldn't stand to put on paper yet.

Subject: I need help. I'll give you what you want.

She stared at the sentence. It felt like a trade she would never forgive herself for making, a bridge no one should have to cross. She pictured Jake at the porch rail, counting zeros until his eyes burned. She pictured the herd lying quiet in the new pasture, peace they had earned together. She pressed send.

The message left with a little whoosh that sounded like defeat and relief in the same breath. She felt very tall and very small. She put the phone in her pocket and went back to the chairs because there wasn't anywhere else to be. Tommy had found a blanket and folded it in a neat square like that could help. Maria handed over a fresh cup. Annie wrapped both hands around it and let the heat give her something to do.

A doctor came through the doors with a face that had learned the right pace. Not slow enough to scare you. Not fast enough to lie. He spoke to Annie and used words like stable and watching and scans. He said they'd know more soon. He said rest if you can. She nodded like a person who could take instruction and then didn't rest at all.

She went back to Jake's side when they allowed it. Machines breathed their small, important breaths. She took his hand and spoke into the noise. "I'm here," she said. "I'm not leaving." She told him the exact hour, the way he liked things measured. She told him Blue was probably trying to fire the night nurse. She told him there would be coffee when he wanted it. She told him he could be mad later.

The vows came out quiet. They didn't need volume. They needed truth. "Not now," she said. "Not ever." She said it for him. She said it for this stubborn place that had crawled under her skin and made a home. She said it for herself, the girl who had walked out of marble floors and into mud and found that mud could hold you up just fine.

Sirens faded from her ears. The white light was still too bright, but it felt less like judgment and more like work. Annie kept his hand in hers, and when fear tried to climb back into the room, she would force a smile and remember how she felt about him. She had sent the email. She had chosen the fight. Now she waited and kept her word.

Morning found them in the same hard chairs with the same paper cups. The window over the parking lot held a slice of gray sky and a gull that looked lost this far from river or field. Machines kept their quiet rhythm. Jake slept with the stubborn kind of sleep that does not ask your permission.

The sheriff came with a folder and a tired nod. He took off his hat because Maria stood up when he walked in. Respect knows how to teach a room its manners. He held the folder against his chest for a second, then opened it like a door that sticks.

"We've got movement," he said. "Tire casts from your drive match a set off a rental out of town. The rental ties to Ricardo's office. We pulled video from the feed store and found a purchase that shouldn't have happened, cash and a name that got sloppy on the form. We've got a witness who saw a man with city shoes near your barn the afternoon before. I'm taking this to the county attorney. An arrest is next."

The words were the right ones. The room did not cheer. Annie felt relief arrive like rain on dust. The ground darkened, then it wanted more. She looked at Jake, at the pale line of his mouth, at the tape on his arm. The truth, at last, but it felt small beside the beeping monitor.

"Thank you," she said.

The sheriff nodded. "You'll likely need to give one more statement when he's stable enough to talk. I can push it if you want."

"We'll be ready," Tommy said. He was still in yesterday's jeans. He had a smear of someone else's blood on his cuff, and he did not seem to notice.

Maria crossed her arms and tilted her head. "About time," she said. "Tell your county man to wear his good tie. I'd like the arrest to look tidy."

"I will," the sheriff said. His smile was short, a man borrowing the light for a second before he carried the folder back into his day. He put his hat on and left them with the soft click of a door that knew how to behave.

Silence came back and pulled up a chair. The machine ticked. Air moved. People in scrubs passed by with clipboards and faces that had learned not to break. Annie sat, then stood, then sat again. She checked her phone and ignored the answer she wanted and the answer she feared. She deleted three new cancellations and filed them where they belonged, outside the room.

She went to Jake's side and took his hand. His skin felt warm and clean and strange without dust on it. She traced one knuckle with her. He did not wake. He breathed, steady now, and that steadiness was the only music she cared about.

She leaned close to his ear. The sheet rustled. The monitor kept time. "I am not leaving," she whispered. "Not now. Not ever."

Her breath moved the small hairs at his temple. If he heard, he did not show it. The words had their own work to do. She said them again, a little louder, then softer, until they settled where vows live when nobody else is watching.

Maria put a sweatshirt over Annie's shoulders and smoothed it the way mothers do. "Eat a bite," she said. "Not for you. For him."

Annie nodded and lifted the cup. It tasted like cardboard and courage. She swallowed and went on holding Jake's hand. Tommy pulled the chair closer. The hospital hummed its neutral song. The day advanced by inches.

Out in the lot a gull found something worth the trip. In the room a man kept breathing. A woman kept her promise. The truth had a name and a folder. The future had a fight and a face. Annie set her cheek against the back of Jake's hand and closed her eyes, not to sleep, to keep the words in place.

"I am not leaving," she said again. "Not now. Not ever."

CHAPTER TWENTY-SIX

I'M STAYING

Annie signed her name in careful strokes, the notary's stamp clicking like a small hammer. The conference room had a view of a parking lot and a cottonwood that knew how to make its own weather. Papers slid across the desk, one after another, a clean break written in ink. The notary checked her license, checked the dates, and pressed that stamp again. Click. Proof that a door had closed.

Days earlier the email to her father had done its damage. She had asked for help and named a price. Now the price stood in a neat stack. No claim to the trust. No voting rights. No strings. The deal was struck. She was signing away a safety net she had never loved, and it felt like both a loss and a freedom.

"Initial here, and here," the notary said.

Annie wrote A.C. in the boxes, then her full name where the space asked for it. Antoinette Contadelucci. The letters named a woman she recognized, one she had decided not to live as anymore. She wasn't running from that girl. She was setting her free, pointed in a different direction.

Maria stood beside her, hand light on her shoulder. No speeches. Just a steady weight that said keep going. Maria's presence smelled like soap and cinnamon, the scent of every kitchen that had forgiven a bad day and fed you anyway.

A small firm lawyer cleared his throat and summarized one last time. "Release of claims to the Contadelucci Trust. Assignment of voting rights. Waiver of future distributions. In consideration, the trustee wires funds to the bank to cure present default and withdraw the foreclosure notice. There are no additional conditions."

"No leash," Annie said. She wanted it spoken.

"No leash," he said, and slid the pen back to her.

She signed the last page. The notary stamped. Click. The sound landed hard.

Maria leaned in and kissed her hair. "Now you're truly one of us."

The words settled warm and steady in Annie's chest. She had been wearing boots for weeks. This was different. This was the oath that did not need a church.

The lawyer gathered the papers and handed her a single copy. "You'll receive a PDF by email. The wire is in motion. The bank should post within the hour."

"Thank you," Annie said. She meant it, even if the thanks tasted like a long journey in a short word.

They stepped into the thin hallway with the beige carpet that every small office seems to love. Outside, the cottonwood tossed its leaves and made the light flicker. Annie's phone buzzed once, then twice. She glanced at the screen. One email from the trustee's office. Wire confirmation attached. One email from Mr. Davidson.

She opened Davidson's first. Funds received. Acceleration withdrawn. Review remains at sixty days. Weekly snapshots continue. His writing always wore a suit, even in an email. Annie let out a breath she didn't know she had been rationing.

The second email was shorter. The trustee confirmed finality and wished her well. She didn't read it twice. She did not need to.

She put the phone away and felt lighter and a little strange, the way a person feels when a cast comes off and the limb is still learning what to do with air.

"Did it land?" Maria asked, already knowing.

"It landed," Annie said. "Attention Mr. Davidson."

Maria smiled at that. "Good. I like a man who reads his mail."

They crossed the parking lot. Gravel popped under their boots. Sun found the backs of Annie's hands and warmed the places the office lights had missed. A breeze pushed through the cottonwood and shook little pieces of shade loose. The world was still the same world, which felt like a blessing. A pickup rolled by slow and a neighbor lifted two fingers in a wave that said I see you and I approve.

At the truck, Annie paused and reached into the pocket of her jacket. Her fingers found the carved bridle piece, the single letter smooth from the worry and the wanting. A. She pressed it to her palm and closed her hand. She did not need luck, not exactly. She needed a reminder that choices have weight, and she could carry this one.

"Hungry," Maria asked.

"Always," Annie said.

"We'll eat," Maria said. "Then we'll work."

They drove back on the county road. Fences went by in neat lines. A hawk wrote its name on the sky and did not ask for permission. Annie watched the land she had chosen, the land that had chosen her right back. The road bent and the ridge came into view, the dark edge of it as familiar as a palm.

She rolled her shoulders and felt something loosen. The trust was no longer hers, and for the first time the word trust meant people, not paper. Maria with a hand on her shoulder. Tommy with a joke at the exact right moment. Mr. Davidson with a sentence that said keep going and meant it. A yard full of neighbors who could swing a hammer and hold a vow.

They pulled into the drive. The gate creaked and then

behaved. Annie could see the string lights coiled on the porch rail like quiet snakes waiting for dusk. She could see the chalkboard inside the door with TODAY'S TERMS still pinned above it. Tell the truth. Take the help. Keep the doors open. Count the cash. Count the stars.

"Ready," Maria asked.

"I'm staying," Annie said. The words came out simple and right. They were a flag without fabric, a stake without a hammer. They did not need proof. They were the proof.

Her phone buzzed again. A short line from Davidson. Confirmed, he'd written. Thank you for the transparency. See you soon.

She typed back. You will. And she would.

Over the next few weeks, Jake's condition kept inching the right way. Color returned. Jokes returned, small and crooked, the kind that ride on a breath and prove a person is still them. The doctor's rules were strict, no lifting, no climbing, no being a hero, and Jake kept to them. When the last set of stitches came out and the bruises turned the harmless yellow of old lemons, everyone agreed. Barn raising day could begin.

Annie took point. She was at the gate before sunrise with a clipboard and a pocket full of pencils. Right on schedule, trucks started rolling into the yard. Coffee arrived in paper cups and a cooler that sloshed when someone laughed. Blue trotted his welcome circuit with a seriousness that made children grin. Maria pinned a sign on the porch that read CHECK IN, and another under it that said EAT FIRST.

Ladders went up. Fresh boards thudded into place and made the ground answer. Levels appeared. Chalk lines snapped. Kids painted fence posts in pairs while Tommy told jokes so bad you wanted to hand him a broom just to keep his mouth busy. Maria ran food like a general, brisk and kind, directing plates to hands and hands to work.

Annie moved shoulder to shoulder with her neighbors. She

measured twice. She hauled without hurry. She set braces square, then checked again. If someone offered better, she took the better. When a choice needed a voice, she gave it. She did not stop moving. She didn't try to be the loudest person in the yard. She aimed for the truest.

The hospital had released Jake the day before, conditional on rest. He had argued, softly, then signed, because he hadn't forgotten what pain can do when pride runs the show. Today he sat in the shade of the cottonwoods with a chair Maria insisted on and a cooler Tommy insisted on, and he watched.

He saw how people looked to her, not because she asked for it, because she kept the rhythm. She split the job into parts that fit in a person's hands. She caught small mistakes before they turned mean. She sent the careful up the ladders and the brave to the far side where the footing still lied sometimes. She wrote names on sawhorses. She wrote times on a whiteboard, so nobody got left on a roof when lunch appeared.

The sheriff stopped by in his truck, hat in hand, and left with a plate and a promise to swing back with cones for the road. The volunteer fire chief drifted through and checked the extinguisher that Tommy had placed smart and plain at the edge of the work. Two teens from church showed up late with a speaker and asked if music was allowed. Annie smiled and said yes, if it behaved. The first song tried to show off. The second found the beat.

By midmorning, the skeleton stood. Posts true, ridge line clean, the shape of a barn where ruin had been. Someone cheered and then everyone did, loud enough to shake a few leaves loose. Annie laughed and clapped, then raised her hand and the yard settled like a good horse. "Water break," she called. "Then we sheet the windward side."

Jake felt his chest loosen, one careful breath at a time. Stunned didn't cover it. Pride wasn't the word either. Pride can be sharp. This was round and deep. It was the feeling a man gets when he watches a thing he loves refuse to die.

Maria walked across the grass and handed him a sandwich like it was medicine. "Eat," she said. "Then sit and keep eating. Doctor's orders as interpreted by me."

He smiled and obeyed. Blue parked at his boot and sigh-snored. Jake's hand fell into the dog's ruff by habit and stayed there.

An older neighbor came and sat on the cooler. "She's got the knack," he said, tipping his head toward Annie. "Talks like a fore-man, listens like a neighbor."

Jake looked down at his cup to hide the look in his eyes. "She does."

"You did alright lettin' her," Walt said.

Jake gave half a nod. Letting hadn't been the right word and it had been. He sipped and let the old man have his opinion in peace.

Back at the frame, Annie counted heads, then handed out tasks. "Fast hands with me on rafters. Careful hands at the cut station. If you've got knees that complain, you're the stair crew. If your knees are liars, you're still the stair crew." Laughter kept the splinters from making anyone mean. She set Tommy at the generator and the east wall because he worked happy where wires had opinions. She kept the kids near the paint and the water. She put Maria in charge of breaks, which meant no one dared skip one.

The day warmed, then got honest about it. Shirts stuck. The air filled with the sweet, bright smell of new pine. You could taste sawdust when you breathed. Annie's hat brim was white with salt at the edge, and she didn't notice. She climbed halfway up a ladder to mark a notch, came down, checked a measurement, climbed again. A neighbor asked if she wanted a break. She said later and meant it.

At noon, they blessed the build by sitting down. Maria's long tables felt as if a parade had paused there for lunch. Chili and cornbread. Sliced peaches that tasted like sunshine from three summers ago. Someone passed a jar of pickles that made a man close his eyes. Annie took the last bench only when every plate was full. She ate fast and smiled slow, checked her list, then tucked the pencil behind her ear and stood.

"Back at it," she called. Her voice wasn't loud. It didn't need to be. She had the rhythm, and the yard moved to it.

Afternoon brought the kind of wind that tests decisions. The crew braced and held and learned each other's names if they hadn't yet. Tommy's bad joke quota ran dry, which meant he'd worked. The teens found the song that kept hammers steady. Annie swapped out crews before arms turned sloppy. She kept a tally in her head and on the board. Wood up. Screws seated. Cuts clean. She wrote THANK YOU in big letters at the bottom because gratitude makes people stronger.

Under the cottonwoods, Jake watched the barn take itself seriously. He watched the way men twice Annie's age nodded when she spoke, the way girls half her age watched her hands as if those hands were the map. He watched a mistake get fixed in the same breath as it was made because nobody wanted to waste her time. He watched her look at a diagonal and see the whole day.

The sun slid toward the ridge and turned the new lumber gold. The shadow of a barn appeared on the ground where the barn would cast it tomorrow. Annie called the last set, then the last cut, then the last sweep. People clapped for themselves and for each other. Someone whooped and wasn't embarrassed by it.

"You did it," Maria said in his ear, so close he didn't have to turn.

"She did it," he said.

Maria's hand touched his shoulder, light and proud. "You both did."

He didn't argue. He didn't have to. The shape stood Annie lifted a hand and the whole crew waved back. Jake felt another careful breath arrive and stay. The barn rose. So did he.

By the time the last sheet of plywood was stacked, and the sweepers had chased the sawdust into neat piles, the light had gone honey colored. Neighbors stood in little knots, admiring the bones of the new barn, trading last jokes, promising tomorrow. Trucks eased down the lane with two-finger waves out the window. Kids climbed into back seats with paint on their wrists that would take a week to leave. Maria handed out foil packets "for later" and hugged even the men who pretend they don't like hugs. Tommy flicked off the generator and the yard exhaled.

A sedan turned in from the road and rolled to a stop by the porch. Not the sheriff. Not a neighbor. Mr. Davidson stepped out, jacket off, sleeves rolled, an envelope under his arm. He looked at the frame and smiled the small, true smile of a man who likes to see a thing stand that was trying to fall.

"Evening," he said. "I was nearby. Thought I'd make this a handoff and not a PDF." He lifted the envelope a little. "Deeds and titles released from hold. Withdrawal of acceleration. Reinstatement letter. Copies for your files."

Annie met him halfway, palms dusty, hair escaping the bandana in cheerful defeat. "You came to the party late," she said, and there was so much thanks in her voice the joke melted and left only gratitude.

"Work smells better than my office," he said. He glanced to the cottonwoods. "Mr. Spyker."

Jake pushed himself up from the chair Maria had forced on him and came to the porch step. He felt steady enough to do it with dignity. "Sir."

Davidson's eyes ticked over the yard, the new lines, the people waving from trucks. He handed Annie the envelope and then, politely, handed Jake the same. "You're current," he said. "Review stays at sixty days. Your snapshots have been useful. Thank you for the transparency. Enjoy the peace of this piece of paper."

"Thank you," Annie said.

"Thank you," Jake said, slower. The weight of the envelope sat wrong in one hand and right in the other. He looked at the seals, the stamps, the words that had been trying to decide his life without ever stepping in his yard. They had a different look now. They looked tamed.

"I'll get out of your way," Davidson said. He touched the brim he wasn't wearing, saw his mistake, and laughed at himself. "See you."

"See you," Annie said.

He left the way he'd come, careful, respectful of the gravel. The last neighbor honked twice and disappeared down the bend. Evening settled for real. The string lights came on as if they had been waiting for quiet.

Jake stood a few steps back and finally understood what had just happened. Not luck. Not charity. All Annie. Her plan. Her grit. Her choice. While he'd been flat on a hospital bed and then tied to a chair by doctor's orders, the world had kept turning because she had grabbed it and made it. She'd written emails he didn't know how to write. She'd called men he didn't know how to face. She'd stood in a room and signed away a safety net that was supposed to be forever, and she'd done it for a place that wasn't hers on paper and was hers in every other way that matters.

What have you done, Annie? What have you sacrificed? Why?

He looked at her and every answer landed at once. She'd saved the ranch. She'd saved him, whether he deserved it or not. The barn bones stood because of her. The bank paper behaved because of her. The people kept coming because she told the truth out loud and then matched it with work. His throat had that tight ache that belongs to pride and sorrow and a joy so strong it scares a man the first time he feels it.

Annie set the envelope on the table by the door and wrote BANK on it with a blunt pencil. She brushed a smear of pine dust off her forearm. Blue did what Blue did best. Maria watched from the porch with a look a mother gives a child who's found the right house at last. Tommy whistled something out of tune and decided it counted as music.

Jake walked to Annie and stopped a breath away. He didn't know if he was supposed to say thank you or sorry or both. Words lined up and none of them were big enough.

"What did you give up?" he asked, quiet.

She held his gaze. "What I didn't need anymore," she said. "What I didn't want to need."

He felt that like a hand on his chest. He nodded once, because anything louder might break him. Wind pushed through the ranch and shook a little shade loose. The new frame threw a long shadow that touched their boots and kept going.

"I thought I was the one who kept this place standing," he said. "Turns out I was just one more board."

"You're a load bearing wall," she said, and smiled, tired and radiant.

He laughed, helpless and happy in a way that made his shoulder remind him to behave. The laugh slid into something quieter. He saw her the way a man finally sees a thing he's been looking at for weeks and not seeing right. He saw the long braid that never stayed put. He saw sawdust on her cheekbone like high noon freckles. He saw the way her eyes held the line and the horizon at the same time. He saw a life he wanted and, for the first time, believed he could keep.

Oh, he thought. Oh. It came in simple and absolute. He loved her.

The knowledge didn't ask permission. It didn't check his bank balance or his scars. It just arrived, settled, and made the next breath easier.

He reached for her hand, and she let him take it. No ceremony. No speech. Skin warm, pulse strong. The barn stood behind them. The yard was theirs again. The lights were small and stubborn and kind.

"Annie," he said, and her name sounded like a promise that had finally found its voice.

She squeezed his fingers. "Jake."

"I'm slow sometimes," he said. "I'm not slow now."

She didn't ask what he meant. She saw it. She had been seeing him all along. She stepped closer so their shoulders touched, and the day clicked into place.

"You're staying," she said.

"I am," he said. "For the ranch. For you. For all of it."

They stood in the soft dark while the frame drew its first night lines across the ground. The wind eased. The last truck's taillights went out beyond the bend. The envelope on the table kept its own very quiet watch. Love, finally named, kept a better one.

CHAPTER TWENTY-SEVEN

THE HARDEST WORDS

They climbed to the ridge before sunrise, the same place where she had once looked down at the stubborn lights and chosen to stay. Cold air lifted the hair on her arms. The grass held a lace of frost that would be gone by breakfast. The sky pinked at the edges, patient and sure. Below them the barn stood almost finished, ribs straight, roof line clean, a promise with lumber.

Blue followed halfway, decided the view was for people, and curled up at a juniper with his nose on his paws. The world was quiet enough to hear ants walking. Annie wrapped her hands around a mug she had carried up like a talisman. The steam rose and made a small ghost between them.

Jake stood with his hat in his hands and let the words come. He did not try to dress them up. He looked at the barn, then at the valley, then at her.

"I need to say what I didn't say," he began. "The day the letter came, I opened it, and it hurt me bad. I put it in the drawer and told no one. I counted cattle to try to make the numbers work. I told myself I was protecting you. I wasn't. I was protecting my pride."

He turned the hat, brim against palm. "I know I pushed you away when you tried to reach out to me. I said save yourself when I meant I don't know how to save any of us."

The words hung with the fog and did not drift. He let the next breath steady him.

"I told myself I was born to take hits and keep quiet. That's how I learned to be a man. It's not how I want to be with you. I'm sorry I didn't tell you about the denial. I'm sorry I kept you on the outside while I tried to figure it out on my own. I'm sorry my pride is the way it is."

Annie felt the apology settle in her chest like a warm rock, heavy in a good way. She kept still. She didn't hurry him. The ridge had its own time.

He lifted his head and met her eyes. "When Davidson came with the papers, I finally saw it clear. It wasn't luck. It wasn't charity. It was you. Your plan. Your grit. Your choice. You signed away a safety net because you decided this place was as much yours as it is mine. You decided I was yours too. I don't know if I deserve that, but I see it."

He swallowed and the last of the night slipped out of his voice. "I'm sorry for what you gave up. I'm sorry for the ways I made it harder. I said the ranch comes first like that meant you come second. That was wrong."

The sky deepened to rose. The ridge kept its old silence. A meadowlark tried a few notes.

Jake took one more breath. When he spoke again, his voice was steady.

"Annie, I love you. I think I always have."

The words moved through her like heat after cold. Annie closed her eyes and felt the truth of them find every sharp place and smooth it. She set the mug on a flat rock and stepped closer. Her fingers touched his jaw, light as breath.

"Say it again," she said.

"I really do love you," he said. "I know it took me a while to realize it, but now I know I always will."

She smiled, not wide, not shy, full. "I love you too," she said. "I think I knew it the first night I stood up here and looked down at those stubborn lights and didn't leave. I'm not sorry for what I gave up. I chose what I wanted. I chose you. I chose this."

He let out a sound that might have been a laugh or a prayer. He pulled her in, careful of healing bones, and set his forehead to hers. The hat hung loose at his side. The valley smelled like cold water and pine.

"I have to say my hardest words too," she whispered. "No more secrets. No more hidden letters. If a letter comes, we read it together. If fear shows up, we handle it together."

"Yes," he said. "Together. One problem at a time, this time with both of us in the same room."

"Good," she said. "Then kiss me and let the day start right."

He did. It tasted like steam and winter and relief. Below them the barn caught the first clean stripe of sunlight and wore it proudly. Blue lifted his head, saw that the people had decided the important thing, and put his nose back on his paws.

They stood with the ridge at their backs and the ranch below, and they let the morning choose its colors. The hardest words had been spoken. The truest ones could carry them now.

Back at the bunkhouse table they pulled out scrap paper, old magazines, a dull jar of pencils, and a basket of sticky notes that Maria had been saving for grocery lists. The table still smelled like smoke and saddle soap. Morning light fell in a clean stripe across the boards. Blue settled under the benches.

"Let's build it," Annie said. "On paper first."

They started with shapes. Jake drew a cabin the way a boy draws a house, square and simple. Annie leaned in and added a small porch, two chairs, and a kettle on a hook. She shaded the window so it looked like lamplight, then sketched a little path that ran to the edge of the page.

"A small tasting room here," she said, penciling a rectangle near the barn site. "Nothing fancy. A counter, three stools, jars of Maria's pickles, a cooler for the cuts. People taste, then take a little of the ranch home with them."

"Like a fancy steak dinner doggy bag," Jake said. He grinned at his own joke even though he knew it was a bad one.

She laughed anyway. "Exactly like that."

They cut pictures out of the magazines. Quilts in colors that did not try too hard. Tin cups on a rail. Stars that looked close enough to touch. Annie clipped a photo of a hand with soil in the palm. Jake found an image of a steaming skillet, tore it free, and said, "Maria can make a pan look like a holiday."

"Label," Annie said, writing as she talked. "Spyker Ranch Beef. Raised right. Finished right. A story on every tag."

She drafted a tag on a scrap, neat and simple. Harvest date. Pasture origin. A short line about the steer that did not turn him into a cartoon. Just respect in black ink. She pressed the scrap to the board with a strip of tape and nodded to herself.

They circled stargazing tours and slow evenings under quilts. Annie wrote "Sky Cabin nights" in her tidy hand, then added small notes around it. Star map in drawer. Kettle and cocoa. Lantern path from bunkhouse. She drew a dotted line that made the path feel like a promise.

Jake finally smiled, full and unguarded. "This is amazing."

Annie looked up and felt the warmth hit her cheeks. The barn bones stood outside. The future bones were lining up on paper. It felt like the same kind of good.

"Alright," she said, hands on her hips. "Hard truth and good news. I need to tell you something."

His eyes narrowed, not with suspicion, with attention. "Shoot."

She rolled a sticky note between her fingers. "Investors. I told you about the conditional. We had two. Then one pulled out when things looked rough. He wrote danger like it was a dirty word." She lifted her chin and smiled. "Now we have three, all in, one hundred percent committed. Two more are sniffing around. They want to see three weekends of profit, then they will try to fight the others for a spot."

Jake stared, then laughed once under his breath, almost in disbelief. "You're good at this stuff."

She felt the small burst of pride and let it show. "I am."

He reached across the table and touched her wrist. "Thank you for telling me. Thank you for doing it."

Her eyes went soft. She looked at him the way you look at a sunrise you did not expect to catch. "I love you too."

The words were simple. They landed clean. He closed his hand over her fingers and held on a second longer than he needed to, then let go because there was work to finish and the day did not plan to slow for kisses on a vision board.

"So," Jake said, clearing his throat and picking up a pair of safety scissors. "What do we call it? I have a few ideas. Star Nights. Spike and Blue. Annie's Place."

"Absolutely not," she said, smiling. "Too much pressure to live up to the name if you put mine on it."

"Spike and Blue are solid," he said. The dog thumped his tail like he agreed.

"It is also a risk when Spike decides to eat someone's hat on a Tuesday," she said. "People will blame the brand."

He leaned back and considered the wall of scraps. "Star Nights has a nice sound."

"It does," she said. "But it feels like a calendar. I want something that feels like a choice."

Annie cocked a crooked grin. She printed on a bright sticky note in firm block letters and pressed it at the center of the board.

Boots and Stilettos.

Jake laughed, the sound easy for once. "That is either brilliant or trouble."

"Both," she said. "It's us. Work and polish. Mud and glass. You and me. The ranch and the city. It tells people what they are buying. Grit that cleans up nice."

He looked at the sticky note again and shook his head in happy surrender. "It fits."

"Then it is settled," she said. She wrote it again on the top of the whiteboard and boxed it so no one could miss it. "A sub line here," she added, thinking out loud. "Bring your boots. Bring your best. We will handle the sky."

He watched her as she wrote. The letters were neat and strong. The words were clear. The board looked messy and perfect. Color tucked among pencil. Tape holding down corners that wanted to lift. Plans that would become receipts and receipts that would become a roof.

Tommy poked his head in, saw the chaos, and grinned. "You two doing arts and crafts or saving the county?"

"Both," Jake said. "Come look. You are the first audience."

Tommy came around the table with reverence and hands held like he was in a museum. "I like the beef tag," he said. "People will eat the story along with the steak. And this part with the quilts. Smart. City folks think quilts are a personality trait."

"They are," Maria said from the doorway. She carried a tray of coffee and the kind of cookies that taste like butter and childhood. "I approve the name."

"Already?" Annie said. "That is a record."

Maria set the tray down and tapped the sticky note. "This tells me you know who you are," she said. "That is all a name has to do."

They ate cookies and circled three more ideas that came out of the sugar. A small porch concert in late summer. A winter program for stargazing with thermoses and hand warmers. A postcard wall where guests can pin a note and a wish.

Jake leaned back and let the sound of them soak in. The

bunkhouse had been a place of bad news and good work for weeks. Today it felt like a beginning with flour on its face.

He reached for a sticky note and wrote his first real contribution in careful print. "No fake," he wrote, then added a second line, "No rush." He pressed it next to the name and looked at Annie.

"That is the whole brand," she said.

He nodded. "Then hold me to it."

"I will," she said. "You hold me to the rest."

Blue sneezed like a stamp of approval. The late sun came through the window and lit the board until every scrap looked important. Annie took a photo, then another from farther back so the mess and the perfection both made it into the frame.

"Do we tell the investors and the bank the name?" Jake asked.

"They will hear it when we print the receipt paper," she said. "They'll like that the best."

Jake stood and offered his hand. She took it and rose. The bunkhouse door opened towards the yard. The ridge wore a soft rim of light. The almost barn sat proud and patient.

"Boots and Stilettos," he said again, testing the sound in the air.

"Home," she answered, simple and sure.

They stood at the fence where the new barn threw a long, clean shadow across the yard. Blue patrolled a slow circle, then flopped.

Jake reached into his pocket and set a small box on the rail of the fence. The lid creaked a little when he opened it. Inside sat his mother's turquoise ring, old silver worn with wear, a thin band shaped by years of honest hands. He didn't kneel. He didn't make a speech. He watched her face instead.

"No pressure," he said. "Just wear it when you're ready."

Annie's breath lifted and fell, steady. She slid the ring onto her right hand and turned it in the light. The stone caught the sky and kept a piece of it. Her mouth curved. She looked at Jake, then at the yard, then back at the ring as if listening for an answer she already knew.

She slipped it onto her left-hand ring finger. "Looks like you didn't have to wait too long," she said, smiling.

Then with those eyes looking up at him, she said, "I do."

The words were simple. They landed the way rain lands on thirsty ground. Jake nodded and felt his chest find a new way to be. He grinned back. "I've learned patience."

"Me too," she said. "At least the useful kind."

Blue thumped his tail and pretended not to stare. Maria paused at the porch with a dish towel over her shoulder and read the scene from fifty feet, then turned the first strand of lights on and left the rest of the moment alone. The bulbs bloomed soft along the eave, one after another, a necklace of small suns.

Jake lifted Annie's hand and looked at the ring in its proper place. The silver fit her like it had been waiting. He touched the edge of the stone with a fingertip and felt the warmth it had borrowed from her skin.

"Was this your mother's ring?" she said.

"It was," he answered. "She'd like where it landed."

"I'll take good care of it," she said.

"I know," he said.

They stood with their shoulders touching, elbows easy on the rail. The barn bones looked less like a project and more like a promise. Tomorrow would be full of ladders and lists again, but tonight had room for a pause the size of a life.

"Tell me one more thing," he said, not letting go of her hand. "Remember our deal? No secrets. No hidden letters."

"No secrets!" she said.

"Deal!" he said.

The sunset took shape, gold turning to peach, then to the blue that makes stars bold enough to show themselves. Two birds lifted from the cottonwoods and flew side by side across the last light of the day. Annie tipped her face up. Jake met her halfway. The kiss tasted like forever.

When they parted, the yard had settled. The lights hummed. The ridge held the first pinpricks of night. Annie looked at the barn, then at Jake, and the smile stayed. He felt the quiet answer rise in him, simple and certain. Home, he thought. Home with her.

They turned toward the porch together, steps in time, Blue trotting ahead as if he had planned the route. Behind them the ring caught the last stripe of sun and flashed once, quick as a wink, then rested where it belonged. The hardest words had been spoken. The truest ones would carry them the rest of the way.

BOOTS AND STILETTOS

Six months later the ranch breathed like it had a new set of lungs. The barn stood straight and sure, fresh paint catching morning light. A new gate swung clean on its hinges. The sign over the drive read Boots and Stilettos in hand carved cedar, the letters dark and glossy, the little star brand tucked in the corner like a wink. A town car rolled past the gate and up the lane, then another behind it, tires whispering on gravel that had been raked that morning. Beyond the barn a tight row of cabins shone as crews finished trim and steps. Lanterns glowed along the path even in daylight, a soft promise for later.

Annie walked the yard in scuffed boots and turquoise stiletto earrings. Her hair was braided and tucked, then already loosening because the day liked her better that way. The turquoise ring caught sun whenever she turned her hand to point or wave. She had a clipboard in one palm and a coffee she kept forgetting to drink in the other. She greeted guests by name, through the real smile of someone who means it. She asked after a grandmother, a new job, a long drive. She laughed with the staff. She straightened a quilt on a porch rail. She checked a lantern wick and fixed it. The rhythm of the place matched the rhythm of her steps.

The Sky Cabin had a new roof and a stargazer's map in the drawer. Reservations were full through winter. The tasting room smelled like cedar and coffee. Maria had stacked jars of peaches and pickles in a soldier line and started a pot of chili that could make a person cry. Tommy had found a tall ladder somewhere and was using it to fix a thing that probably did not need fixing, which let him hold court and tell jokes from a higher altitude. Mr. Davidson had been by earlier for a quick coffee. He walked the yard with Jake, nodded at the weekly snapshot, and said the kind of sentences that meant peace. The sheriff stopped for a pastry and a handshake on his way to the highway. The postcard wall had gone from three hopeful notes to a hundred small squares, each one a quick thank you from a weekend that had landed just right.

The town cars parked under the cottonwoods. One stood out without trying. Dante Contadelucci stepped out, jacket open, tie neat, hair sharper than wind should allow. No lawyers. No assistants. No Ricardo, because Ricardo was in jail and learning in the slow way what a consequence feels like. Dante looked around and his eyes took in everything the way a math mind takes in a page of numbers. The barns. The cabins. The paths. The people. His gaze settled on his daughter and he watched her move through the crowd.

Annie touched a guest's elbow and pointed out the ridge where sunset would sit, then turned. Dante crossed to Jake first. Their handshake was firm and simple. Two men who had both lost and kept things, who had both decided to keep going. They didn't compare scars. They didn't trade speeches. They held eye contact, then let it go.

Dante turned to Annie and gave a single nod. "You did good," he said.

No list. No counsel. No fine print. Just the sentence she had wanted a father to say and to mean. It landed in her chest and held. He smiled, a true smile, the kind a father saves for a beloved daughter who has found the door that opens and the room that fits.

He reached into his jacket and pulled a thick stack of notarized papers. She knew them fast. They were the copies of the documents that had revoked her trust and her votes. The papers she had used and sold to save the ranch when the letter was heavy, and time was short. He met her eyes as he tore the top sheet in half. He tore the next. He crumpled, then handed the pieces to her. One by one he made the stack into something small enough to carry.

He leaned in and spoke for her alone. "I trust you, not a trust."

Her breath caught. She did not cry. She tucked the torn halves into the pocket of her jacket and felt their weight change. It was like closing a door that had stayed cracked too long, then seeing the room you had chosen bloom brighter for it.

"Thank you, Daddy." she said softly.

He tipped his head again and stepped back, now a guest like any other. He had booked a cabin like he was nobody special. Paid in full. Black American Express card, no drama. He walked toward the tasting room, paused for a cookie, then stood by the porch rail and let the place work on him.

A local band tuned on the flatbed under the string lights. Fiddle, guitar, a stand-up bass, and a snare with a soft hand. People drifted to the packed earth and started to dance. Boots scuffed. Kids clipped around the edge and copied the steps. Maria clapped time from the porch, then shushed herself and cried a little where no one could see. Tommy cut in on a laugh and spun a guest who looked like she had been waiting her whole life to be spun.

Jake touched Annie's hand and waited. Annie smiled and let him pull her in. The two-step felt like walking and breathing at once. They moved easy and sure. The band found a sweet groove.

No whispers. Only clapping, bright faces, and the clean sound of joy. People closed the circles around them, not to trap them, to bless the moment with their attention and then get back to their own fun.

They danced through one song, then two. Jake did a small move at the turn that made Annie laugh out loud. He had practiced it with Tommy behind the barn when no one was looking. He leaned in close at the end of the third song. "You make the ranch feel simple," he said.

"You make me safe," she said.

The sun reached for the ridge. The string lights grew braver. The cabins lit one by one like small homes in a model town. A couple from Chicago kissed under the porch lantern. A grandmother from Billings taught a teenager from Austin how to hold a partner without stepping on toes. Mr. Davidson and Maria argued gently about the correct ratio of coffee to cream, then settled it with laughter and another cup. Dante watched his daughter be the center without reaching for the center.

At sunset they slipped away from the noise. Nobody stopped them. The yard had already accepted that sometimes the people who hold it together need to be held by quiet. They walked toward the arena, which lay warm and empty. The dirt had been raked that morning and wore neat lines. The bleachers smelled like sun on wood. Spike trotted behind them, head high, pleased with his shadow. Blue walked a little ahead, then circled back, eyes bright, tongue out. If a dog can smile, he did.

They climbed the rail and sat like they had sat a hundred times, hips close, boots hooked. The sky moved from gold to pink to the honest blue that stars love. The cabins were far enough that the music became a hum, and the hum became a memory of a very good day.

"What next?" Annie asked. She rested her chin on her forearm and watched Spike chase nothing but joy across the open. Her earrings caught the last light. The ring did too.

Jake tipped his hat back and let the smile spread. "Whatever we want, darlin'. Whatever we want."

They let that live between them. Then they began to talk about the small next things, the kind that make a life. A Sunday sunset ride for guests who want to say goodbye slow. A winter plan for hot cocoa and hot stones by the fire ring. A spring seed day where kids can plant a row and come back to see what grew. A scholarship jar in the tasting room for the ag class at the high school. A new coat of paint for the sign when summer breaks its first sweat. The big next things could wait. The big ones always can if the small ones are true.

Annie leaned her shoulder into Jake's and watched Blue roll on his back in pure goofy bliss. "I used to think happy ever after was a fairy tale," she said.

"It is," he said. "We live on a ranch. We do fairy tales with chores."

She laughed and put her hand on his knee. "That should be the new subline."

"Print it," he said. "Everyone will love it."

They sat until the first star took its place, then the next, then the rest. The ridge went dark and friendly. The lights along the path blinked in a calm row for anyone who needed to find their way back. The band struck a soft last song, and the crowd lifted the kind of cheer that wraps around a person and makes them brave.

They climbed down and walked to the tasting room for a bourbon nightcap. Inside, a chalkboard listed tomorrow's plan in neat letters. Breakfast at seven. Trail talk at eight. Blue is allowed in the tasting room, if he minds his manners. Bathrooms sparkle. Annie added one more line and underlined it. Thank you for being here.

Dante stood by the postcard wall and read a handful. He nodded for himself, then for her. He did not say more. He did not have to. He wandered out to his cabin like a man who had learned that a daughter's life can make sense even if it is not the one he wrote in his head. The door shut soft. A porch light clicked on. Quiet settled.

Tommy leaned on the window and asked if anyone wanted one last slice of apple pie. The answer was always yes. Maria boxed two pieces in a split second.

Annie rested her head on Jakes shoulder. "Do you ever think about the girl in Milan?" she asked, voice easy, not sad.

"Only when I want to thank her," he said. "She brought you here."

"She did," Annie said. "She is happy for us too."

They sat with that. Then they rose because the night asked them to take a short walk under the lights before sleep. They went past the postcard wall and read three notes out loud. 'Thank you for the stars.' 'Thank you for the quiet.' 'Thank you for reminding us to breathe.' They added their own, a small slip that said, 'We promise to keep this true.'

At the gate they paused. The sign over them looked older already, which is how a sign is supposed to look when it belongs. Annie touched the carved letters. Jake covered her hand with his. Blue leaned on both of them, so they had to laugh.

"Home," he said.

"Home," she answered.

They turned off the porch lamp on his grandmother's old home. The cabin Annie stayed in when she first got there. But they let the lanterns keep their gentle vigil. Together, hand in hand, they walked toward the big house just over the ridge. The ring winked once at a friendly star. The earrings swung and caught a little song only she could hear.

Happy ever after didn't make a loud noise. It made a small one. The click of a latch that fits. The hush of quilts. The soft pad of a dog at the foot of the bed. The quiet promise of two people who chose the same life and kept choosing it. That was Boots and Stilettos. That was them. And it was enough.

. . .

The Beginning.

* * *

IF YOU ENJOYED **Boots and Stilettos**, I'd truly appreciate an honest review on BookBub or Goodreads. Even a few words can help other readers decide if this story is right for them.

You can find more about my books at **KirkVoclain.com**, and you're welcome to join my newsletter for updates on new stories, bonus content, and future promotions.

ABOUT THE AUTHOR

Kirk Voclain writes stories about grit, heart, and the trouble we get into when we follow both. He believes books should move fast, feel true, and leave you a little lighter when you turn the last page. South Louisiana is home. That rhythm shows up in his voice. So do porch conversations, strong coffee, and people who keep their promises.

By day, Kirk does for a living what most call a hobby. By night, he does for a hobby what most call a profession. Photography pays the bills. Writing feeds the fire. He is happiest when the scene on the page clicks into focus and the characters refuse to stand still.

His debut thriller, **Double Exposure**, introduced readers to high stakes and a hero who never blinks. **Boots and Stilettos** shows another side of his storytelling, where romance, people, land, and second chances take the lead. More novels are in the works... because of course they are.

Kirk also runs Pro4uM.com, a long-running creative community where working pros swap ideas, sharpen skills, and say the quiet parts out loud. Teaching and encouraging others is part of his DNA.

That same drive to help creators led him to launch FiiP.net (Fresh Indie Ink Promotions). FiiP is a platform built for authors who are tired of shouting into the void. It's about real visibility, honest contests, and helping indie voices find the readers they deserve. No fake hype, just fresh ink and the spotlight it earns.

For news, extras, and contact info, visit kirkvoclain.com. If you enjoyed this book, a short review helps more than you know. Thank you for reading… truly.

Connect with him personally on any of his social accounts.

instagram.com/kirkvoclain
facebook.com/kirk.voclain
tiktok.com/@kirkvoclain
linkedin.com/in/kirkvoclain
x.com/kirkvoclain
youtube.com/kirkvoclain
goodreads.com/kirkvoclain
bookbub.com/authors/kirk-voclain

Dust and Inheritance

Read the prequel here now.

And more to come! Join our mailing list to be notified of future releases:
https://kirkvoclain.com

DUST AND INHERITANCE

PREQUEL TO BOOTS AND STILETTOS

THE BUS TICKET

She almost didn't get on the bus.

The ticket sat on the seat beside her like it belonged to someone braver. Millie checked her watch. 7:17 a.m. Saturday, August 31, 1957. Thirty minutes before departure, in a depot that smelled like stale coffee and old leather.

It was a one-way ticket from Ohio to Montana that promised sixty-seven hours on the road, two cheap hotel stays, and over two thousand miles of thinking time.

Montana.

An entire state that sounded like dust, cattle, and men who didn't smile unless they meant it.

Mildred Caldwell. Millie to the handful of people who still had permission to call her that. She stared at the ticket and tried to make sense of herself. What was she doing? This wasn't a vacation. It wasn't a business trip. It wasn't even a clean obligation.

It was a borderline favor.

Her uncle's last plea kept looping in her head. Again. And again.

Don't let it vanish.

She told herself it was about him. About paperwork and land

and doing the right thing. But the truth sat closer to her ribs than she liked.

She'd bought the ticket herself.

Nobody forced her. Nobody begged her, not in person. She could've stayed home and let the world handle its own mess. She could've folded his letter, put it in a drawer, and let it go quiet.

But Millie didn't fold easily.

The bus rolled into the depot with a hiss and a tired shudder. Doors opened. People moved. The whole place shifted like it had decided time was leaving with or without her.

Millie took a breath, smoothed her dress, and grabbed her suitcase. She took two steps, then stopped.

She turned back. Picked up the ticket. Held it between her fingers like it might burn.

Then she walked straight toward the bus, chin up, shoulders squared, stubbornness leading the way.

She didn't know the man waiting in Montana was a liar, or that she was about to fall for a place that didn't care who she was. She stepped onto the bus anyway.

CHAPTER ONE

THE ARRIVAL

Clem leaned against the fender of his red truck, watching the dust settle at the edge of town. Beside him, Wade spat into the dirt, not bothering to look at the approaching bus.

"You sure about this one?" Wade asked, his voice low.

"I'm sure," Clem said. His eyes were fixed on the depot. "Her uncle was desperate before he died. That makes her desperate now. We get her to trust me, we get the deed, we sell it to Halverson for a premium."

Wade smirked. "And if she's smart?"

"Smart doesn't matter when you are out of time and out of help," Clem replied, his tone flat. He opened the truck door. "You wait by the post. Signal me when you spot her with the folder. Give me one tap of your boot on the porch. I will signal you back with a brake light flashing twice."

Wade tipped his hat. "Easy money."

Clem climbed in and started the engine. "Only if we do it right. Do not miss the signal."

* * *

MILLIE STEPPED DOWN from the bus with a suitcase in one hand and stubbornness in the other. Exhaustion sat behind her eyes, but she didn't have time for it.

Montana was wide and quiet, and it didn't care who noticed. The air felt different, thinner maybe, and it carried dust the way some places carried humidity, steady and unavoidable. Millie blinked once, then twice, and decided her eyes weren't going to water. Not here. Not now.

Her one suitcase was scuffed at the corners, the latch stubborn enough to need a smack from the heel of her hand. But the other thing she carried mattered more. A folder, thick and tired, tied with string. It was a folder opened too many times, and it always ended the same way.

Behind her, the bus hissed, then it was already gone, leaving her with a gust of grit and the sound of her own breathing. The little depot wasn't much. A bench. A bulletin board with curled notices. A man leaning against the post like he'd been there since the first fence went up. He looked her over, not rude, just curious, the way people did when you weren't part of the scenery.

Millie adjusted her grip on the folder. Tightened the string. Tightened herself.

Her uncle had written three letters before he died. Three. Like he knew he didn't have many left. The first letter had been hopeful. The second one sounded tired. The third was a hurry, written hard and fast, like he didn't have the breath for a fourth.

Millie, I started something I can't finish. You're the only one I trust with it. Don't let them take it. Don't let it vanish.

He hadn't said who "them" was, but the letters had carried a name anyway, like smoke clinging to fabric. A neighbor. A man with land already, but always wanting more. A man who knew how slow paperwork moved and how fast a grieving family could lose their nerve.

Millie wasn't the grieving type. Not in public.

She reached up and smoothed her hair, as if that could smooth the rest of her life. It was pinned back tight for a reason, so the wind wouldn't take it. Her dress was simple, travel-stained, and she'd chosen it for one reason. It didn't wrinkle much. She'd needed that little lie of control.

A red truck rolled past, slow, then slower, then it kept going. She felt the eyes on her back like a hand. She turned just enough to show she noticed, then looked away again, like she didn't care.

The man by the post shifted his weight, spat into the dust without a second thought, then tapped his boot heel once against the wood. Not loud. Not for her. Just enough. Driving by just then, the red truck didn't slow, but its brake lights flashed twice.

Inside the folder was a mess, organized just enough to look official.

A homestead claim. Dates. A rough map drawn by hand. Receipts for supplies her uncle had bought, maybe to prove he'd worked the land. On the map, her uncle had circled the spring twice, hard enough to score the paper. The note beside it was short. *Water holds this place together.* Letters with official stamps that looked important, until you read them and realized they said almost nothing. The words "prove up" appeared more than once, underlined hard, as if her uncle could press the law into obedience with a pencil.

Millie knew the basics. She'd read everything twice. She'd asked questions back home and gotten answers that sounded like shrugs.

A claimant had to live on the land. Improve it. Build something. Work it. Then, if the government believed you, it became yours. It sounded simple when people explained it across a counter. It wasn't simple when the person who started it was buried two states away and all you had was a folder full of notes.

The clock was not polite about it either. If she missed the land office deadline, the claim would go soft, then disappear.

She hadn't come all this way to be pushed around.

Her uncle had been close to finishing. Close enough that it made her angry. Close enough that it made her hopeful.

Hope was dangerous out here. She could feel that already.

A woman came out of the depot office, wiping her hands on her apron like the dust was her fault. She was middle-aged, strong in the shoulders, and she had the look of someone who'd watched a thousand people arrive with dreams, then leave without them.

"You need a room?" the woman asked.

Millie nodded. "Just for a night. I'll check in after I handle some business."

The bus ride had been brutal. She'd slept in pieces through potholes, crying babies, and strangers who didn't know the meaning of quiet. Her body wanted a bed, but her mind stayed on the job in front of her.

The woman tilted her head. "You got family in town?"

"No, ma'am."

"Work?"

Millie hesitated, then decided honesty would cost less than pretending. "Land."

That word changed the air. Not much, just enough. The woman's eyes shifted toward the folder in Millie's hand, then back to her face.

"What kind of land?" she asked, like she already knew there were kinds, and some of them brought trouble with them.

Millie swallowed. "A claim. My uncle's."

The woman's mouth tightened, then relaxed again. "You're late in the season for starting over."

"I didn't come to start over," Millie said. The words came out sharper than she meant. She softened her tone, but not the meaning. "I came to finish."

The woman studied her for a long moment, then agreed like she respected that, or at least understood it.

"You'll want the county office," she said. "And you'll want directions that don't get you lost."

"I'd appreciate both," Millie replied.

The woman wiped her hands again, then pointed. "There's a diner on Main. You can get a hot meal, and you can ask questions without folks pretending they don't hear you. Just don't ask the wrong person."

Millie almost smiled. Almost. "How do I tell the difference?"

The woman gave her a look that held a dry sort of humor. "You won't. Not at first. Just pay attention."

Millie turned her suitcase upright and started toward the street, the folder still tucked tight to her ribs, held close the way you held something you couldn't afford to lose. She'd barely taken three steps when a voice behind her called out. It was quiet, but curious enough to stop her.

"Miss," the man at the post said.

Millie stopped and looked back. He wasn't old, but he had lines like he'd argued with the sun more than once. Hat pulled low, hands relaxed in a way that suggested he didn't waste energy, or words.

He nodded toward the folder, then toward the open land beyond town, like he could see exactly where she was headed.

"You headed out there alone?" he asked.

Millie lifted her chin. "Yes."

He didn't argue. He just watched her a second longer.

"Road doesn't care about brave," he said quietly. "It'll still swallow you."

Millie held his gaze. "Then I'll drive slower."

The man's mouth twitched, not quite a smile, more like approval that tried to pretend it wasn't.

He tipped his hat a fraction. "Suit yourself."

Millie turned away, but she felt his eyes follow her, steady and measuring, as if he'd already started counting her chances.

And, worse, as if he'd already started counting what she might be worth.

Millie didn't look back again.

If she did, she'd have to admit the man had gotten under her skin, and she had no time for that. She had a county office to find, a diner to stomach, and a piece of land waiting out there like a test she didn't get to study for.

Main Street was short and dusty. A few storefronts. A feed store. A diner with a window full of pie that looked like it had been sitting there since breakfast and didn't care who judged it. Millie walked in anyway. She ate, asked a couple careful questions, and listened twice as hard as she spoke. She didn't say "homestead" to just anybody. She said, "my uncle's place" and watched faces, watched pauses, watched the way people answered without answering.

She left with directions that sounded like a riddle and a key detail that sat heavy in her stomach.

"Don't miss the turn," the waitress had said, wiping down the counter like she'd seen too many folks miss it. "If you hit the dry creek bed, you went too far."

Millie nodded like she understood, even though she didn't.

Behind the diner, in an empty lot next to the feed store, a man with a pencil behind his ear rented her a truck that had seen better years and didn't care who knew it. The paint was sun-faded, the seat cracked, and the floorboard held a fine layer of dust that looked like it paid rent. Millie climbed in and set her suitcase on the floorboard. She set the folder on the seat beside her and rested one hand on it for a moment, like it could jump out and run. It started on the second try. The engine shuddered, then settled into a steady rattle that sounded almost confident.

The town fell away behind her. Not dramatically, just quietly, like Montana had a lot of room and didn't waste it on goodbyes.

The land opened up in front of her, and she tried not to show her reaction, even to herself.

It was big. Bigger than she expected. Not just distance, but emptiness. The kind that made you feel small without insulting you. The sky stretched wide and clean, and the light had a sharpness to it.

Millie tightened her grip on the wheel. Her knuckles weren't white, but they were thinking about it.

The first few miles were fine. Hard-packed road, a few scattered fence lines, a couple of cattle that looked up with slow interest and then went back to their business. Millie followed the directions in her head. Left at the leaning cottonwood. Past the old windmill. Keep going until you think you've gone too far.

Then keep going anyway.

The road narrowed. Gravel turned to ruts. Ruts turned to two pale tracks through grass and dirt. The signage, if it had ever existed, gave up and disappeared. The wind picked up, pushing dust across the hood in low sheets. It made the world look like an old faded photograph.

Millie swallowed. She told herself she was fine.

She told herself she'd driven worse.

She told herself a lot of things.

A gust hit the truck broadside and it drifted just enough to make her breath catch. The tires spat gravel. She corrected, too fast, then eased it back. Her heart settled. Her pride did not.

Out here, there were no landmarks that felt friendly. Just land and sky and a road that could vanish if it felt like it.

She slowed. The waitress had said don't miss the turn, but she hadn't said what the turn looked like. Millie watched for anything that might be a sign. A break in the grass. A post. A fence corner. She saw a dry creek bed ahead and felt her stomach drop.

That's when the tire went.

It wasn't a dramatic blowout. It was a sharp crack, then a heavy thump-thump-thump that pulled the wheel hard to the right. Millie fought it, brought the truck down to a crawl, and guided it off onto what looked like the shoulder. Except it wasn't really a shoulder. It was just ground that happened to be a little flatter.

She sat there for a second, both hands on the wheel, breathing through her nose like that could keep her from saying something she'd regret.

Then she got out.

The wind hit her immediately. Dust stung her eyes. She blinked it away and walked around to the front right tire.

Flat.

Of course.

Millie looked up and around like the land might offer an apology. Nothing. No other vehicles. No house. No help. Just the road behind her and the road ahead, and both of them looking equally unconcerned.

She opened the driver's side door and grabbed the folder off the seat. That was instinct. She hated that it was instinct. She set it carefully on the floorboard, tucked under the seat edge, out of the wind and out of sight. Then she popped the hood, as if the hood had anything to do with the tire. She didn't know why she did it. Maybe because it made her feel like she was doing something.

She moved to the back and found the jack. Found the lug wrench. Found the spare, and her first real problem.

The spare was there. It was also bald, worn down like it had been dragged across stone, and the sidewall had a crack that made her stomach tighten.

Millie stared at it, then glanced back toward the flat tire like she might negotiate with it.

No.

She wasn't going back. Not today.

She hooked the bumper jack into place and started pumping the handle. The first few strokes were easy, then it began to click and bite, lifting the truck one stubborn notch at a time. She kept at it until the flat tire hovered just off the dirt.

The lug nuts fought her.

Millie planted her feet, put her weight into the wrench, and pulled. Nothing. She repositioned and pulled again. Still nothing. Her hands slipped and scraped, and she hissed through her teeth, more angry at herself than the truck.

"Come on," she muttered, and leaned into it again.

The wrench finally gave, and the lug nut moved a fraction. Millie exhaled hard like she'd won a small war.

She didn't see the red truck at first.

It came over the rise behind her, slow enough that it didn't throw much dust. Just a low, steady roll like the driver wasn't in a hurry and didn't want to announce himself. It crept closer, then stopped a good distance back.

Millie kept working, but her shoulders tightened.

The driver sat for a moment. Watching.

Then the door opened.

Boots hit the ground. The man who stepped out didn't walk fast. He didn't wave. He took in the road, the sky, the truck, and Millie beside it, like he was looking at a scene that needed decoding.

He approached at an angle, not straight on, and he didn't speak until he was close enough that she could hear him over the wind.

"You're a long way from town for a bad tire," he said.

Millie kept the wrench in her hand. She didn't aim it. She didn't put it down either.

"I'm handling it," she replied.

His gaze dropped, quick and quiet, not lingering. Clean hands with a smear of grease now. Dress hem dusty. A folder on the floorboard, barely visible. He didn't stare at it, but he saw it. His eyes flicked back to her face.

"Looks like it," he said, dry as the dirt. "You got a spare that'll hold?"

Millie straightened, wiped her palm on her skirt without thinking, and instantly regretted it. "It'll have to."

He agreed, like that was an answer he respected.

Relief tried to creep in. Pride stepped on it.

The man looked down the road, then back at her rented truck. "Leave it here. We'll come back with a real tire."

Millie stiffened. "I'm not leaving my truck on the side of the road."

"You already did," he said, calm. "Only difference is, now it won't be your problem alone."

Millie lifted her chin and went back to the lug nuts like she didn't need him, like she hadn't been alone out here two minutes ago with the wind clawing at her nerves.

The man watched her work, calm and quiet, and for the first time since she stepped off that bus, Millie had the distinct feeling that Montana had finally noticed her.

She leaned into the wrench again. The lug nut gave a fraction, then stopped, like it wanted to argue.

Millie set her jaw and pulled harder.

Behind her, the man said nothing. No helpful suggestions. No fake coughing to announce he was still there. Just a steady presence and the sound of wind through the grass.

When the lug nut finally turned, she let out a breath she didn't mean to share.

"Stubborn," the man said.

"So am I," Millie replied, and went back to work.

She got two lug nuts loose. The third one laughed at her. The wrench slipped, her hand slid, and pain flashed across her knuckles. She hissed, shook it once, then grabbed the wrench again like she wasn't going to give the world the satisfaction of watching her bleed.

The man took one step closer.

"I can break it loose," he said.

"I didn't ask."

He nodded like he expected that. He crouched near the tire anyway, not touching anything, just looking.

"You're using your arms," he said. "Put your weight on it. Use your heel."

Millie stared at him. "You always give instructions to strangers on the side of the road?"

"Only the ones who look like they'll throw the wrench at me."

She tightened her grip. "Don't tempt me."

His mouth twitched again, almost a smile, but it didn't reach his eyes. Those stayed careful.

Millie repositioned the wrench, put her foot on it, and leaned down. The lug nut popped loose with a sharp snap that made her heart jump.

She didn't look pleased. She did feel pleased.

The man stood back up. "There you go."

Millie bent and loosened the rest, working faster now, breath steady. She didn't need him. Not technically. Not yet.

But she did need the spare to hold.

She dragged it out, rolled it closer, and her stomach tightened when she saw the cracked sidewall again. A crack that didn't care about hope, or stubbornness, or the fact that she'd come too far.

The man's eyes went to it.

"That won't make it," he said.

"It'll make it to the claim," Millie answered.

"That's not what you need it to do."

Millie straightened. "And what do you think I need?"

He looked past her, down the road she'd come from. Then he glanced toward the horizon where the land lay open and quiet, as if it couldn't hear a thing.

"You need to get back to town," he said. "You need a real tire. And if you're headed where I think you're headed, you need to get there before you lose daylight."

Millie bristled. "I didn't ask for a weather report."

He shook his head, still calm. "No. You didn't."

He walked to his red truck and opened the passenger door, then leaned inside and came out with a tire iron that looked like it had lived through a few bad days. He tossed it lightly from one hand to the other.

"I can help," he said. "But it's not free."

There it was. Not romance. Not charm. Just a transaction, clean and honest.

Millie narrowed her eyes. "What do you want?"

"Gas money," he said, like he'd already decided it was the most reasonable thing in the world. "And a look at the map you're using."

Millie's hand went instinctively toward the folder on the floorboard, like she could cover it with her palm from five feet away.

"No."

He didn't argue. He just watched her, patient, like he'd wait all day if he had to, and that made her more uncomfortable than any pressure.

"I'm not asking for your papers," he said. "I'm asking for the map. You can hold it the whole time."

Millie stared at him. The wind pushed dust between them, and for a second she felt how alone she was out here. Not helpless. Just alone.

She didn't like that feeling. She liked it even less that he knew it.

"How much gas money?" she asked, sharp.

He shrugged. "Enough to make it worth stopping."

"That's not a number."

"It's a negotiation."

Millie let out a slow breath, like she was counting to ten and deciding to stop at six.

"How much?" she asked.

He didn't glance at her purse. He didn't glance anywhere that would look greedy. He just leaned against his red truck and let the wind do the talking for him.

"Five dollars," he said.

Millie laughed once, short and sharp, like the sound surprised even her. "For what, exactly? A conversation and a tire iron?"

"For stopping," he said. "For turning around. For the miles. For the fact that you're not walking."

"That's not gas money," she said.

"It's gas," he replied, "and it's my time."

Millie narrowed her eyes. "Your time must be precious."

He shrugged, calm as ever. "Depends on who's asking for it."

"I didn't ask," she reminded him.

"No," he said, "but you're thinking about it."

Millie stared at him a long moment. Then she reached into her purse and drew out bills one at a time, slow, like she wanted him to feel every second of it.

She held up four dollars. Not hidden. Not folded. Four clean bills pinched between two fingers.

"That's what I've got for gas," she said. "Take it or keep driving."

He looked at the money, then at her face, like he was weighing more than the bills.

For a moment, Millie thought he might leave. Thought he might try to make her blink first.

Instead, he reached out and took the four dollars without brushing her fingers. Quick, careful. Like manners still mattered, even out here.

"All right," he said, pocketing it. "Four."

Millie didn't relax. She didn't thank him.

But something in her shifted anyway, just a hair. Not trust. Not yet.

He wasn't a saint.

Which, oddly, made him feel safer than one.

"Now the map," he said.

Millie hesitated, then slid the folder out and untied the string. She didn't hand it over. She opened it herself, flipped to the rough page with her uncle's penciled lines, and held it up so he could see.

The man leaned in, but not too close. His eyes moved quick, taking in the road marks, the creek bed, the circled spring.

"County won't care how hard you want it," he said. "They'll bounce you if your dates don't match their book."

Millie went still. That sounded too true.

"I need the county office," she admitted, and hated that she'd said it out loud.

He nodded, already knowing. "Then you need to get back to town first."

Millie lifted her chin. "I'm not turning around."

The man's gaze held steady, and in it she saw something that looked like calculation, but also something else, buried under it.

"You will," he said, quiet and sure. "You just haven't realized it yet."

Millie snugged every loosened lug back down before she lowered the rented truck off the jack and locked it. She grabbed her suitcase and the folder, then hesitated long enough to hate herself for hesitating.

The man opened the passenger door of his red truck and stepped back, giving her space, leaving the choice where it belonged.

She climbed in anyway.

She noticed it the moment she climbed into his red truck. He didn't bark orders, didn't act like he owned the road, didn't treat her like a problem to be managed. He just drove. Steady hands. Eyes always up. Like the land could change its mind at any moment and he'd rather be ready than surprised.

Millie sat stiff in the passenger seat with her folder on her lap, one arm wrapped around it like it might try to escape. Her rented truck was still out there behind them, sitting lopsided in the dirt like a bad decision. Millie tried not to think about it. Every mile back to town felt like she was leaving something exposed.

"You always carry paperwork like it's gold?" the man asked, voice dry, not looking at her.

"It's not paperwork," Millie said.

He glanced over once, quick, then back to the road. "That a fact?"

"It's my uncle's life," she replied, and immediately wished she hadn't given him that much.

The man didn't smile. He didn't soften either. He just nodded, filing the information away in a drawer he kept locked.

Then he surprised her.

He stuck out his hand, more business than kindness. His palm was rough, knuckles scarred in the quiet way of work.

"Name's Spyker," he said. "Clement Spyker, but folks just call me Clem."

Millie looked at his hand for a second too long. Out here, a handshake could mean anything. A deal. A promise. A trap.

She gave him her hand anyway, firm enough to make her point.

"Mildred Caldwell," she said. Millie was for family, and for the version of herself that still lived back home. "You can call me Mildred."

Clem's grip was brief, polite, and gone before it could turn familiar. His eyes stayed on her a second, then went back to the road.

"Mildred," he repeated, like he was testing whether the name fit her.

He put his eyes back on the road. "You headed to the claim first, or you trying to straighten the papers before you go?"

Millie didn't answer right away.

"County office closes early," he said. "If you're trying to get anything done, you'll want to move."

Millie watched the road. "I'm moving."

"No," he said. "You're riding."

She shot him a look. "You like correcting people?"

"I like people staying out of trouble," he answered.

Millie almost laughed at that. Almost. It didn't sound like concern. It sounded like experience.

www.ingramcontent.com/pod-product-compliance
Lightning Source LLC
Chambersburg PA
CBHW061917130726
47908CB00016B/519